THE SINS OF SISTERS

Emma Bradley

For Sammy and Talie, because sometimes
families are difficult, but their hearts are in
the right place.

And for Kainen, who is taking the whole 'wise
uncle of the woods' thing far too seriously.

CHAPTER ONE

MOLLY

"Careful!"

Molly lifted her head as the tower of multi-coloured fabric teetering above her head veered sideways. The explosion of dresses was stacked in the centre of her enormous room at the Illusion Court, and wasn't so much a pile as a disgustingly expensive mass determined to conquer every inch of the pale marble floor.

She leaned forward with one arm out as the pile twitched somewhere in the middle, followed by a flurry of clothing exploding upwards as Reyan's flushed face appeared.

"Almost drowned in the velvet thing at the bottom," Reyan panted as she swiped her messy blonde hair behind her ears.

Molly grimaced. "It's um... yeah. We definitely don't need all these. The entire court couldn't get through all of these."

Reyan clambered out of the pile and gave the edge of it a weary kick.

"You'd be surprised," she muttered. "Just pick one and be done with it."

Molly eyed the fabric landslide again, then glanced around at the cavernous room. Her room. Everyone had insisted she take the royal room when she arrived at court, and now Molly understood why nobody else was keen to claim it. The stone walls were echoingly far apart and painted ice white, and the shadows never fully receded no matter where she set the bedside lantern. Being underneath a mountain, the Illusion Court was nearly always firelit, and she had adjusted to the softness and the shadows.

"I'm sorry this has kind of hijacked your birthday though," Reyan added.

Molly shrugged. "I don't mind. Easier to slide under the radar that way. It's been four months since I left the citadel and I'm still not used to all the attention."

"I get that. I'm not sure I'm even used to it yet, but Kainen insisted on a wedding for all of Faerie and midsummer is meant to be the luckiest."

"Please, it took all my persuasion to convince him I didn't want a party, wedding or not," Molly said.

Reyan smiled with nerves still dancing in her smoky grey eyes. Some courtiers had almost mistaken her and Molly for sisters at the beginning, but Molly's hair was a longer and brighter blonde, and where Reyan was graceful, she was solidly practical.

"Lucky that he listened then." Reyan sighed. "The whole elite of Faerie will be in attendance today."

All morning she'd been the epitome of calm, but she folded the same dress three times before putting it back on the pile and picking up another to fold without even looking at it.

"Yeah, so shouldn't you be getting ready?"

"Orbs, probably. Pick a dress, then I can go and shove myself into mine."

The bedroom door swung open before Molly could grab the first dress that looked the least objectionable within reaching distance.

She smiled as the queen of Faerie strode in, a vision in a dark green ballgown sprinkled with red berries and lined with a web of lace frost.

"Ever heard of knocking?" Reyan asked with a smile.

Demi shrugged. "Queen. This was also technically my room before Molly moved in. Anyway, Kainen's convinced himself you're not going to show up."

Reyan snorted. "Typical. Is Taz with him?"

"Of course. Who do you think put the idea in his head?"

Demi smoothed down her skirt and reached up a hand to shove the circlet of silver and holly sprigs back into her black curls.

"Doesn't that hurt?" Molly asked.

Demi nodded. "Yep, but I owe Milo and he looked like he was about to cry when I mentioned wearing a normal one."

"How is he? And Ace?"

"They're fine. On top secret royal court business, but they're here for the wedding." She frowned at Reyan. "Speaking of the wedding, aren't you supposed to be ready by now?"

"I just want to make sure Molly finds a dress."

"Stalling?"

"Maybe."

"Don't want to marry him anymore?" Demi barely managed to hide her smile.

"Of course I do. I just hate all the staring, and I'm convinced Glennoria is going to throw something at me when I go past, or try to trip me up, or-"

"She won't," Molly promised.

"You can't know that!"

"I can. I made her promise."

Reyan stared. "How?"

"Promised her first tea with the princess, remember? All those months ago, and one of my caveats was that she had to be nice to you before the wedding. Make the most of it though, it'll expire at midnight."

She revelled in the impressed looks passing between the other two. Her four months at court had taught her many things, mainly how to avoid people without being rude, but Kainen was right when he said you could convince more Fae with flattery than fighting. Most of the time.

"Not princess of Faerie my behind," Reyan muttered. "You're as crafty as any of them."

"Hey!"

Demi clapped her hands. "Right, dresses, now. Reyan, go and get yours on. Molly, grab whatever fits."

Molly did as she was told and dug through the pile until she unearthed the least objectionable excuse for a dress she could without pulling the lot down on top of her. It was a deep blush pink with no sleeves and a flared long skirt that rustled. It would do.

She brushed out her hair and left it loose, then grudgingly grabbed the slender circlet of gold inlaid with pale pink gemstones. It was on loan and mandatory apparently, a sign of her status, but she was learning to pick her battles. Refusing to wear it would no doubt sour the fragile relationship she was being forced to build with her grandmother, the Oak Queen.

With a matching-if-you-looked-in-the-right-light pair of slipper shoes, she left the room in time to meet Demi and Reyan coming out of the one opposite.

Reyan's wedding dress was long-sleeved but left her shoulders bare, made of dark grey satin that sparkled with swirls of lilac gemstones. The fitted body gave way to sweeping silk and lace skirts that trailed behind her, and the veil covering her face was made entirely from pearlescent white shadow.

"It's- wow." Molly smiled. "Kainen might even be speechless."

Reyan pulled a face. "I knew I should have gone with the other one."

"Too late now," Demi said cheerfully. "Come on, you wanted me to give you away so let me get it done. Then I can go and sit on the floating bed thing and pretend to be too important to talk to anyone."

Molly grinned. "I didn't realise that was an option. I'm going to do that as well."

She followed them along the hall, familiar with the bare rock walls and the shining hard-wood floors underfoot. Crowd noise echoed from beyond the stone archway that led to the court's main reception hall, until Reyan muttered something into her hand and elegant music swelled.

"Last chance to back out," Demi said. "We'd hide you."

Reyan laughed. "And start a war? It's less hassle just to marry him and be done with it."

The music circled from announcement to soft attention, and Molly kept pace with them as they walked under the archway and down the stone steps toward the sea of silent faces.

Faelight bounced off the rocky walls, shimmering thanks to the pool of water that dominated one half of the room. Plants climbed toward skylights in the rock above and Molly sucked in a deep breath of soft lilac scent before focusing forwards.

She had a bet going with Meri, Head Manager of the court, over whether Kainen would cry. His suit matched Reyan's dress in dark grey and lilac, his brown hair swept back and his smile broad, but given the constant blinking he was doing, she was going to lose the bet.

She stepped aside to join Taz, her uncle, and her grandmother the Oak Queen behind the royal enclosure, separated from the crowd by a length of purple and gold rope. Demi slid in alongside her as Reyan reached Kainen's side.

Molly risked a wary glance at both Taz and the Oak Queen, her blood family that she still didn't really know all that well, but she had to admit there were similarities. Her nose and the queen's, her hair a similar shade of gold to Taz's, although he'd aligned with Demi's court over his mother's. It was a tangled web of family and obligation, one that Molly still couldn't believe she was stuck in.

The officiant, a face Molly didn't know, cleared her throat and the music fell silent.

"Welcome honoured guests to the union of Lady Reyan of the Illusion Court and Lord Kainen Hawthorn Merrytree Hemlock-"

"Hawthorn?" Taz hissed under his breath, his turquoise eyes wide.

Molly pressed a hand to her mouth. "Merrytree?"

She didn't dare look Taz's way, but his choked breath mirrored her helpless giggle. Demi gave them both a look but she couldn't keep the smirk off her face either.

Molly missed most of the short address the officiant made, but the moment kisses were exchanged and cheers went up, she sagged with relief. The couple faced the crowd and Kainen raised a hand for attention.

"Thank you all for joining and celebrating with us. All who mean us and ours no harm are welcome here."

"Bit formal isn't it?" Molly muttered.

Taz shook his head. "Has to be. The tiresome dance of court politics and not trusting a single soul inside your own home."

"Those who know us even remotely will remember how much effort I put in to convincing her to date me, let alone marry me," Kainen continued. "However, she's the one in charge of the both of us these days and I promised not to go on and on. So, from my fiancée and-"

"She's your wife now, idiot!" Taz shouted.

Kainen's eyes lit up. "My wife! *Awesome*. From my wife and I, thank you for joining us to celebrate the best day of my life. Hopefully hers as well, but I know when not to push my luck."

The crowd roared appreciatively and Molly looked around at those assembled. She'd fought with everything she had to avoid needing a guard following her, which had seemed like a good idea at the time. Now she realised that there was one circulating anyway but she had no idea who it would be.

She looked around for a familiar face as Taz and Demi dipped into the crowd and the Oak Queen appeared at her side. Her dress looked almost half the size of the mammoth pile in Molly's room, made of peach blush satin, full-skirted with a train of tangling golden vines that wrapped around her arms as well.

Molly managed a grimace in her grandmother's direction. Beyond a few excruciatingly awkward tea dates over the past couple of months, they'd not had any reason to see each other much.

No point letting her suck me in for whatever manipulations she's planning next.

"Oh!" She raised a hand and rushed past the rope. "Beryl!"

"Molinia."

The Oak Queen's voice was like iron, unyielding and full of command. Molly turned to face her warily.

"Yes?"

The queen frowned. "Yes, grandmother."

"Er... okay. My friends-"

"I have a gift for you."

Molly blinked in surprise. "Oh, that's kind but I don't need gifts. I've already got-"

"It's exceedingly rude to refuse a gift."

Tiny pinpoints of pink hit the queen's cheeks and the air began to pinch with untamed energy.

"What if it's a gift that's meant to harm you?" Molly countered.

"Do you think I intend to harm my only grandchild? The future of our family line?"

"Well…"

The queen pressed a delicate middle finger to the bridge of her nose and closed her eyes momentarily.

"It isn't a gift that will harm you. Give me your hand."

Molly bit her lip on all her usual retorts. She wanted to demand the queen give the gift to someone else, or be more supportive of Demi's initiatives to ensure that all Fae got a gift as standard when they came of age. Instead, she held out her hand with a belligerent glower.

The queen swiped her thumb over Molly's wrist, then frowned at the silvery tattoo of a spiralling cage.

"A princess should not be tattooed like some miscreant," she said.

Molly thought of May, the queen's youngest daughter, who was laden with tattoos and spent her time glamouring to hide them.

"This princess didn't grow up knowing that," she retorted. "I didn't have a choice. Well, I did, but I probably wouldn't be here if I'd refused. Celeste saw to that. Remember?"

Mentioning her mother was as close to antagonism as she could get, and the queen's unspoken part in the chaos that had happened to the citadel months ago still lingered like a bad smell between them.

"Hmm. I gift you with enhanced sight."

Molly froze as a chill fluttered over her skin and multi-faceted light dazzled her eyes. She closed them as a surge of magic tingled through her system and the new gift settled across her face like a veil. Her sun gift warmed in her chest to welcome the new flow of magic, and her stealth gift was more like a tingle on her palms when she used it, but now her whole upper body came alive with the exhilarating rush of gifts.

She opened her eyes as the queen dropped her wrist and a gasp tumbled from her lips. It took some adjustment, but she could see the tiniest hint of nicks and grooves in the wooden posts of the mini-decks floating in the iridescent water pool, and each individual sparkle on Reyan's wedding dress danced in the flickering firelight.

"Wow."

"Indeed." The queen's lips twitched. "Use it well."

She swept off toward Kainen and Reyan, and the crowd scattered out of her way like rain over chimneypots.

Rain. Molly grimaced. *I wonder…*

"Princess."

She lifted her head to find a beautiful young woman in front of her, tall with a crown of deep auburn hair, a sun-dusting of freckles and bright green eyes.

Is she this vivid because of my gift?

Molly shook the thought away and her cheeks burned as the woman curtsied low. She held the almost automatic grimace in with great restraint and bit her lip. With no hope of knowing who the woman was, she settled for simplicity.

"Hi?"

"Lady Violetta, how lovely to see you." Reyan swooped in before the woman had even finished rising from her curtsey. "Lady Violetta patronises the Court of Revels, Molly, and her family is most likely in some part responsible for these decorations."

The three of them made the obligatory sweep of the room and Molly managed a weak smile.

"They're very fine." She hesitated. "I particularly like the arbor towers. Very sturdy, well-built. I can see the screws are level, although that may be the new gift the queen just gave me."

Lady Violetta laughed. "Call me Vi, please. And I should hope the towers are sturdy enough. We're not known for poor craftsmanship in our family."

"You're crafters?"

"Of a sort. My mother is the engineer and the muscle, while my father comes up with most of the concepts."

Molly glanced doubtfully at Violetta's exceptionally smooth hands. Violetta crinkled her nose and held one up, vanishing a glamour to reveal chewed nails and work-worn fingers.

"Appearances are a must apparently. A pain, but still."

Molly accepted a drink from Kainen as he swirled past and whisked Reyan straight into a dance.

"And you?" she asked. "You mentioned your parents are crafters."

Violetta smiled. "I dabble in much of everything. I carve woodwork when needed, I paint, and more often than not I sing badly while I do. But I hear you're handy too?"

"I used to be, in another life before all... this."

"Not a fan of frippery?"

Molly shrugged. "I'm more a fan of making and fixing things. Kainen and Reyan have been kind enough to give me a workshop here and I spend far more time in there than I should. All of this seems to mean very little though when it gets to this level of excess."

She eyed the sweeping curve of Violetta's one-shouldered gown, a paler pink than her own with a sparkling bodice and skirts that swished to her ankles. Large flowers, real ones, wove diagonally from the shoulder ruffle to the hem but instead of looking flouncy, it looked stunning.

Molly bit her lip and glanced doubtfully down at the puff of pink she'd chosen.

"Your dress is very nice," she said.

Violetta laughed. "It does to make a spectacle among the Fae. Not all of us can have the privilege of royal blood to give us dress freedoms."

"Freedom?" Molly arced a hand around the hall. "You call this freedom?"

"No, I call it an orbing pain, but a necessary one. I meant no offense, Princess."

Molly eyed the amused quirk of Violetta's berry red lips.

"Nobody ever does," she muttered.

Violetta tutted and removed the goblet from Molly's hand with a bold swipe. She took a long sip, placed it on a nearby table and held her hand out.

"A birthday party is the one acceptable excuse for

excess and minor offences. Will you honour me with your first dance?"

Molly stared at the outstretched hand, the long, manicured fingers utterly steady. She had no reason to refuse.

"Just one."

She slid her hand over Violetta's, surprised that it didn't feel awkward.

Violetta grinned as she tangled their fingers together.

"I do like a challenge."

CHAPTER TWO

TALIE

"Happy birthday, princess," Talie whispered.

She sat beside the window of Molly's briefly occupied bedroom in the Menagerie, staring out at the vast glass that hemmed in the citadel tower. Somewhere out there in Faerie, Molly would be celebrating her birthday with Kainen and Reyan, perhaps with the entirety of the Fae nobility.

She lifted a finger and traced the path of a raindrop coursing down the glass outside, then sighed at her faint reflection in the window. Aside from her dark hair hanging in a longer ponytail, and the smudges under her hazel-grey eyes, she looked much the same as she had the day Molly left.

Sammy hadn't asked why she wanted the tiny wrapped parcel that sat on the sill beside her, but Talie had to do something to mark Molly's birthday, if only to torture herself.

The parcel was full of hair-ribbons, a symbolic gesture, because of course she'd done the noble thing and decided to encase herself back in the citadel to keep an eye on Phoenix and find out what his true intentions were. He'd also dangled the possibility of finding out who Sammy's family were, something Sammy had wondered aloud often, and Talie knew she had to give Sammy that shot if she could.

Then again, Sammy seems completely set with all her new friends.

Sammy had embraced the enhanced life Phoenix had offered them, almost always out with some new face. Talie didn't need new friends. She wanted Molly, but Molly was outside living a fancy new life. She lost count of how many times a day she daydreamed about walking down the countless levels to the now sparsely populated noble area and finding some way through a forgotten window into the wilds beyond.

Even just to orb her and say happy birthday, but I can't risk it.

Drawing Molly back into the vortex of the citadel's problems wasn't something she wanted to do under any circumstances.

The tiny cupcake she'd begged from the Menagerie kitchen had a candle on it and the flame flickered against the gloom outside. She leaned down and blew it out. Molly would likely have tiers of cake now for her birthday celebration, but again, symbolic.

She almost smacked the cake into the window as the bedroom door swung open and Phoenix strode in. He'd exchanged his familiar gym clothes that everyone knew him for and taken to wearing smart jeans and a shirt, but his silver hair was still long down his back and his expressions were sharper than ever.

"You really need to learn to knock," she muttered.

Phoenix sighed. "Sorry to interrupt the pity party, but we have things to do. Also, the rain really needs to stop."

"I'm trying. It's linked to my mood."

"Then you need to cheer up." He hesitated. "You really think she's out there thinking about you in return? I get it, but we have so much to do here. She's gone, we're not."

Talie slid her hands into the long sleeves of her sweatshirt. She'd found it among the endless rails of clothes in the walk-in dressing room, not sure if it was one Molly had worn or just a concession Celeste had made among the countless dresses during Molly's brief captivity. Either way, she'd adopted it as her own.

Not like she's coming back for it.

She sucked in a sharp breath and stood.

"What's the plan?"

Phoenix grimaced. "It's getting fraught now. The other towers are refusing to assist unless I give away things I'm not willing to give."

"Like what?"

She followed him out of the room and along the opulent corridor full of potted plants and weird dried perfume bowls toward the wide, curving staircase that led down into the entrance hall of the Menagerie. Phoenix had all but disbanded the Menagerie, in name at least, but she wouldn't be able to think of the place as anything else. He'd even had the stained glass window at the far end fixed, and she had no idea how considering most of their

16

citadel tower was struggling to source enough food, let alone resources to rebuild.

"Never mind that for now." Phoenix waved her questions aside. "We won't get help from the other towers, not yet, so we need to figure out how to get our tower fully functional again by ourselves."

Talie frowned as they left the Menagerie and walked out to the main lane that led up and down the circling levels of their tower. The core of the tower circled on the right-hand side with larger buildings and warehouses built against the central column. On the other side of the lane, the glass side, were alleys of houses and smaller businesses that led to the vast planes of glass hemming the tower inside. Talie had no idea if the wards that stopped people going in and out of the tower were somehow to do with the glass or just Fae gift magic, but either way the wards were the first thing Phoenix made sure of after she returned.

He nodded to people as they passed, apparently not aware of the wary looks they gave him or the way some of them scurried inside like frightened mice. She didn't blame them either. He'd promised change and provided nothing. Several of the cobbles and paving stones underfoot were still chipped after the explosion four months ago, roofs were missing tiles, and she didn't need to look up to see the huge gap in the level above. It had been patched up, but the thick wooden beams running across the metal girders had been laid with flimsy boards to shore up the hole. Other levels had fared worse but those gaps were now roped off and everyone was trying to function around the mess.

17

The only thing the other towers had donated was endless sheets of glass to replace the shattered ones, lifted and bracketed into place by an astonishing combination of gift-use and effort.

Molly would have loved to be a part of that.

Talie dug her fingernails into her palms as they started going up the levels at a smart pace and her emotions caused the drizzle of her rain gift to intensify.

"It looks like people are at least trying to help fix some windows and shore up broken foundations for others," she said.

Phoenix shoved his hands in his pockets.

"Good for them. That doesn't fix the halt in grain production flow from the upper levels or return the milk beasts that escaped."

Talie's mood sank even further at his dismissive tone. He was in a foul mood, which meant she had to be even more careful about what she said and how firmly she sought for answers. He'd given her almost nothing useful over the past four months, too obsessed with fixing up the citadel and his reputation within it. He didn't know she'd seen him slipping behind the large doors at the back of the Menagerie's entrance hall late at night though, or that she could guess exactly where he was going when he entered the labyrinth beyond.

"I've managed to keep the nobles quiet about their involvement," he continued. "The last thing we need is them flapping lips and assuming they can take control."

Talie frowned. "Their involvement?"

"Some of the supplies we needed to rebuild were

brought in through nobility trade."

She squelched down the instant question brewing. Phoenix had insisted they didn't want outside help, and it was his insistence about walling them all in again that had sent Molly fleeing to the courts and realms beyond.

"So the citadel isn't self-sustaining like everyone was led to believe," she said.

He slowed to a halt and glanced around before facing her with a frown. The lane and alleys branching off it were deserted, but he was increasingly paranoid about appearances and who might be listening.

"Don't be naïve," he snapped. "Why else would nobles have had the lower levels in the first place if not to provide? We simply can't let those in production get wind of it. If they find out the nobles are trading with us, then they'll start asking why the nobles can't trade with them directly. The citadel functions when we control the production flow. Why else would the Menagerie have been in the middle between the two instead of down with the luxury?"

Talie nodded bitterly. "Makes sense."

Because it did. She didn't have to like it, she didn't have to think it was right. She just had to get close enough to find out the truth.

"I've called the towers to another meeting," he added. "They're likely to approve my continued rule now that Celeste is no longer here, so I'll try asking them to assist again, but until then we need to control the damage ourselves."

Talie slouched along behind him as he led the way to

the gym, their previous headquarters, and swung the door open. A few people were scattered around, working out and training, but Phoenix headed straight toward the door near the back. That meant it was time for her to go to work, to earn her keep and Sammy's, but she hated doing it.

She followed him through the door and into the studio room beyond. Her jaw dropped. Instead of one person waiting to have their mind wiped, maybe two, there were several.

"Take your time," Phoenix said, as if he was doing her a kindness. "If you need to take a break that's fine, but don't leave until they're all done. Most are from various guilds but I've written you a list."

Talie took the piece of paper he held out to her, with a neat list of the names, the guild they belonged to, and what he wanted her to erase from their minds.

"Why are we here?" one demanded.

A smooth smile fell over Phoenix's face and he held his hands up as muttering swept across the studio.

"I've asked Talie here to put a couple of questions to you, nothing more. We're interested in the function of the guilds. If you answer honestly and support the process you'll be out again in no time."

"And if we don't?" someone else asked.

Good point. Talie couldn't bring herself to smile, but she focused on keeping her expression neutral. *If you don't, I bet he'll find a way to make more than your memories disappear.*

"Why wouldn't you want to assist us?" Phoenix asked, his head tilted and a mask of soft bafflement firmly in place. "We're doing our best to rebuild the tower and we need to know if the guilds are in a position to help."

Another round of weary and wary looks passed through the gathered Fae, thin faces and soul-broken eyes narrowed up at him.

"Nobody's forcing anyone to do anything," he added. "If that's what you're saying, nobody's keeping you here."

Talie glanced at the two guards that appeared either side of the door, sturdy chested with muscled arms. A shiver ran down her back as nobody else answered, the room ominously silent.

Phoenix's smile widened.

"Good. Remember, you're all contributing to the new future we're building, a fairer future for all."

Talie didn't move as he walked toward the door, or when the two guards saluted him. That was a new one, both men standing with their right arm hooked in front of their chest, their left fist thumping twice on their right shoulder. Nobody had saluted Celeste that she could remember. She'd never seen Molly do it, and Phoenix had never expected that when they were a resistance fighting the powers in control.

But then, he was always on both sides. All of this is part of his wider game.

She turned her attention to the crowd as Phoenix left and one of the guards shut the door to trap them all in.

Talie strode toward the storage cupboard she had been 'given' to use for her mind-wiping. It was big enough for a small round table and a couple of chairs now that the training equipment had been removed, but every time she stepped inside and flicked on the Faelight, she thought about Molly out in the wider realms of Faerie and wished with everything she had that she'd left with her instead.

She scanned the list. Phoenix would expect it back, each line neatly ticked to confirm it had been done, but she needed to assess if there was anything useful tucked among the questions she was supposed to use to drag their memories from them.

Most were from the Artificer's Guild and a couple from the Refuse Guild. She frowned.

He wants me to remove the memory of exports made three days ago? What exports?

She rubbed a hand over her mouth, her gaze stuck on the vague wording. As far as she knew, the Refuse Guild were the only few that exited the citadel on any kind of regular basis to take the waste out that couldn't be re-used or recycled.

What would he want wiped about rubbish?

It was typical Phoenix, especially lately, to leave her with the job of deciding which questions she needed to ask. A lot of the Fae were belligerent about being questioned by a sixteen-year-old, but more recently they whispered as she passed, no doubt assuming that she was part of Phoenix's inner circle and just as to blame for the citadel's more recent issues as he was.

She scanned further down and another line jumped out at her. Even though four months had passed, constant thoughts of Molly sometimes triggered thoughts of her old friend Ru. Talie couldn't bring herself to be overly distraught that he'd died, but she guessed Molly still missed him even after his treachery. She stared at his name right there on Phoenix's list alongside Celeste's as part of questions to be asked, and chilly discomfort danced across her skin.

She had no idea if Phoenix would have had Ru's room in the Menagerie cleared out by now or not, but it was worth checking. He might have written down or saved something she could use.

Either way, she would need to get her task done first. With a loud sigh that told everyone outside exactly how she felt about having to question them, she eyed the list and called out the first name.

CHAPTER THREE

MOLLY

"We'll honeymoon later, honestly."

Molly bit her lip as Reyan reassured her, but she couldn't push aside the nagging feeling that she was at least a small part of the reason Reyan and Kainen were postponing their honeymoon. She'd insisted she didn't need to be sent to the royal court for a few weeks after the wedding, and suddenly they "weren't that fussed" about going away and had far too much court research to get on with.

"You'd rather be having this meeting than having some alone time for yourselves?" she asked.

Reyan sighed. "I'd rather be eaten by Betty than have this particular meeting, but other than that, I've told you we don't mind."

Betty uttered a soft hiss from the shadows in the corner of Reyan's office, which was technically Kainen's office first but nobody called it that anymore. The snake was in her shadow form and invisible but Molly often heard her hissing or slithering around the halls, so often that she suspected Reyan had chosen Betty to keep an eye on her.

Unless that's why Violetta was so overly friendly. She said she would be hanging around court a while, and she wanted to see the workshop.

Molly shook the thoughts of Violetta aside as a sharp knock echoed on the office door.

Reyan groaned and swiped her hands over her hair, then sat back against her chair.

"Come in."

Molly smiled as Glennoria Featherdown strode into the room in a sparkling black velvet pantsuit, her black hair gelled back into a tight bun and her brown eyes sharp with wicked amusement.

"I was summoned," she said sniffily.

Reyan nodded, her relaxed posture nothing more than a mask as she pointed to the chair on the other side of the desk.

"What news from the citadel?" she asked.

Glennoria spared the briefest twitch of her lips for Molly before taking a seat. She unbuttoned the front of her jacket and tapped a deep red fingernail on the edge of the desk.

"Oh. Well, Lord Chivestem is the current leader in the ongoing card tournament. Lady Ivy has come to tea twice with her newborn. Surprisingly quiet for a baby. Let's see…"

"We've no interest in random lords and ladies," Reyan said. "What news do we need to know?"

Glennoria tilted her head with a supremely irritating frown.

"Well, how do I know what news you deem worthy of your knowledge, Lady?"

The honorific dripped with sarcasm and Molly stood torn between amusement and loyalty.

"Is the Menagerie still operational?" she asked.

Loyalty won and Reyan gave her the briefest look of weary gratitude.

Glennoria nodded. "In a way. Phoenix has disbanded the name of course but it stills runs on much the same. He's moved his closest into the Menagerie halls and they're working on rebuilding, but from what I hear they're struggling to get support."

"The towers are self-sustaining." Molly sighed. "They won't accept outside help easily."

"Oh what rot. Since when have the towers not accepted outside help? Orbs, the nobles have been funding and propping up parts of all of them for as long as the citadel's been a going concern."

"What do you mean?"

Glennoria plucked a pen from the edge of the desk and tilted it diagonally between them.

"The upper levels control production and the produce trickles down, yes? So if the produce trickles down, and funds trickle up to buy them, where do those funds come from in the first place? Where do the supplies for those production centres come from?"

Molly frowned. "We only produce what we can sustain though, everyone knows that."

"Who mines the iron for repairs to the levels? Who cuts down the wood to replace those hulking great beams?

Where do all the mysterious potions and ingredients the artificers tout about with grow? Self-sustainment is a myth."

Molly frowned. "But the guilds, the grain guild and the transports, they're all feeding and funding the citadel, aren't they?"

"I'm sure on a small scale it can be managed, but to compete with the other towers?" Glennoria scoffed gently. "No, Phoenix and Celeste always walked a very thin rope between keeping the nobles investing and the production centres producing, and by all accounts Phoenix is struggling to bridge that gap since Celeste left."

Molly wiped a hand over her face. She'd known all her life that the citadel was untouched by outside influence, and she'd never stopped to wonder how the nobles could come and go as they pleased. They arrived, spent coin and that somehow travelled upward, but she'd never even thought of it as manipulatable, only 'the way things were'.

"So Phoenix is struggling?"

Glennoria smiled. "It would seem so. All these whispers about Celeste chasing tall tales have died down and she's been suitably forgotten, but so many nobles are still wary to invest in the citadel and Phoenix needs their money. I wouldn't be surprised if he agrees to the demand to reinstate gift-battle arenas. A bit of entertainment would draw the nobles in, and a bit of glory and prestige for lesser Fae."

Molly gulped down the instant urge to challenge the 'lesser Fae' comment. She was stuck between being born royalty but raised as lesser Fae, and people were always hanging around to remind her she should be grateful and apologetic for both.

"Is that all?" Glennoria asked.

Reyan nodded. "For now. Are you enjoying the top dog spot here at court still?"

Glennoria's smugness iced over ever so slightly, barely noticeable except for the sudden tension in her shoulders.

"It has its uses."

Reyan smiled as the shadows drew closer, along with the echo of a warning hiss somewhere in the near vicinity.

"You may go. Perhaps congratulate Lord Chivestem on his card game with our compliments next time you're in the citadel."

Glennoria stood, her lips pressed thin despite her smile.

"Of course, Lady." She took a step back and her smile softened slightly as she eyed Molly next. "Princess."

Molly pulled a face and both of them laughed. The moment Glennoria left and shut the door behind her, Reyan sagged over with her head on the desk.

"She hates me," she muttered.

Molly nodded. "Kind of, but that could have gone worse. More importantly, Phoenix is struggling. He never should have warded the tower off again."

"And why would he do that unless he has something to hide?" Reyan sat up as the door swung open again and Kainen strode in. "You have the most uncanny timing."

He grinned and swept a hand through his messy brown hair as he rounded the desk to kiss her. Molly wrinkled her nose and looked away.

"I saw her come in and waited around until she left," he

admitted with a grin.

"Nice," Reyan muttered. "Thanks for that."

He perched on the edge of the desk. "What news?"

"Phoenix is struggling," Molly said.

He shrugged. "We expected that. Any sign of him digging any deeper into the citadel's core?"

"She didn't say anything about that, but she reckons he'll allow some kind of tournament? Something about gift-battles?"

"They're outlawed."

"So's coalbane, didn't stop Celeste using it. For all we know, he is as well."

"It'd be hard to come by," Reyan said gently. "We've about exhausted the books in our library, and Milo's not unearthed anything helpful in the Arcanium one."

Molly sighed. "It was the Oak Queen's personal library we found the coalbane mention in. She's the oldest out of the lot of us and didn't she set up Arcanium, or fund it or something? I doubt there'd be anything in that library she wouldn't have herself."

"True, and Queenie would probably have to concede to give her anything truly valuable," Kainen said.

Molly had met Queenie twice since finding out about her own heritage, and she still couldn't figure out if Queenie was meant to be her great aunt or aunt once removed, or just another aunt. As the Oak Queen's sister though, she commanded her own kind of respect and Molly was quietly awed by her.

"I suppose we could orchestrate a situation to get Molly invited for tea…" Reyan suggested. "We do have certain sneaking abilities through the shadows that not everyone knows about yet. You could go and have a snoop around in the library while we do the exhausting social battle."

Kainen's eyes lit up. "I wonder if Taz's wings have fixed themselves yet."

"That was mean," Molly said, amused. "But yeah, I'll orb him and it's probably time for me to visit May anyway."

She pulled her orb from her pocket and held it up in front of her face.

"Taz Darcy."

Kainen pulled a face. "Still can't get used to him taking Demi's last name."

"It's her crown," Reyan reminded him. "Her court. Her title. He never liked his princely connections much anyway."

Taz's face materialised in front of them in pearlescent grey quality. He smiled then his gaze flicked sideways at Kainen and his expression soured.

"Still not talking to him," he muttered.

Molly nodded. "Understandable. Are the... um..."

"My wings are almost back to normal now thankfully. The orange is still a bit dull and the fire sputters now and then, but at least they're not bright green butterfly ones anymore."

"Well that's good," she said diplomatically. "I'm just orbing because it's probably time to arrange a-" She struggled over the words for a long moment. "-family meet-up."

It was code for 'we need an excuse to either interrogate

the Oak Queen or talk without being on the orb-waves'. So far they hadn't had much reason to use it, but sneaking into a royal library definitely counted as a need for code words.

"Ah." Taz glanced over his shoulder. "I'll orb May. Expect an invitation in the next couple of minutes. I'm sure the queen will drop whatever she's doing for her favourite granddaughter."

Molly groaned. "Don't, I'm her only granddaughter and barely that beyond blood."

"Don't say that to her face," Taz said with a grin.

He disappeared and Molly pocketed her orb. Kainen was still grinning like a fiend, no doubt revelling at glamouring Taz's wings after too much *Beast* during the wedding.

"Wipe that smirk off your face," Reyan said. "Go get something suitable for a royal visit on. You too, Molly."

Molly shook her head. "Nope, she takes me as I am or not at all. Might as well start lowering her expectations early."

Kainen glanced down over his black jeans and leather jacket.

"And I look every inch the lord of a court that deals in mischief and trickery."

"I give up." Reyan sighed. "Oh. That was quick."

The air shivered and a purple card embossed with gold lettering and much detailing of oak leaves and acorns dropped onto the desk.

Reyan grabbed the card and stood with one hand held out to Kainen. He took it then extended his to Molly.

"Remember, anything about gift extraction, the citadel

or the Omens is what we need," Reyan said. "If Phoenix is continuing Celeste's work, then we need to be prepared."

Kainen nodded. "Yes, sweetheart. You know, sometimes I worry you don't have much faith in me. Don't answer that."

The nether wrapped around them as he whisked them into realm-skipping, a swirl of purple and grey haziness that swept the office away and resolidified moments later as the Oak Queen's throne room. White marble floors inlaid with black swirls stretched in all directions, the walls covered with tapestries and climbing vines flanked by enormous marble pillars.

Molly shook her hand free of Kainen's and firmed a warding around herself, just in case. Even as Taz popped into existence beside her and May sauntered out from a side door with a grin on her face, Molly's focus was on the large wooden throne at the far end of the hall, ornately carved with oak motifs and towering over all atop a marble plinth of steps. The Oak Queen didn't rise but her power emanated around the room like a spring morning warning of potential further chills.

"I must say I'm surprised my children are calling me to gather them together," she announced. "If I were a suspicious person, I'd assume something underhand was going on."

May snorted. "You are a suspicious person."

"Careful, Mayflower."

"It's a queen's job to be suspicious, isn't it?" May countered, flicking her loose blonde curls over one shoulder. "Hi Molly, don't you dare call me auntie."

Molly lowered her warding long enough to let May get a firm hug in, then raised it again as they stood together facing the queen, the sides and allegiances being drawn with excruciating obviousness.

"Well, I'm happy to see you," May continued.

Molly nodded. "Same."

"I thought it'd be a good idea to get family together," Taz said.

The queen pursed her lips. "I'd question your use of the word family."

Taz rolled his eyes and folded his arms across his chest, and May smirked in his direction as they faced their mother.

"I changed my name," he said. "If I were a female noble you wouldn't bat an eyelid, let it go. My loyalty is to the family I'm building, sure, but that doesn't mean people can't choose to be a part of that."

"You assume anyone wants to choose to be a part of that," May retorted.

He pulled a face at her as she stuck her tongue out in return.

"I don't know much about family-" Molly winced. "I mean the family, this one, whatever. It'd be good to get to know everyone better."

If only to find out what side they're on.

She focused on Taz and May as she said it but Kainen raised a hand.

"I'm not family, so I'll go and find the facilities," he announced. "Actually, I think I am technically family, if only distantly, but still."

The queen smiled, a thing of beauty and cunning, and the pointing of verbal knives.

"I'll have someone come to escort you both."

Kainen set off toward the main doors leading out of the throne room with an airy wave of his hand.

"No need, I've been here before. Reyan stays with Molly while she's under the protection of our court, you understand. I only need to pee."

He was out of sight before the queen could refuse, although she pulled a disgusted face at his parting retort. Molly took the opportunity to shuffle closer to Reyan's side. The queen would be more than prepared for any questioning, but Molly got the sense there were more similarities that ran in the family than just sibling bickering.

"How's Celeste and the baby?" she asked.

The queen's eyes widened the tiniest amount.

Blunt, good. Get her rattled. Keep her mind off...

She cut the thought about what Kainen was doing before it could run through her head. She had no guarantee that a queen couldn't read her thoughts as easily as she could blast her off the face of Faerie.

"They are adjusting," the queen said. "Celeste's memories are gone and she cannot tell us who the baby's father is, so the lineage may well be tainted for all we know."

Molly scoffed. "That's the thing you're upset about? Must have been a delight to find out about me."

She caught the glance that passed between Taz and May, incredulous disbelief on his face and undisguised delight on hers. The subtle fizzle of energy increased around her as wardings were strengthened.

"All grandchildren are a blessing," the queen said. "But heritage is also important for a royal line. The baby is unharmed and is due to be born in around four months' time."

Molly thought back five months or so and her chest squeezed, her gut clenching tight.

Around the time Talie and I were climbing around the Artificers Guild looking for clues. Oh orbs, what if it's Phoenix while he was pretending to be Marcus?

She caught herself before any emotion showed on her face as the conversation stalled again, but the thought lodged inside her head. Phoenix had spent years pretending to be the head of the Menagerie as well as the head of the resistance, enough that he was in Celeste's inner circle while she hunted for the well of power and harnessed the Omens to advance her own gifts. As Marcus, Phoenix would likely have known all about the well and what lurked within the prison it had been formed as.

"We should hold a ball soon, I think," the queen announced.

Molly held in her groan but Taz didn't bother.

"Why? Why are Fae obsessed with holding balls?"

May opened her mouth with a lethal grin, but one sharp look from the queen and she closed it again.

"Molly hasn't officially been introduced into our society yet," the queen reminded them. "They've met her yes, unavoidable thanks to circumstances." She gave Reyan an even more dismissive glance next. "But we've not announced her as family or brought her under the protection that offers."

May shrugged. "They know. She's our niece but you forget she's also friends with Demi, which carries its own power, and currently under the protection of the Illusion Court. She's fine."

"I forget nothing. She needs to be introduced to the right sort of nobility and given the right opportunities to make connections."

"Are you saying my court isn't the 'right sort' now?" Taz asked.

The air around him turned icy and Molly stared in awe at the hint of pale crystallisation creeping across his cheeks as his wings flared fiery behind him.

"I am honestly fine, I don't need a ball," she insisted. "It's all the arrangement and frippery for not much. I can make my own connections if I need them."

The queen shifted on her throne and spiky nettles climbed up the sides as she levelled Molly with a piercing gaze.

"Not the right ones, clearly. Perhaps we should reconvene to discuss a family event at least." The nettles crept back down as her mood settled. "It needn't be a ball. We could arrange a picnic in the far meadow if that suits, just for a select few from each of the courts."

Taz and May exchanged another startled look, but Molly had no hope of working out what that one meant. She bit her lip, torn between compromise and social exhaustion.

"I guess... a picnic wouldn't be the worst thing?" she

said.

"Excellent. My court will handle everything and send out the invitations. How about Thursday?"

"Thursday?"

"For the picnic? I must say, your Lord of Illusions has outdone himself and disappeared it seems. For all his flaws, he at least seems to understand the necessity of social obligation."

Molly tensed at the insinuation, because Kainen would likely have made it to the queen's library by now but without much chance to read yet.

"Too many oia berry pies." Kainen's voice echoed behind them. "I doubt I need to caution your majesty against the woes of excess however. That said, those crystalline tarts at the last ball were exceptional. You must allow your kitchens to share the recipe with mine."

Molly had seen the true depth of what Kainen's charm could do so rarely that it stunned her to see it now. His eyes sparkled with amusement and the devilish smile was a thing of deception so finely crafted she almost fell for it.

The queen merely smirked.

"I'm sure some arrangement can be agreed upon," she agreed.

"Perhaps you'll be able to provide them for the picnic then," he added smoothly. "And allow us to contribute some of our reserved label wine? It's the least we can do for Molly's social debut."

The queen nodded. "It is said to be the best. I suppose you'll expect me to invite your friends, Molinia?"

Molly grimaced. "First of all, everyone calls me Molly.

I won't reply to Molinia so let's squash that one straight away. Secondly, yes, if you're not going to invite my friends then don't bother inviting me. Also, I never got a chance to get a look at the library in the citadel because it was carded, and Arcanium can be a bit loud, and I've exhausted all the stories at the Illusion Court now, so could I maybe have a look at the library here next?"

It was pure desperation and she firmed her warding as tight as she could around her, because of course the queen was probably going to blast her into a million pieces, granddaughter or not.

After a tense moment where she could feel the edge of several protection wardings fighting each other to squeeze around her own, the queen offered a tiny tip of her chin.

"Fine."

"WHAT?!" Taz and May exploded in unison.

"How come she gets to be called by the name she wants?!"

"Why does she get to have her friends over when you can't stand half of mine?"

"You never let us go into the library without the librarian hovering over us!"

Kainen folded his arms with a huge grin, visible even when he opened his mouth wide, but Reyan slapped a pre-emptive hand over it.

"Are you quite finished?" the queen snapped. "Adults and you're throwing tantrums like squalling babies. Now, are we agreed on Thursday for our celebration of bringing Molly into the family?"

Taz frowned. "We have gift-ball on Thursday."

"Oh right yeah." Kainen nodded. "Don't want to miss that. Can we do Friday?"

The queen pressed a finger to her nose and closed her eyes in torment.

"You can't miss gift-ball for one week?"

"Of course not! It's the inter-court regional quarter finals!"

She clenched her fist against the edge of the throne, then released it slowly.

"*Fine.* Friday then. Any objections?"

Taz and Kainen both dutifully shook their heads as Reyan leaned close to Molly.

"The bromance is still fairly new," she whispered. "I almost miss the days they were threatening each other."

"I'll consider this family meeting concluded," the queen announced. "Once this picnic is done with too, we can start looking for a suitable marriage alliance for you, *Molly.*"

Without another word, she rose from the throne and swept from the room.

Molly froze.

"I can't believe you aren't in pieces," Taz muttered.

May nodded. "It's true what they say, cruddy mothers make over-indulgent grandparents. If either of us made demands like that, she'd have us locked up or doing weeks of ritual humiliation."

"Sorry, what did she say about marriage?" Molly asked. "I'm not… she can't…"

"Oh she does that," May said.

Taz nodded sagely. "Yeah, I wouldn't worry about it. I was to be married off to six different ladies and one distant lord before I married Demi."

"And I'm on number nine." May shrugged. "The secret is to chase them off without her realising how you've done it. It's when she starts asking you to wear velvet that you really have to worry, because that's her way of signalling to society that you're basically open for business."

"Kainen wears velvet," Molly retorted. "Nobody accuses him of being open for business."

"No I don't!"

"Not even a bit?" Taz asked.

"Once, but that's it."

Taz rolled his eyes. "Oh come on. We're all friends here, kind of."

"Fine, I have been known to wear velvet suits on occasion." Kainen threw up his hands, his voice dripping with sarcasm. "There are even flouncy velvet suits with lace and ruffles, is that what you wanted to hear?"

Taz held up an orb. "Music to my ears."

He and his feral grin twisted around and broke into a run down the hall, almost crashing into Marthe as she came in through the doorway. Kainen stared in horror for several seconds before giving chase.

"Come back here and delete that right now or I'll snap you like a broken limb!"

Molly stared until a hysterical laugh choked out of her, then she doubled over and continued struggling to breathe. As she wiped the laughter from the corners of her eyes, she eyed Reyan, who had her hands over her face in mortification.

"Every time," she muttered. "Every orbing time we

come here, I swear."

Molly sighed. "It didn't even do us any good and now we have to go to this picnic thing."

Reyan glanced around and leaned closer. May eyed them with her head cocked, but after a moment she shrugged and walked off toward the doors leading out of the throne room.

"I've cast a bubble warding to keep sound in. No guarantees it'll hold here but enough to say Kainen managed to use his speed gift."

"And?"

Reyan grimaced. "There were a couple of books on the return cart and one was the *Potions Most Foul* or whatever it was called, the one you found the gift extraction recipe in."

"That's not good. Why have that one out if the gift extraction in the citadel has stopped?"

Reyan glanced around again.

"It could be innocent," she said. "Academic interest, but still, it's questionable at the very least. The other book he noticed was *Histories and Heritages of the Nether*. Considering the Omens are meant to be spawned from excess nether hotspots, someone's doing some very in-depth research."

"Might not be her though." Molly nodded to the empty throne.

"Maybe not, but it's been four months so someone's fishing around still, and he said there was a bookmark in the Potions book for gift replication."

Molly wiped a hand over her face and let the weariness

slump over her shoulders as Kainen came back into the room.

Reyan pressed a finger to her lips and moments later the sound of Kainen's footsteps blossomed around them.

"All good?" she asked.

He scowled. "Taz is an arse, but then what else is new?"

CHAPTER FOUR

TALIE

Talie hesitated outside one of the many doors inside the Menagerie and glanced up and down the hallway.

Sneaking into a boy's bedroom, there's a new one.

She pushed the handle down to the room the maids had told her used to belong to Ru and eased the door open. The scent of dust and something faint but unpleasant wafted up as she slipped inside, and she lifted the neck of her t-shirt over her nose.

The room was neat but she guessed Celeste or Phoenix-as-Marcus would have at least done a sweep of it already.

She pulled a couple of desk drawers open, all full of clothes, and grabbed a pencil to push them gingerly back and forth.

"Eww." She wrinkled her nose and picked up a questionable sock with the pencil.

Beneath the sock was a dark grey orb, and her pulse picked up as she fished it out. She swiped her thumb over the shiny sphere and it turned red.

"Crud," she muttered to herself. "What would someone

like Ru have chosen as their password?"

Another look around at the room and she went to the stack of tiny papers pinned above the head of the bed. As she scanned them, a random drawing of an acorn caught her eye.

She lifted the orb up to her face. "Acorn."

Nothing happened. She eyed the board again and tried Molly's pre-royalty name.

"Molly Acorn."

Nothing.

With a frown, she tried to remember what Molly's royal name was.

"Molinia Elverhill."

The red cloud disappeared from the surface and she grimaced. He'd known the whole time, or long enough to use the truth as a password to his orb. She couldn't fathom how Phoenix hadn't found it, but then perhaps Celeste had been the one to give it.

She thumbed across the surface of the orb through old messages and saved orb channels, until she reached Ru's notes and projected them into the air in front of her.

"-plans about Molly," she muttered aloud. "Celeste ruthless, need to handle emotions on both sides. Celeste going to hurt her, approach- approach Talie? Really? *Idiot*. As if I'd ever help him. Get 'resistance bloke' to get her out."

She shook her head at the increasingly chaotic ramblings and skimmed over the bulk of his conflicted feelings about the Menagerie and how Molly hated him for being used to kill.

Phoenix had been pretending to be Marcus the whole time, and Molly had said at some point that he was fond of Ru. So many would probably tell her about how 'fond' Phoenix was of her too.

Her insides chilled and she eyed a slip of notes at the very bottom.

"Worse than I thought..." she murmured. "Gift extraction and replication being used alongside physical duplication... transfers haven't fully taken... duplicate minds untethered..."

She frowned. Duplicate minds sounded ominous and she hadn't ever heard of anyone saying gifts had minds in any form, or that they had any kind of sentience attached. The closest she'd ever come to sentient giftery were the whole Omens in the nether thing, and she had no desire to revisit them again.

The faintest echo of noise crept through the tiny gap she'd left between the door and the frame. She dropped the orb back into the drawer, shunted it shut with a grimace at the noise and slipped back into the hall.

She would need to find a place to hole up and think. If she could get the information out of the tower somehow, to Molly or even just to someone like Kainen, they might be able to do something.

"Talie."

She tensed at the sound of Phoenix's voice and let a warding creep around her as she turned to face him. Her pulse picked up and her skin flushed hot as he eyed her up and down, like he could sense the misdeeds on her somehow.

45

"With me," he said. "I have someone to meet and may need you to do your thing."

"Watch for the nod?" she asked drily.

"Exactly."

"Who is it?"

Phoenix led the way toward the entrance hall, where an unfamiliar woman was standing dressed in a large hat with a big pink feather, and a maroon velvet dress with so many ruffles that it could have clothed at least four people.

Talie flinched as he leaned close to whisper.

"Betula. The leader of sunrise tower." He straightened up with his most charming smile. "Betula! Welcome. May I introduce my second right-hand woman, Talie."

Talie lowered her head in grudging deference. Sunrise tower, so called because the rays of sunlight hit it first in the mornings, was profitable. It ran much of the recycled metal production, a trade all towers needed. Morning and day towers were middling in their trades and produces but sunset, where they were, was a chaotic mess of agriculture, unlike the night tower who dealt in glass and refused to do or divulge much of anything else.

"Our meeting is long overdue," Betula said, her voice low and seductively lyrical.

Talie shook her head and risked a small step back. Charm was a common gift among nobles, she'd found that out during her brief time stuck outside the citadel, but she'd not had anyone use it on her before.

Something calming settled in her chest.

Means Molly never tried to use hers on me.

Betula smiled. "Heart's gone a-wandering already, has

it? Come along then. I'm intrigued to see these grain setups you have. We could use some extra reserves now the costs elsewhere are getting higher."

"Night court keep raising their costs," Phoenix agreed.

Talie followed them out of the Menagerie and onto the main thoroughfare of the lanes. Either Betula could read minds or hearts, or more likely saw her charm wasn't landing properly, but Talie couldn't do anything about either.

Phoenix lifted a hand to hail a cart and Talie squeezed in opposite them on the narrow bench seat back to back with the driver. As the Arumpii between the shook its spined neck and set off in a clatter of hooves, Talie sank into the wind that ruffled her hair.

The cart rumbled up levels and she focused on counting them as Phoenix pointed things out to Betula. They passed Molly's workshop, the park, the gym, Talie's old room she hadn't been back to since moving into the Menagerie. After a while longer, they moved up past the children's home she'd grown in.

Long gone where the signs of anything green, and the old shop had grills on the front. A couple of alleys passed with shadowed groups lurking in them and Betula's gaze narrowed.

"Do you often venture this far up, Talie?" she asked as the cart rattled to a halt outside the ranks of stone silos towering above them.

"No, I don't really need to. Most of the production that happens up here is the grain grinding."

She waited while Phoenix sprang out of the cart and

extended his hand, but Betula didn't take it as she stepped down.

"So this is where our shipment will be produced?" she asked with a doubtful tone.

Phoenix nodded. "And realm-skipped to you direct from source. There are-"

A deafening shriek stole his words away a second before the ground shook beneath the cart.

Talie cast a warding around herself as the Arumpii between the spokes snorted and reared onto his hind legs, and Phoenix veered away from the cart as the spokes splintered under the weight. The Arumpii broke free and shot away back down the levels like the beasts of ancient tales were snapping at his hocks.

The cart driver called after him but her voice was lost in the cacophonous rumbling that shook the sides of the nearest grain silo.

Betula twisted into nothing and reappeared beside Phoenix out of harm's way, but Talie clung to the cart as a sea of beige tumbled towards them. The grain explosion cascaded past the cart and she prepared to jump, but a flicker of colour caught her eye.

On the side of the metal silo was a bird painted in white, its neck at a hung angle with gashes of red slashed across it.

Phoenix saw it too and his mouth twisted thin as the grain flow from the silo steadied then slowed. The spillage would likely keep tumbling down for any passing person to run out and grab.

Maybe with the recent shortages that's no bad thing.

A sizzle tore through the air before the grain frow could even level out. As the scent of burning matches filled her nose, the painted bird burst into flame.

A Phoenix. She bit her lip. *Can't be any clearer threat than that.*

She risked a glance his way and shuddered as the blaze reflected in his eyes turned them white. The cascade slowed almost as quickly as it exploded free, but there would be no easy recollecting as the wave continued tumbling down the lanes behind them.

"Are accidents common?" Betula asked. "I wouldn't have thought grain could cause much calamity."

"You'd be surprised," Talie muttered.

People from the nearby processing plant spilled out into the lane as the fire burned away to leave the Phoenix sigil charred against the metal, a brand that still hadn't lost the slashes of red paint.

Phoenix eyed the gathering crowd and smiled wide.

"We'll need an investigation into this," he announced. "Gather what you can and secure the silo. Betula, let me find us another cart back down."

Talie gave the astounded driver a weary grimace as she clambered down. Ankle-deep in shifting grain, she wondered who exactly would be behind the sigil.

The resistance becomes the next oppressor and a new resistance forms. Does it ever stop?

She wiped a hand over her face and almost scraped half her eyebrow off as a scream bounced around the lane. A small streak of dark brown flitted toward the cart, closely followed by a sturdy-armed woman holding a huge knife.

"Stupid waste of- Oh!" The woman tumbled to a halt in front of them. "Phoenix, forgive me. I was chasing one of our barrel rats that escaped in the chaos."

Given the hint of blood the woman slid her sleeve down to hide and the knife in her hand, the creature didn't want to be chased, much less found.

Irritation flared and Talie sucked in a breath as moisture beaded over her palms. A soft chittering noise, almost mournful, crept out from under the cart.

"Now, the creatures that carry the barrels are usually well trained," Phoenix said.

The woman sighed. "Most yes but that one's scrawny. Doubt it'll grow sturdy enough, and they become vermin if they can't work."

Talie clenched her fist against the side of the cart as memories from the children's home flashed in her head. She jumped down from the cart and scanned the space until a pair of large dark grey eyes blinked back at her. The creature chattered again and she held out a hand.

She'd never had much to do with barrel rats before but everyone knew about them. They carried barrels of grain in and down the levels through an inner network of air and water pipes. The poor thing was shaking but it looked more like one of the otters that Finola sometimes had in the gym with her.

"It's okay, I won't hurt you," she muttered.

The otter inched toward her while clinging onto the underside of the cart.

"You must have sticky feet or something, good for climbing. Reminds me of... Never mind, come on."

She tried to make a kissing noise like Finola usually did, but the barrel rat, otter, whatever it was, took a flying leap into her arms and the breath whooshed out of her mouth as a grunt.

Scrawny my behind. I'm going to regret this.

She edged out from under the cart and cradled the creature to her chest.

"If you don't have use for him, I'll take him."

She couldn't be sure about the 'him' bit, but she was adamant he wasn't going anywhere near the woman's shiny blade. The woman glanced at Phoenix. He shrugged.

Talie eyed the sleek brown coat and the patchy bits around his legs that looked like bite marks, while the creature gazed up at her with endless grey orbs for eyes.

"You'd be responsible for him," Phoenix warned, then frowned. "What am I saying? I'm not your father."

The barrel runner clapped her hands and the otter tried to climb under the neck of Talie's top.

"I'll be back to my task then," the woman said. "You'll catch the orb munchers that did this? Who knows how much grain's been lost or spoiled, and we're suff-"

"Yes, off you go, Hostia," Phoenix said with a bite to his tone behind the smile.

The woman hesitated then strode off swinging her knife, and Talie glowered daggers into her back as she walked away. Despite the otter bring hefty to hold, when he wriggled against her shoulder, his body stretched remarkably thin.

Like an arrow from the old stories, finding his way tight into my chest. Oh well, I've named him now.

"Do you want to see inside?" Phoenix asked. "We have other silos and the production centre."

Betula laughed. "Grain is grain for what we need it for, so no. I have to say, this does bring into question how likely it is you'll be able to provide the quantity we require."

Talie clung to Arrow with one hand and focused on checking him over as Phoenix shrugged.

"As I say, we have other silos, and as you say, grain is grain for what you need it for. An educated guess would say you need the grain in place of sand to douse glass fires."

Betula cocked her head. "Our need isn't relevant, but I think given the state your tower is in and the evident discontent, we'll probably need to stagger our order to be safe. We'll take one unit for now."

"One unit?" Phoenix frowned. "It'd be nonsensical to navigate the realm-skips for any less than three."

Talie had no idea how big a unit was, but Phoenix didn't sound happy about it.

"Two to start and that is my final offer. We can't spare any coin either right now, but I'd reckon you need influence over currency anyway."

"I'll take a favour from your tower, certainly."

"No favour. Influence is what you're lacking with the other towers and you'll need one on your side at the next communal moot."

Talie could almost feel Phoenix seething even though he smiled readily enough. He wasn't in a position to refuse any offer, although she didn't see what influence with other towers would get them when they already refused aid before.

He seemed to still be deliberating a suitable answer when another cart waded through the grain to stop alongside the first. The man aboard seethed through his teeth.

"I can tow you down, Sal," he offered.

Before Sal could agree, given her desperate look of gratitude, Phoenix shook his head.

"Never mind that, you take us straight to the Menagerie. You can come back up and start bringing the grain up while you're at it."

Talie grimaced at the snap in his tone. The carts didn't have a guild of their own but they were a tight-knit group and didn't operate under anyone's control.

The man didn't argue but given the tiny smirk on Betula's face, Phoenix's rule was unravelling fast and everyone could see it. Word would get round to the other towers who would all be knocking soon for discounts and ultimatums, probably while the cart drivers and guilds and nobles alike threatened to revolt from the inside.

Talie slid into the new cart and bunched herself into the tiniest corner possible as it set off down the levels.

"There's always an adjustment period," Phoenix said smoothly.

Betula smiled. "So they say. You won't win with common sense though, not in the long run. That was always your ideal, yes? Fae don't understand it and nobles won't want it. Fairness, kindness, they're illusions."

"Of course they are, but it has to be a gradual descent.

Our tower would never choose direct rule willingly because it's overtly punitive. Nothing in it for them but more hardship."

"The way things always have been." Betula didn't bother to hide her disdain as she eyed the lanes they passed. "The sooner they accept control, the better it will be for you."

Talie focused on Arrow contorting himself into coils on her lap as a chill set in her chest.

Phoenix shrugged. "Perhaps. Think of it this way then. Celeste drained our tower of resources placating the nobles for her gift extraction project. The normal Fae were too afraid of reprisals to fight back. I then offer them hope but with necessary evils to see it through. Those necessary evils further our plans."

Talie held herself as still as she could with her heart sinking and her rain gift lifting droplets of moisture into the air above them. They hung suspended in mid-air, but she still hadn't gotten the hang of drawing them back to her. She could only hold them or let them drop, and if her mood descended any more, holding them wouldn't be an option much longer.

Phoenix was as she'd worried, no better than Celeste. Different maybe but no better.

"Then when they realise your hope is nothing but smoke on the glass?" Betula prodded.

Phoenix smiled as the cart stopped outside the Menagerie.

"Then you swoop in with hard measures and they'll have no strength left, no choice but to fold in submission.

Gradual descent into our control, that's what gets them under heel in the end."

Talie focused on Arrow as he chased a falling droplet of rain so he could roll in it. She couldn't rule out Phoenix using this visit as an opportunity to test her loyalties against her morals, but either way he was another problem their tower really couldn't afford.

"You like water I take it," she murmured. "We're matched okay then."

She clambered down from the cart with Arrow clinging to her shoulder, and followed Phoenix and Betula to the Menagerie's entrance hall.

"That's all for today, Talie," Phoenix said over his shoulder. "Now, can I interest you in some of our grain spirit liquor?"

Betula shook her head. "I won't stay, lots to do. Send the two units and I will honour my debt of influence with the other towers at the next meet. Until then."

She gave a little wave, an almost mocking twiddle of her fingers, then vanished.

Phoenix strode toward the side-hall then changed direction toward the doors that led into the core's labyrinth, toward the sneering face of Mulberry, head of the boots that kept order in the tower.

Talie started a slow amble toward the bottom of the stairs where Sammy was hanging from the end of the banister talking to Nia, but she didn't need a hearing gift as Phoenix came to a stop.

Mulberry's hefty shoulders were hunched but he gave Phoenix a suitably chilling smile that could have passed for deference on a less frightening face.

"Get those you trust up to the grain stores," Phoenix said.

Mulberry's gaze narrowed. "To do what?"

"There's been a spillage. Interrogate all of them and have as many as you can sweeping up spilled grain to go to the Sunrise tower."

"By any means necessary?" Mulberry asked, his tone eager.

Phoenix hesitated. "No heavy measures, for now."

He stalked off toward the kitchens and Mulberry's expression twisted back into its usual sneer. Talie watched him disappear into the bowels of the Menagerie, no doubt to issue orders, and sagged as Sammy's gasp drew her attention.

"Cute!" Sammy smiled at Arrow, her brown eyes wide and hopeful. "Who's the rat?"

Talie rubbed a finger over his head as Sammy flicked her black braids over one shoulder.

"They were kicking him out up on the grain levels, so here he is. I called him Arrow."

"Hi, Arrow!"

Sammy held her hand out but Arrow had a firm grip on Talie's shoulders and his nose tucked behind her ear.

"Rude." Sammy shrugged. "Nia introduced me to some people so I'm going to see them. Don't wait up!"

Talie opened her mouth with a hundred warnings and questions bursting to spill out, but Sammy moved quick when she had to and was out of sight in seconds.

"Got yourself another hanger-on already?" Nia teased.

"Sammy's off on her own so you got a pet?"

Talie pulled a face. "Ha-ha. These friends of yours..."

"All above board. They're good kids from my defence classes. She's growing up, you can't protect her forever."

Talie frowned. Everyone kept telling her that but it was a hard habit to break, especially when Sammy was the reason she was walled behind the glass and not outside it wherever Molly was.

"These guys can be trained, can't they?" she asked. "Is Finola around?"

Nia nodded. "She's due in the gym tonight, but I have no idea if your barrel-rat would be any good at boxing. Looks more like a yoga kid."

She nodded at Arrow and Talie rolled her eyes.

If Arrow was trainable, then she would train him to navigate the tower's barrel tunnels.

Right out of the citadel to Molly with a message.

CHAPTER FIVE

MOLLY

~Royal Family~

Taz has added Demi, May and Molly to the ~Royal Family~ group chat

Taz: *I thought it'd be good to have an orb channel for just us.*

May: Spectacular idea.

May has added Kainen to the ~Royal Family~ group chat

Taz: WHY.

Kainen: I am utterly unsurprised to be here.

Molly: he's not, he squealed over the breakfast table

Kainen: Traitor.

Taz: This was meant to be for family only.

Kainen: I am family.

Taz: blood family.

Kainen: we're thirteenth cousins four times removed, or something.

Taz: immediate blood family.

Kainen: I've adopted Molly, logistically speaking. That makes me as immediate as it gets. You're just her uncle.

Taz has removed Kainen from the ~Royal Family~ group chat

"This is going to be fun." Kainen grinned wickedly.

Molly slumped over the breakfast table in Kainen and Reyan's bedroom with a groan.

"Be careful he doesn't get you uninvited from this picnic," she warned.

"The queen would never allow it. She actually respects me, as much as a reigning monarch is capable of respect for lowly Fae."

"Why?"

"I'll pretend that wasn't said with such disbelief. She sees me exactly as I am, Fae enough to trick and charm accordingly, and one who will be smart enough to play the ancient game of Fae politics rather than revolutionising it."

"But you're best friends with Demi."

"She sees that as strategy no doubt, keep the sides of power sweet until the tide turns one way or the other."

Molly sat back in her chair. "And are you?"

"Am I?" Kainen mimicked her stance, one eyebrow cocked. "Are you? If I were loyal to Demi over power, what's to say you won't run to the Oak Queen the moment she offers you something you want?"

Molly stared, heat similar to shame creeping over her shoulders and up to her cheeks.

"I would never!"

Kainen eyed her for a second then slammed a hand to his forehead.

"You're not supposed to admit that though, haven't I taught you anything? We're entering into the political shark tank of Fae nobility and you need to learn to smile sweetly and talk pretty. Can you flirt?"

She grimaced. "I doubt it."

Unnerved by the unexpected disappointment on his face, Molly looked up as Reyan walked in.

"Time to go. You look great, Molly."

Molly looked down at the simple muted pink linen trousers and shirt. The shirt was more like a long-sleeved t-shirt than anything formal, so she felt comfortable enough.

"Don't I look great, sweetheart?" Kainen asked.

Reyan rolled her eyes. "You know the answer to that."

She held out her hands and Molly took one while Kainen took the other.

"Oh, before I forget, the queen sent a summons for us to arrive in the entrance hall not the picnic ground." Kainen grinned as the nether swirled purple and grey mist around them. "Something about dressing Molly. So sad I remembered to forget or some such."

The bedroom disappeared in a swirl of nether and dissipated into a vast forest glade. Warm sunlight dappled the trees, the tables and chairs too, all decorated with gold and purple bows. Strategically placed picnic mats lay on the perfectly trimmed grass, and the scent of cake permeated the air even though no food had been laid out yet.

"There you are!" A familiar voice filled the air. "Look at you, pretty as a picture."

Molly smiled weakly as Marthe, the Oak Queen's head housekeeper, swept toward them and patted her cheek. Marthe had her silvery hair bunned up tight and her pale pink shirt and trousers were utterly crease-free.

"Think of this as a proper birthday celebration at the queen's command," she added.

A shiver flickered through the air and the Oak Queen appeared, her blonde curls left loose and her sharp eyes bright with determination. Although she wore a flowing dress of oak leaves and gold, the softness stopped at the hems. Molly almost forgot to bow until Kainen and Reyan lowered beside her.

"You were supposed to bring her to the entrance hall,"

the queen admonished.

Kainen sighed. "I take full responsibility, your majesty. The message came direct to me, an oversight indeed as I'm known to forget things on occasion."

The queen's lips pressed thin but another shiver of air brought Taz and Demi to them in much more casual clothing, along with other familiar faces. A round of bowing later, and Molly grinned as Ace and Milo gave her a joint hug, which Beryl spoiled by piling on top of.

"Where's Aurora?" Molly asked.

Beryl huffed. "Motherhood sucks. Nobody asks where I am anymore."

"Nobody asked that before either," Taz retorted.

Beryl stuck her tongue out at him and held out a beautifully ribboned pink gift bag to Molly.

"The tradition is to give you Fae gifts but I figured you'll need things to keep for your own as well."

Molly smiled. "Thank you, and you're right. A present without obligation or manipulation or debt is a true gift."

"We sent ours to the Illusion Court already," Ace said. "Everyone should have their own book collection."

Molly's smile widened as May hurried toward them, her arms glamoured to hide the tattoos and a suspiciously velvety gold dress with acorns draped around her.

"I also got you something physical, mainly because we can't gift others." She gave the queen a sour look.

"That's enough, Mayflower," the queen said. "Now, Molinia, there's time enough yet for you to change."

Molly sidled ever so slightly closer to the space between Kainen and Taz.

"No thanks, I'm good. Also, it's Molly."

"If you insist, but *I* must insist on proper attire. As part of the royal family, you are held to the most impeccable of standards."

"It's fine, Kainen's taught me which forks to use when."

The queen blinked. Hard.

"Knowledge of etiquette is a start, but-"

"Absolutely." Kainen slapped a hand on Molly's shoulder. "As I'm sure you'll remember, you crowned my sister Diana as Youth Etiquette Champion. Three times. We nobles must adhere to standards."

"And recognise the best of the noble traditions." Taz caught on fast.

"Although some could do with refreshing to be fair."

"Like the need to have thirty-six forks in the first place."

"Most of them are the same basic fork."

"Except that weird one-pronged one you use with all the others."

"You mean the knife."

Taz smiled sweetly. "Oh. Yeah. Also, Molly's too young to be in velvet."

"I was in velvet when I was twelve," May grumbled.

And you're still wearing it now," he retorted. "A clear sign it doesn't work."

"Probably not a wise idea to alienate the poor girl on her birthday either." Demi joined in.

Reyan nodded. "It's not like the nobles don't already have their sights honed and their claws ready."

Molly snuck a glance at the Oak Queen, who looked supremely unruffled by the mayhem except for the almost absent lips.

If they get any thinner, she's going to need them drawing on.

Molly cleared her throat, determined to stand her ground on at least one thing.

"I'll decide when and if I get married," she announced. "It certainly won't be happening today. I never asked to be royal."

Taz grinned. "You could always-"

A crack of thunder boomed overhead and drowned out the 'A' word no doubt tumbling from his lips.

"If any of you even *thinks* the word 'abdicate', there will be no mercy," the Oak Queen warned.

Marthe rushed over like a shining beacon of motherly calm, no doubt having heard or sensed her mistress's wrath. Molly tensed as Marthe lifted a hand between them, a simple golden crown carved into the shape of a many-layered daisy chain hanging from her fingers.

"Every princess should have a first tiara," Marthe said. "Arlo from the kitchens and a couple of the girls you worked with when you were here before wanted to chip in too."

Touched, Molly ducked her chin obediently so Marthe could settle the tiara on her head.

"There now. I tried to get it exactly like the daisies you planted."

Molly froze. She had completely forgotten planting a seed that Aurora had given her after their first meeting in a pot outside the royal Court palace kitchens. She'd assumed it was an acorn given the shape of it, but daisies were a welcome change to the royal emblem.

"Suits you," Reyan said. "I don't think any royal has ever had daisies as their sigil before. Just in time too."

Nobles appeared in the glade like a tidal wave of fine clothing and a ridiculous abundance of feathers.

No velvet, no feathers, ever.

Molly fixed a smile on her face as the Oak Queen snapped her fingers and the tables were suddenly groaning with the finest pastries, cakes and fruits.

She didn't recognise most of the nobles assembled but sank into the exhausting rounds of greetings and gratitudes, relieved that no matter who the Oak Queen led her to next, there was always Kainen or Taz or May at her side.

"I do believe it's customary for the princess to choose a noble to offer her first bite," one young man announced hopefully.

Molly had no hope of remembering his name let alone his title, but given the way he was looking at her she was glad she wasn't in velvet after all.

"A rudimentary principle," Kainen countered smoothly. "Several have been eating already, so it hardly matters now. Besides, as pretty as the princess is, you wouldn't want to miss the entertainment."

"There's entertainment?" Molly asked.

Kainen winked. "I'd estimate in three, two-"

"Kainen Hawthorn Merrytree Hemlock get your sorry excuse for a self here right now!"

Reyan's irate voice filled the glade and his eyes widened, a-glitter with sudden promise as his lips curved wickedly.

The trees burst into song a moment later, and what looked like very expensive fountains of wine appeared.

"I love it when she full names me." He pressed a hand to his chest. "Coming, sweetheart!"

"I'm going to make you suffer a very slow and agonising fate!"

Molly stared at his retreating back and a bubble of laughter escaped as he hurried in the direction of Reyan's fury. Before another random lord could step any closer, Taz appeared at his side and engaged him in determined conversation. That left Molly at the mercy of a woman decked entirely in periwinkle blue satin complete with a huge blue hat full of feathers. The woman waited for all of two seconds before loudly clearing her throat.

Taz turned his head with a smile that didn't quite meet his eyes.

"Lady Birchberry," he greeted her.

"Your majesty. I must say your mother does put on a very elegant show."

Taz shrugged. "One thing she's good at, sure. Molly, allow me to introduce Lady Birchberry, one of the nobility at the Nether Court."

Molly hesitated at the mention of nether, because she'd mostly forgotten the names of the courts she hadn't met yet, but she dutifully put on a smile as Lady Birchberry ducked her chin briefly.

"I understand you grew up with your mother in the citadel, Princess?" Lady Birchberry asked.

Molly shook her head. "Not entirely, but I was raised in

the citadel."

A blonde eyebrow lifted beneath the enormous hat.

"Not entirely? I must say, her majesty has kept everyone on tenterhooks for every little bit of information about you."

"Adds to the drama Fae love so much," Taz said.

"Quite. And you enjoyed citadel life, Princess? I have heard the calibre of the place has declined since the explosion."

Molly smiled. "There are so many different things to be heard that I have no time to establish what to believe. The citadel has been my home though, and I am hopeful they'll be able to rebuild and finally open the wards to the wider realms of Faerie one day."

Lady Birchberry's eyes widened. "You think that might be possible someday?"

"I have no idea, but I'm hopeful all the same."

"There is tell of secrets hidden within that even the citadel nobility don't have access to. I'm sure everyone would love to get their hands on that kind of leverage."

Molly gulped down the indignant huff brewing and clung desperately to her smile instead.

"Everywhere has its own secrets. The Nether Court must have plenty that you can't divulge, surely?"

"Well, certainly, but we are an ancient court full of scholars and we hold a lot of intimately arcane knowledge."

"Speaking of intimacies, you must meet Lord Bryson," Taz said. "He's Lord of the Nether Court, Molly, and his trusted team are friends of ours."

"There certainly have been a lot of peculiar choices of promotion recently." Lady Birchberry sniffed.

"Like what?" Molly asked.

The woman's cheeks tinged pink ever so slightly.

"Well, it's generally accepted that nobility and accession to title is a generational matter, to keep the bloodlines managed."

Molly sank into the ridiculousness of it as her irritability turned to wickedness.

"Why do they need to be managed? Is there some kind of deviancy that forms otherwise? Too many cousins, that sort of thing?"

"Well, I don't believe this is a proper topic of conversation for one so young."

Taz grinned. "Ah, Molly's good at flustering the nobility. She's like a cat among pigeons."

"It's all that climbing practice I had to do," Molly agreed, keeping her expression as grave as she could manage without bursting into laughter.

"Climbing practice?" Lady Birchberry gasped. "Surely as a princess, you wouldn't be expected to do anything physical."

"Faerie forbid," Taz agreed with a serious nod. "Molly, you be very careful that other people don't expect you to do anything physical."

"Okay. So, the Nether Court, do you only study the nether, or do you have any control over it?"

Lady Birchberry frowned. "Nobody controls the nether, but there are some ways of swaying it on occasion. The great mysteries of Faerie and beyond are known only to a select few across the various courts. Why, time was we had Fae investigating the likelihood of cloning. It was something to do with gift replication gone wrong."

Molly tensed, aware of Taz going deceptively still beside her.

"How so?" she asked.

"Well, the research suggests that some tried to replicate gifts using a complex process of gift-use and various potions, but they accidentally duplicated the Fae along with them."

"That might be considered somewhat far-fetched," Molly said quietly.

By anyone who hasn't seen and heard what I have.

"It wasn't actual duplication of course, that would be non-sensical, but given the supposed process for extracting the gifts to replicate, I'd say-"

"Molinia."

The queen's command cut across the entire glade enough that everyone fell silent for several seconds. The crowd noise rose again soon enough, but Molly almost screamed with frustration. She gave Taz a meaningful look but she couldn't disobey the queen in her own domain.

She crossed the grass toward where the queen stood and hovered in front of her.

"You need to make wider connections," the queen said.

Molly hesitated. "I am. I know a lot of people at the Illusion Court now, and Demi's. I know Marthe and some of the kitchen staff here, at least a little bit. I've spoken to some man whose name I don't remember, and then there's Lady Birchberry who was talking to me."

"The other queen's court is full of FDPs not the nobility, and the same goes for my kitchens in terms of lack of title."

"So people are only worth knowing if they're nobles?" Molly asked.

"The nobility are the sort of connections you can mould and trade on. You will one day need to call on favours as much you'll inspire loyalty."

"But not trust. Celeste said much the same and we all know what happened to her."

The queen hummed under her breath and surveyed the mass of nobles circling them at a respectful distance.

"Even Celeste, for all her arrogance, was part of a wider plan."

"So that was your doing then?" Molly folded her arms across her chest. "You placed her in the citadel with a view to taking over?"

The queen was silent for a long moment and Molly scoped out the running distance between herself and several of her friends.

"Celeste was a failsafe. The citadel has functioned outside of royal control and we agreed she would abdicate to keep an eye on it."

"But you had to know she'd try and take over."

"What she did was her doing."

Molly snorted. "A calculated placement by you, wind them up and let them do your dirty work for you."

"Be careful." The queen's tone was soft with warning. "You are the first of a new generation in the oak line and I have already given you several allowances I would not tolerate in my own children."

"You sound like her," Molly couldn't stop herself.

"Celeste? I would imagine so. She was the first I took great pains to educate. I seem to have drifted since with the rest." The queen's gaze moved to where Taz and May were smiling with Beryl and Demi. "Belladonna was always the ruthless one and her spitefulness spilled over. You likely won't meet her, but never say never. Blossom… she could have been a great asset. Her social skills were unmatched. Then Mayflower and Oakthorn have strayed. Mayflower tries to defy me at every turn, and Oakthorn is more of a burdensome emissary than a son. They're more likely to adhere to Demi's governance now."

Molly snorted. "Ever asked yourself why?"

The hint of pink edged its way across the royal cheeks and Molly firmed her warding as tight as she could.

"You might consider how much benefit you could gain from allowing some small measure of socialness," the queen replied. "There will always need to be an Oak Queen, or king I suppose, but there's nothing saying the crown can't skip a generation."

Molly frowned. "May should have it. I don't want a crown. I spent most of my life being raised as normal and then I got sucked into debt with Celeste and the Menagerie. I'm done being used for politics. I want to be free."

The queen lifted a hand and the crowd noise vanished, as though an invisible bubble had dropped around them. Utterly at her mercy, Molly's guts twisted into knots.

"Not even to help your friends? Whatever our reasons for ruling, whether those are to do with power or morality or simply out of duty, we can use our power to do good as much as anything else."

An image flickered in front of them, half-see through like an orb-cast, but Molly could see it clearly enough. She recognised the familiar stone lane curving around on itself with the metal beams and vast panes of glass. It didn't look like a level she knew of, but there were patched up gaps in the edges of the lane and a huge hole fenced off so the carts could go around. Several people sat on the edge of the lane, dishevelled with utter desolation on their weary faces.

"That's not real, it can't be."

"Isn't it? The tower came down and it takes a lot to rebuild such a large structure. The other towers aren't likely to be charitable either, not when there's profit to be had. You could change all that."

Molly shuddered. "You know what the Omens are, right?"

"I've heard many a tell of them. Demerara has told me what happened to you and Celeste, although I have no way of knowing exactly what transpired."

"You could have asked," Molly muttered.

She reached out a hand and felt the subtle zing of a warding domed around them.

"Perhaps. I'm more accustomed to being approached than approaching. I do so want this to be a fruitful partnership between us."

Molly assessed her options, the only immediate one being getting out of the queen's bubble warding.

"I'll consider it." *For like a second.*

The crowd noise swelled back around her but she couldn't even bring herself to look back as she darted across the grass toward Kainen, Reyan and Demi.

"Not here," Demi murmured. "Don't say a word. We'll convene. For now, play the part. Socialise. Agree to nothing."

Kainen nodded. "Thankfully, socialising is my forte. Molly, let me introduce you to the better half of the Fae nobility."

She let him put an arm around her shoulder as Reyan settled on her other side. Taking the queen's offer, if it was even that, wasn't an option but if the orb-cast of the citadel being in such a dire state was real, she had to do something.

"Lady Tira, Lady Lolly, Lord Tyren, may I present her royal highness, Princess Molly."

Molly couldn't stop the hysterical snort leaping out of her nose, but the gathered group grinned welcomingly enough in return.

She glanced around and took a deep breath. Given the small groups immediately edging closer to theirs, it was going to be a long afternoon.

CHAPTER SIX

TALIE

"Wrap your hands," Nia insisted.

Talie wiped her sweaty face on her bare arm and clung to the rope around the training ring with her other hand. An hour of training in the gym and she still couldn't shake the relentless frustration. Nia had agreed to spar with her but given the indignant chittering from Arrow, he didn't like the violence.

"Don't need to."

"You think I want your blood on me when you're done beating out your issues?" Nia scoffed. "Wrap your hands."

Talie grabbed wraps from her bag and wound them tight around her hands and wrists.

I did this for Molly. She's safe with her family, as she should be. And I'm in here with mine.

It didn't make her feel any better.

Nia took a stance as Talie ducked back into the ring.

"So, think you made the right decision?" Nia asked.

She ducked a punch and Talie gritted her teeth in preparation for a retaliation.

"How do you mean?"

Nia shrugged and swung, barely scraping Talie's shoulder.

"You chose to wall yourself back in here with us, instead of follow Molly to the great outdoors."

"What does it matter?"

"You don't exactly look... blooming."

"So? My hair's a bit longer but I can't be bothered to have it cut, so what."

"You're skinnier. Barely sleep given the circles under your eyes. Snap at anyone who dares spend more than the bare minimum of time with you."

"What is this, a mother's meeting?"

Nia grimaced. "Orbs no."

"Did Phoenix put you up to this?"

Nia stepped back and dropped her hands to her sides.

"Has he ever bothered before?" she asked softly.

No. Talie couldn't remember Phoenix taking much interest in anyone's emotional wellbeing before, now that she thought about it. *I always used to think it was because he was busy, important.*

"Sammy seems happy at least," Nia continued, and from anyone else it would be a taunt. "She's spending a lot of time with Azalea and Coni. Even Phoenix seems fond of her, said he'd invite her to do a couple of little 'favours' for him."

Talie heard the subtle warning in Nia's otherwise conversational tone and blood chilled at the thought. The rest of her burned hot with fury. After all the effort she put in over the years to keep Sammy safe, Sammy seemed more than happy to pull herself right into the things Talie had worked so hard to shield her from.

She hunched into herself and raised her fists ready.

"I'm done talking."

The hit Nia landed to her gut seconds later radiated a satisfying blossom of pain, slicing away the incessant carousel of regret.

She ducked and punched until her skin was streaming sweat and she could barely suck in a breath, but the same restless energy was still carved deep between her ribs.

"You're getting good."

She tensed at the sound of Phoenix's voice and lowered her hands as Nia stepped back. Phoenix stood with his arms braced on the ropes surrounding the ring so Talie tore the wraps from her hands and flexed her aching fingers.

"Work time?" she asked.

He frowned. "No, there's nothing yet."

"Nothing fixed yet either," she muttered.

"Well we are working on it. The start of progress is always slow and fractured. Betula's assistance is one of the first steps."

"All very well, but we've had no real help from the other towers beyond that, and the vents are suddenly 'mysteriously' set to the frostiest rear-end of winter with nobody left in the citadel apparently who knows how to fix them-"

She broke off and fought the need to press her hand to her chest, the ache there swelling enough to choke her.

Molly would figure out a way to fix it.

"These things take time," he insisted, the soothing tone

scraping to the bone.

"People are dying," she snapped. "That man whose mind I wiped from the Refuse Guild said they were getting rid of bodies, and I never even knew they did that. There have been loads, he said. If people are dying then we aren't doing what we're supposed to."

Talie pinned her lips between her teeth as the man from the Refuse Guild's words circled in her mind, words spoken in whispers shortly before she erased them from his.

"It's the missing bodies that worries me, gone before we can move them outside the glass. What would anyone need to take bodies for?"

"There's a lot of rot talked about death, Talie," Phoenix said, his tone scarily calm. "Yes, we've lost some in the fall of the tower, and sadly some since, but they're already dead, that's it. Gone. Any mourning is purely self-serving and those who pretend otherwise are hiding from the brutal beauty of the existence we live."

"Brutal beauty? That's what you call it?"

"There are bound to be casualties in troubled times like these, but we need to be focusing on the living. That's why these minds need clearing, and why the work you do for me is so vital. Can you imagine if they went around saying anything they liked to people with high emotions like yours? There'd be anarchy before we can get anything under control."

Talie held herself steady, her limbs never shaking even though her insides were bubbling hot with fury.

"And are we getting anything under control? We don't

seem to be doing much more than wiping minds and registering everyone. Besides, it's arrogance for anyone to assume they know best. All we get is a choice and taking that from people is wrong no matter the excuse."

Phoenix laughed but the sound had no humour in it. Talie didn't miss the subtle shuffle Nia made toward her, perhaps to defend. In a few short months that had lasted longer than lifetimes, she hated Phoenix as much as she feared him.

"I can still hear Molly's opinions speaking through you," he said. "It's not about taking choice, it's about loyalty."

"Blind loyalty without question? Does it have to be earned at least first? What's loyalty anyway? Fae expect you to pay homage to whoever you're born to, like some supplicant pet, or belonging. What about those who sacrifice things for you, or hold you up when you're about to fall?"

Phoenix sighed. "So many lofty words. I never should have given you that library card."

"Oh behave," Nia said, her tone stricken under a veil of forced friendliness. "Talie, we get you miss Molly and those who went with her, but we need to think of the greater good of the citadel. There are so many Fae still in here who deserve to live in a safe place with a fair shot at a good life."

"What's a good life without choice?"

"You think we should have held the walls open after all?" Phoenix's tone turned quiet. Contemplative. Dangerous. "Let the queens in with their whims and wants and opinions? Do you think they'd give people a choice?"

Talie's blood fizzled in her veins, her pulse pounding in her ears as she struggled to restrain her temper. She shoved her hands in her pockets to hide clenched fists and shrugged.

"I don't think. I know what I know, and I'm not anyone special to be knowing it." She scowled back at him while fighting to keep her control.

Too much vehemence and he'd remove her from the centre, not enough and he'd assume she was plotting behind his back while smiling to his face. She took a deep breath before continuing.

"Thinking's meant to be your job. If you're truly intent on the good of all the people in this tower, that can only be proven with actions. All I'm asking is what happens to the Fae who don't agree with your actions when you take them."

Silence swelled between them, a cavernous void that suffocated all the goodwill from the room, until Nia cleared her throat.

"I think we've all been overdoing it," she said. "It's late. I'll ask the kitchens to send food to our rooms and we can try again tomorrow."

Phoenix inhaled sharply, some kind of disagreement no doubt brewing on his tongue. After some hesitation, he nodded.

"As it is, perhaps we should hand out an olive branch of sorts," he suggested. "We'll call in the royals and perhaps there can be some trade they can offer us."

Talie guessed it was as much a test for her as it would

be for the royals to strike a deal for aid, but the thought of maybe seeing Molly again had that ache between her ribs easing slightly.

"If anyone can convince them, it'd probably be you," she muttered.

Phoenix cocked his head. "I'll *choose* to take that as a compliment."

Talie didn't risk an answer. She turned on her heel and stalked out of the gym with Arrow scampering at her heels before he could anger her further. The moment she was out of sight, she let her gift explode and the sudden deluge of rain from the vents sent people dashing inside, but she powered on until she reached a familiar turning.

The door to Molly's workshop was still shut, and the small house at the far end of the alleyway in darkness. The lane was too still, too silent, even with the faint hum of the vents above.

She had no key to either building, but that didn't stop her lingering. If only one of the doors would fly open and someone could come stomping out. If only she could find out Molly was okay, it would be enough.

No, it wouldn't.

She would probably beg whoever to get her out of the citadel and to Molly's side. Sammy never tired lately of telling her how self-sufficient she was, how she didn't need to be "smothered" anymore.

Screw the citadel. Phoenix is selling another tower of sand and they're all buying it, that's on them.

She wiped a hand over her face, her fingers welding to her cheek as a flicker of shadow caught her eye. Arrow chittered a warning and she squinted, unable to control her gift enough to stop the rain in time as the shadow took a half-form.

The vague outline of a woman she recognised became half-visible in the darkness.

The shadow turned her way and wavered.

Then it vanished.

Talie ignored the sinking sensation in her chest, used to the realisations that seemed to be stalking her lately.

Reyan had no reason to linger and talk to her, but the fact she had been inside the citadel meant Phoenix's tower of sand wasn't the fortress he thought it was. If Reyan was shadowing in, it meant those outside the citadel hadn't forgotten it.

Maybe even Molly hadn't forgotten it.

If she were to choose one of their Courts to stay at, I bet she'd choose Kainen and Reyan's.

Talie bit her lip and waited, but the shadows were utterly still so she set off back toward the main lane. She tried to rein in the not-so-subtle flutter of hope lighting in her chest, but she couldn't stop her gift responding to it.

As the rains dried up overhead, she let the thought of Molly out there somewhere no doubt causing some kind of chaos settle her nerves.

CHAPTER SEVEN

MOLLY

~Royal Family~

Taz: We should discuss a united front before we go into the citadel, especially as the queen is breathing down our necks about the results.

Molly: We were just about to leave. Besides, isn't Kainen taking the lead on all things your-mother-related?

Taz: well, yes...

Molly has added Kainen to the ~Royal Family~ group chat

Taz: stop doing that!

Kainen: you secretly like proving how much you miss me.

Taz has removed Kainen from the ~Royal Family~ group chat

Taz: We'll see you there in a minute.

Molly bit her lip as the flutter of anticipation tore through her gut. Kainen was grinning to himself still as he held out a hand and she took it.

"Let Taz do the talking," he advised. "It's his previous connection with Phoenix we're trading on, not yours."

Molly nodded as the nether wrapped around them and the achingly familiar entrance hall of the Menagerie came into view. She twisted around to look at the doors leading to the lane, but they were almost completely shut so she couldn't see out.

"Molly!"

She tensed on instinct and staggered under the sheer force of Sammy's hug a second later, but her gaze lifted past Sammy's shoulder immediately.

Talie stood with her arms folded over her middle, fighting wraps on her hands and an emotionless expression on her face. If not for the tiny press of her lips, Molly would have assumed Talie didn't even recognise her.

"Molly?"

She snapped her attention back to Sammy, who looked bright-eyed and well-clothed in smart jeans and a t-shirt. Even her hair was sleekly braided in a style Molly hadn't seen before.

"Huh?"

Sammy rolled her eyes. "I said how's life outside the glass but you're clearly distracted. Come on."

Molly flinched as Sammy grabbed her hand and towed her across the short space of the Menagerie entrance hall. Unlike Sammy, Talie's clothing was as worn in as ever, except for a familiar pink sweatshirt. Molly bit her lips between her teeth as she recognised it as *her* sweatshirt from her brief time incarcerated upstairs.

"Talie, Molly. Molly, Talie." Sammy waved a hand between them. "And go."

"We already know each other," Talie muttered.

"Yeah well, the atmosphere was turning pheromonal."

Sammy stalked off to where Taz and Kainen were talking to Phoenix, and Molly fought the tension in her limbs enough to nod awkwardly.

"Hi."

Talie frowned. "Hi."

"You're okay?"

"Do I not look okay?"

Molly bit her lip. "I didn't mean it like that."

"Hmm. How's the fancy new life then?"

"Too fancy," she retorted. "How's the gilded cage?"

"Still standing." Talie's lips twitched ever so subtly.

There was nothing left between them, no outstanding questions to ask or communal friends to enquire about. Molly thought of her workshop but she didn't want the answer, and yet her feet wouldn't move her away.

She cast a glance over the surprising hint of softness she

84

didn't recognise.

"Your hair's grown long."

Talie shrugged. "And yours is the same."

Molly took a step back. She still hadn't fathomed if Talie had a right to be angry with her or not, but she clearly wasn't suffering any heartbreak since they parted.

"You're still wearing that." Talie's voice turned soft.

Molly followed the line of sight down to her own hand and the *Akiai* heart charm she wore on her middle finger.

"Yeah, so?"

"Easy, Princess." Talie's lips lifted at the edges. "Just making an observation."

She lifted her hands in mock defence and her sleeve slid down.

"What's that?" Molly forgot her awkwardness and leaned forward. "A tattoo?"

Talie flinched and shook her sleeve down, but Molly had seen more than enough. A burn crept to her face as her pulse started to thud faster.

Sunshine and moor grass... surely...

"It's rude to stare," Talie snapped with her cheeks flushing. "Besides, that's not the most interesting one."

Molly ignored that and continued staring.

"You've got more?"

Talie nodded and tapped her stomach with two fingers.

"Yeah, but probably too racy for royal sensibilities."

Molly choked over a laugh. "Arrogant much? Don't worry about my sensibilities, Sunshine. Court life definitely isn't all hearts and flowers. I've probably seen stuff that would make your tattoos cower."

She stalked away toward the others with her insides flaring. No need to tell Talie the worst of it was walking in on that group doing naked yoga in the Illusion Court library.

"Welcome all. There are drinks provided in the dining hall, but perhaps we should walk and talk?" Phoenix announced.

Molly didn't bother to meet his gaze. As Kainen had said, Taz was commandeering the meeting so she would simply blend in.

I can't believe she has tattoos. What else don't I know?

She managed a weak smile as Sammy appeared at her side again.

"I would stay and chat but I'm meeting some friends and I can't let them down," she said. "It's all going to be trade talk Phoenix said anyway. Good to see you again, Molly!"

Molly stared as Sammy gave her arm a side-hug then jogged out through the ajar doors to the lane. She wanted to follow, to go and see for herself how bad the situation really was, but the others were waiting for her to join them.

"Well, I can start us off by saying our second-in-command would like access to your library," Taz said. "He sees it more as a demand, but then he's all for book liberation."

Phoenix smiled. "I know the type. There are places in our realms for all types, including the studious."

"What exactly is it you need?" Taz suggested. "Perhaps we should start there."

Molly fell into step with Kainen as they trailed behind

Taz and Phoenix. The whole time she was ever conscious of Talie a few steps behind her.

Is she his second-in-command now then? The thought had her nerves jittering.

"We're hoping to rebuild but costs are high," Phoenix said. "The day tower is asking an exorbitant amount for fresh glass, the other towers too for wood and metal. We supply grain and other things to the towers but those deals are already set, and they won't agree to take more in exchange for aid."

"So your plan is for us to provide it?"

"Nothing so charitable. The nobles are still patronising the lower levels but we need the entirety of their custom back."

"And you'd like us to provide it, to sway the nobility to see this as a prime spot to be?" Taz guessed.

"Exactly that. We wouldn't be able to offer you any power, to put it bluntly, but as you've said our library is one of the best."

"So I've been told. I'd need a few guarantees first."

Molly watched the discussion ping back and forth as the group rambled around the hall, up and down, back and forth. She stopped keeping pace with them, a not-so-tiny part of her wondering if Talie might do the same.

She didn't. If anything she dodged past to walk closer to Phoenix. Molly's heart sank.

She glanced at the doors that were open onto the lanes.

They have my orb details. She bit her lip. *Nobody needs me here anyway.*

The flicker of recklessness grew until her sunshine gift

tingled awake to warm her bones in agreement.

I might never get another chance again.

She waited until the group passed near the doors and slipped into her stealth gift. Kainen seemed studiously engrossed in the Menagerie's ceiling beams, and she knew she'd likely owe him for being so 'remiss' in guarding her later.

Before anyone could look back, she crept out of the Menagerie and into the lane.

The regurgitated air from the vents above was set to a brisk breeze, but the sunlight coming through the glass outside was bright enough to make it seem like spring. She set off past Fae going about their business on the main lane, then glanced to the side.

With a wicked smile, she changed course and hopped onto a nearby crate to scale one of the vast pillars. The climb was one she'd taken many times before and she reached the girders and wooden beams beneath the level above with a smile.

Tracing the familiar route across the rooftops, she continued going up the levels. The park looked much the same from above but her heart crunched when she saw Merry's kiosk with the shutter down.

She moved on with her heart sinking as her enhanced sight toyed with her pattern-seeking mind, and she saw the state of the citadel for herself.

So many loose tiles that would likely dislodge half a roof if they came down.

Several large stones and bits of leftover rubble waiting to upturn a passing cart into the nearest gaping hole onto the level below.

The odd weary face of someone dashing past, head down to hide the clawing fear in their eyes.

She shivered and soldiered on as the chill air from the vents bit through her sweatshirt. By the time she reached her old alley, worry had her insides aching. She dropped down in front of her workshop door and laid a palm on the wood.

There was a bag inside which could hold some of her stuff, and nobody could stop her going in to take it now or say it wasn't safe. She stood frozen for a while, wondering if taking it would be for the best or whether leaving it gave her enough of an excuse to come back.

Then again, what's the point? She sighed. *Talie's clearly moved on.*

She pushed away from the door and climbed back up to the beams. The short walk to where the end of the beam met the citadel's glass was still clear, and nobody had come to remove the cushion she'd put there a long time ago.

She sank down to sit on it and stared through the glass at the vast forest in the realm below.

It's not as if we were anything...

She couldn't finish the thought without lying, at least for her part.

So absorbed in her melancholy, she almost missed the subtle grunt of someone heaving onto the beam behind her.

CHAPTER EIGHT

TALIE

Talie glanced sideways as discreetly as she could manage the moment the group turned a corner, only to find no Molly.

Stealth gift. She smirked. *I wonder where she'll go first.*

She let her step slow but Phoenix didn't notice her disappearing from his side. As they continued on away from the doors, Talie whirled around and hurried straight out of them.

If she didn't know better, she would have assumed Molly completely missed her subtle warnings about not being too friendly in public. It was worth it either way to see her get all snippy.

She tugged her sleeve over her hands and clutched the hem in her fist as she powered up the levels. She couldn't risk Molly seeing the tattoo and figuring out what it meant, not when they hadn't spoken in months.

She turned down the alley and eyed the workshop door. Molly had no reason to hide her visit, but Talie eased the door handle down to check it was still locked before turning to face the orb-forsaken crates and pillar she would have to climb next.

All the mad things I do for this girl.

She eased herself up with quiet movements, still not comfortable despite the secret climbing practice she'd been sneaking out for in the dead of night. She came across Menagerie people on the beams sometimes, but they recognised her as one of Phoenix's chosen few and let her be.

She cocked her head to listen but there wasn't a single sound to suggest Molly, or anyone, was nearby.

Only the subtle scent that reminded her of Molly. She'd caught whiffs of it so fleetingly in the lanes that she'd followed it and spent her first lot of tide-over money from Phoenix on the bottle of body wash that smelled the same.

She smiled as she crept closer to the suspiciously flat cushion near the end of the beam and the citadel glass.

"Hiding, Princess?" she asked.

"What?" Molly's bodiless voice floated toward her. "Oh, right."

A second later she materialised, her legs folded beneath her on the cushion. Talie looked her over for some signs of change or sudden excessive elegance, but Molly looked exactly the same as she always had, right down to the slight quirk of a frown on her face.

"Have they called me back already?"

Talie shoved her hands in her pockets and shook her head.

"No, but I guessed you wouldn't have gone far. Is it all as you remember it?"

A stupid question, because the entire tower was wrecked, but her mind had scrambled.

"Yeah, scarily so."

Talie frowned. "Scary how? Doesn't live up to your expectations now?"

"You really don't think much of me, do you?" Molly shrugged and Talie's heart plummeted at the resignation on her face. "It's scary how being back here feels like I never left."

Talie dropped to sit beside her and Molly shuffled aside to give her half the cushion. Before she could find something to say, a disgruntled chittering filled the air.

Molly flinched as Arrow scampered across her legs.

"Is that…"

"This is Arrow." Talie waited to see if Molly was afraid of barrel-rats like she was birds. "He kind of made me adopt him."

Molly's eyes lit up. "Hi, Arrow."

She held out her forefinger and grinned as Arrow reached out for it with his little sticky paws.

"He's adorable! How did he come about?"

Talie bit down a laugh as Arrow made himself at home in between Molly's crossed legs, rolling around and around.

"Long story, but he leapt at me and I decided to keep him safe."

Molly sighed. "A lot has changed in four months."

"Do you miss it? Or has the glamour of court life managed to seduce you instead?"

"Can't it be both? I like the Illusion Court but it's not

home. Now here doesn't feel like home either but I miss it still, and wherever I go I'll have a title hanging over my head so it's irrelevant anyway. I hate that side of it."

Talie flexed her fingers inside her pocket as the urge to reach out and hold Molly's hand swelled.

"What brings you back here then?"

"Up here where nobody knows me, besides you, or back to the citadel?"

"Let's go with the citadel."

"I still don't agree with a lot of what's happened." Molly shrugged. "Kainen and Taz figured I'd want to come back though, and I'm not going to say no. It looks... not exactly great."

Talie smiled and reached out a finger to stroke Arrow's head, content to have even a fingertip of contact with Molly's jeans.

"How diplomatic. It's not great at all right now to be honest. The other towers aren't supporting us beyond the odd trade tipped in their favour, which is why Phoenix has had to ask for outside help."

"The nobles aren't helping I take it."

"When do they ever?"

Molly stared out over the realm beyond the glass.

How much of Faerie has she seen already? Talie wondered.

"Apparently, nobles have always had a stake in the operation of the citadel. It's not self-sustaining at all. Stuff goes out, stuff comes in, and nobody is ever told about it."

Talie sighed. "Not that long ago I wouldn't have believed you."

Molly tilted her head and Talie sank into the familiar gaze as it landed on her.

"But now?"

"Now, let's just say there are doubts everywhere."

"Is that the Talie equivalent of saying I was right?"

"Don't push it." Talie couldn't stop her lips twitching. "But things aren't rebuilding at all, and I'm having to use my gift on random people for weird things."

"Can you tell me any?" Molly asked.

Talie hesitated. "I can, but I'm not even sure what it all means, if anything. I found mentions of gift extraction in your friend's old room though, you know, Celeste's puppet."

She waited for the inevitable grimace but Molly only bit her lip and looked away through the glass again.

"Oh."

"There's stuff about gift duplication too." She watched the subtle tensing of Molly's shoulders and a tiny flicker of hope lit warmth in her chest. "And then there have been a lot more bodies leaving the citadel via the refuse guild."

Molly frowned. "It's adding up but I can't see the whole puzzle yet. I'm not even really meant to be getting involved anymore."

"Too busy with the royal waves?"

The words were out before she could stop them but Molly only scoffed quietly.

"Too busy avoiding having to do royal waves more like. The Oak Queen despairs every time she has to deal with me, but I'm stuck with it now."

"What happened to seeing all of Faerie then?"

Molly sighed. "I'm waiting for things to calm down so I can find an excuse to leave, but I need to earn enough first."

"You haven't inherited bags of money then?"

"Of course not. Why would they give me money when they could use it to control me instead? No, I'm earning it or not at all. I've taken on commissions at court already, which the nobles think is charmingly eccentric, and Kainen helped me get an account with the bank of Faerie, but several have told me to keep some items like gold or jewels, as if I have any jewels."

Talie smiled. "I'd have thought loads of fancy relatives would be lining up to drape you with stuff."

"Only as a loan which carries an unspoken debt to be owed. Even the Oak Queen tried, but I've not exactly endeared myself by being amenable."

"You not amenable?" Talie didn't even bother to fight the grin that broke free, elation tumbling inside her limbs until the glass in front of them missed with condensation. "Surely not."

Molly lifted a finger and swiped it gently through the damp with a smile, then shunted her shoulder into Talie's.

"Shove off," she muttered.

"Oh strong words from royalty."

"Only the best, Sunshine."

Talie froze as Molly lifted her head which put them inches apart. The daylight picked up the summertime blue shades of her eyes, but the gleam on her golden hair was as much as giftery as it was natural light.

"Still glowing then," she said softly.

Molly shrugged. "Not so much lately. You smell different."

"Fancied a change."

"Is it the one Merry's sister brews?" The tiniest hint of a smile lit on Molly's face. "With the little orange flowers that grow in the park?"

Talie heard the unspoken 'the one I use' tacked on the end of the questioning.

"I guess. Beats the purple one."

She bit her lip, torn beyond reason as Molly glanced her way. Her gaze clicked down momentarily, then back up.

Screw it.

She leaned forward but Molly flinched, then uttered a low feral grumble.

"Of all the-" She hauled an orb from her pocket and the shimmery grey orb-cast of Kainen's amused face bounced between them. "What?"

"His majesty has demanded your return. We're about done here. Also, that is not how one answers an orb call in polite society."

"Well, when I get a call from polite society, I'll try again."

She swiped her thumb across the surface of the orb to clear the image, but Talie was still trying to get her residual panic under control.

"I'd better go," Molly said.

Talie nodded. "Back to your courts and castles and tea parties."

"It's not like that!"

She clambered to her feet and held her hand out. Molly

eyed it for a draw out moment then took it, the firm weight painfully familiar as Talie hauled her up.

"If you say so." Talie started back along the beam. "You have to wear dresses a lot?"

"Rarely. I spend most of my time hiding in the workshop. The court will forget about me soon enough and find a new toy to chase."

Talie hesitated at the edge. It was quicker to take the rooftops down the levels but Molly was already past her and dropping down into the alley.

She doesn't know I've been training with the climbing. I can't assume she's choosing the lanes because they're the slower way back to give us more time either.

She climbed down and settled in to walk at Molly's side. Several people gawked as they past, and a few waved hesitantly.

"Popular, aren't you?" Molly muttered, although she looked uneasy.

Talie smiled. "Not me they're eying up. You've been gone a long while."

She didn't mean it to sound accusatory but Molly grimaced.

"I did think about trying to train Aurora to bring in a letter but I wasn't even sure what I'd say."

Talie's heart lifted. "Well, I don't have birds to send letters, but I would have been glad to know you were okay."

"Didn't think you'd worry all that much. You got what you wanted."

Talie caught the strain of bitterness underneath Molly's

deceptively even tone, but instead of making her relieved, it hurt.

"Phoenix said he might be able to help us find out who Sammy's parents were. It's something she's always wanted to know."

Molly halted and Talie turned to face her.

"Phoenix can see truths and word-tangle enough to almost lie," Molly said sceptically. "Why would you believe him without proof?"

Good question, Princess, but I can't risk telling you the whole truth.

"You might be right, but Sammy's getting drawn more into Phoenix's world and I have to protect her."

"All your life?" Molly sighed. "I understand though, she means everything to you. Well, I'd give you a parting gift if I could but only court nobles and the queens can gift, and I haven't sworn to a court."

"I don't need gifts."

They continued walking and Talie's gut crunched tighter with each step closer to the Menagerie. Molly seemed equally gloomy and Talie couldn't bear it.

As they reached the doors, she grabbed Molly's hand.

"Be careful when it comes to digging too deep." She twitched her gaze toward the group waiting inside for them and widened her eyes meaningfully. "Never know who might be doing the same. If you wanted to send Aurora though, let me know how you're doing, that'd be okay I guess."

It took every ounce of her effort not to bridge the distance and press her mouth to Molly's, but Molly glanced through the doors instead.

"Yeah, I got you. It's been nice seeing you again."

Talie tensed as Molly wrapped a firm arm around her shoulders and the other about her waist, then she did the same and clung on tight as Molly's lips wisped against her jaw.

"Be safe, Sunshine."

Talie managed to let her go, barely, as Molly pulled free and strode through the doors.

"I wanted to see the old haunts one more time," she announced. "Are you finished?"

Talie watched her walk toward the others and the tugging ache, blissfully absent for the past few minutes, crept back between her ribs. Every part of her screamed to go to Molly's side, hold her hand and cling on until they were far outside the citadel. She could find work somewhere, do anything, but she kept a safe distance away as Taz and Phoenix concluded their business.

"Lady Rain." Kainen appeared in front of her with a grin and a flashy bow. "How's life treating you?"

Talie shrugged. "Could be worse. Could be better."

"Sure we can't convince you away for a short holiday to the wonders of the Illusion Court? No debt or obligation."

Talie's chest squeezed.

It would be so easy…

She grimaced. "I can't. Phoenix has me doing a lot and Sammy is here…"

"Ah, yeah. She's clearly settled herself with firm friends here."

The unspoken 'and you clearly haven't' settled between them and Talie rubbed her thumb over the frayed wrapping on her knuckles.

"Speaking of your sister," Kainen announced. "Hello again."

Talie glanced over her shoulder as Sammy hurried past.

"I forgot my coat!"

Talie rolled her eyes and Kainen gave her a rueful smile, very unlike the courtly lord mask she'd often seen on his face.

"I'll be in touch then," Taz said.

Phoenix nodded. "I look forward to a fruitful partnership."

Talie's chest pounded so hard that she struggled to breathe as Molly disappeared along with the others. She fought to keep an emotionless mask over her face, but Phoenix gave her a wary look and Arrow grumbled a warning beside her ear.

"That must have been difficult," he said. "Take today off, no training with Nia either. Go for a walk or something."

Talie bristled instinctively at being directed down to, but Phoenix strode away toward the Menagerie kitchens without a look back. She sighed as Sammy skidded past in her fancy new red coat.

"Don't wait up!"

"Hang on." Talie slid her hands into her pockets. "Who exactly are these friends?"

Sammy frowned. "People Nia knows from the gym. They're my age and we go play games in the park. Why?"

"I'm just looking out for you."

"Well you don't have to." Sammy huffed. "I appreciate it but I'm a grown woman now with friends and a life of my own. This is what we wanted. It's what we came back for."

Talie sighed. "I'm used to worrying. It's what I do."

"You can't mind me for the rest of my life. You can stop now. We're okay. The Menagerie is a safe place and Phoenix has us protected. You need to stop using me as a shield against having emotions. Go live your own life."

The words stabbed against Talie's chest even though they were said gently. She wiped a hand over her face.

"I promised I'd protect you, and I'm still going to do it. Phoenix might be in control but that doesn't mean it's going to be safe forever."

Sammy scoffed loudly. "And you think you can protect us from grown adults with bountiful power? Phoenix was right."

"Right about what?"

"Nothing." Sammy hesitated. "It's nothing."

"Clearly isn't nothing. What is he so right about?"

"It doesn't matter now."

"Sammy." She put every inch of her rising fury behind her tone. "We promised each other no secrets."

"It really doesn't matter now, and I promised not to tell."

Talie folded her arms and used the anchorage to cling tight to her last remaining shreds of control.

"What exactly have you promised not to tell? You're seriously choosing to take someone else's promise over the one we made to each other?"

Sammy glanced around. "I promised I wouldn't say anything because it'll make you feel bad, but fine. You never needed to protect me it turns out, because Phoenix is the man that saved us."

"From what?"

"He's always been looking after us. It's been him all along."

Talie hesitated, the threads of all of Phoenix's machinations over the years tangled in her mind.

"He might think that, but Celeste was the one that chose me," she tried.

"Even before that." Sammy glanced around and lowered her voice. "Do you think we all ended up at that same home by choice? Do you think Celeste chose you randomly? Do you really think my friend at school could manipulate my orb to get through the wards, when even nobles can't get round being tracked through them?"

Talie stared as the horror trickled over her skin in tiny droplets of moisture. Arrow chased one across her cheek, his whiskers tickling her nose, but she brushed gently him aside.

"Phoenix gave you that orb? You said it was someone at school."

"He had the boy at school give it to me. This whole time, he's been protecting us. You said he was part of the Menagerie before in disguise? Well, he's been orchestrating the whole thing all along."

"And he told you this?"

Sammy smiled, a devoted lift of her lips that had Talie's

pulse pounding at a sickening pace.

"He intimated it, and I'm sure one of the boys in my group is one of his chosen ones. He keeps dropping little hints of things that only someone who knew about us when we were little could know."

"Why us then?" She had to ask.

"Not a clue, it's not like Phoenix and I are actually close, not like you and him are. But he has been paying me more attention recently. He even said that everything happening in our tower is his orchestration to keep the citadel in safe hands."

Talie looked around at the Menagerie hall, then at the spot where Molly had just been standing.

I could have gone with them. Sammy's happy to be brainwashed, so anything I say now will bounce right off.

"He even said that if the Oak Queen had gained access the way she always planned to, the whole thing would have been beyond even his skill to save, so we're very lucky he was successful."

Talie let her babble on and sucked in every bit of information. She would need to find Finola and beg her to train Arrow to take a message out to Molly somehow. She would use all her spare time to lurk around the alleyway outside Molly's workshop, maybe find a way to leave an obvious note in case Reyan reappeared again.

"I actually met him when I was really young apparently," Sammy added. "But he says I won't remember."

Talie grimaced. "You did?"

"Yeah, when I was still with Birch, and Birch told me I

could trust Phoenix. I do have a hazy memory of the name, but I asked Phoenix yesterday and he said we were only in that home because Celeste put you there, and that he has been looking after us ever since. That's why he gave you your job too."

Talie nodded, her entire body numb.

This whole time he's been controlling all of it. He probably convinced Celeste to give me my mind-wipe power, had Sammy and Birch put into the home to keep me on side so I'd have someone to stay for.

The entire map of Phoenix's planning unfolded in front of her, the complicated network set out so he could slowly gain power and take over the citadel.

"This was his plan all along," she muttered.

"Well, maybe, but he's still going to set everything right when he can."

"Oh, so he's going to open up the citadel, is he?"

Sammy frowned. "If he's said he will. Until then, he says he needs our support, yours more than anyone's."

"I'll believe it when I see it."

"That's your problem." Sammy took a step back, no doubt thinking of her fancy new friends waiting for her. "You don't trust anyone. Look, I get it's a shock, and now I see why he told me not to tell you. We had a room to ourselves when he stepped in, and you had the gym and I had school. Okay, that first home wasn't great, but we were safe enough."

"Safe?" Talie shook her head in torment. "How naïve can you be? *You* were only safe because- forget it."

"No go on, because you want to have the monopoly on

controlling safety. There's only a year between us and I'm not a child anymore."

"You might as well be if you can't see what's really going on."

Sammy scowled. "No, you just have a saviour complex. Why didn't you stay with Molly? You were happy, but no you abandoned that, abandoned her, because you feel like you have to be the saviour and the sacrifice. But that's your choice because you can't bear the thought of being happy. You're scared."

Talie winced and Sammy sucked in a breath as regret shivered across her face.

"All of this was to give you a chance at a life you wanted, one you could choose," Talie bit out. "Consider me relieved of 'saviour' duty. You have your life free of demons thanks to me but that's it. I'm done."

She shuddered as the memories of long ago swarmed in, nightmares made real from before she grew claws and learned where to punch, back when Sammy was too young to know better. She waited a beat for Sammy to say something, anything.

When nothing came, she stalked away and headed up the stairs. Rain beaded over her head but she didn't even bother to curb the drips forming on her skin as Arrow planted a foot to her neck to keep his balance.

I truly can't trust anyone. She bit her lip hard. *Molly was right all along. I can't call Phoenix out on it either. Sammy will tell him I know, and I need to be in control of myself when he comes to test my loyalty again.*

She needed distraction before facing him and saw Nia

up ahead.

"Do you have time for some artwork?" she called out.

Nia gave her expression the briefest once-over and frowned.

"You want me to draw something for you?"

"On me."

"Oh okay. I can ask Phoenix-"

"Not him. You do it. You've done them before, right?"

Nia's eyes softened in understanding. "I have but Phoenix is better at it than I am, and steadier handed."

"I don't want him doing it. These are just for me."

"Alright. Go to your room and I'll get the bits."

Talie let the recent ideas of what she would get next fill her head to sweep away the worst of the anguish. If Sammy truly was determined to dig herself into the citadel's happy-clappy-pro-Phoenix group, and to keep secrets for him, then she was done with all of it.

"What are we doing then?" Nia appeared and shut the door behind her. "I'll trade you a cover for it. I might need to be absent for a day sometime soon."

Talie wanted to ask why but nodded instead. Covering Nia's responsibilities, whatever they were, would be a cheap cost for free ink.

"You remember Molly's bird?" she asked. Nia nodded. "I want her with a green ribbon in her beak. If you can put acorns on the ribbon, all the better."

Nia hesitated, as if questions were bursting into nothing on her lips for several moments.

"Okay. Where?"

Talie tapped her hipbone.

"That's going to hurt," Nia warned.

Talie settled herself back on the bed and pulled the hem of her trousers down just enough to expose her hipbone.

"Good."

She sank into the distracting bite of pain as Nia got started and let her mind settle.

I might never see Molly again if he finds out what I'm planning but so be it. Then I'm out of here.

CHAPTER NINE

MOLLY

Molly settled the tip of her tongue between her teeth and slipped the wire coil into the setting of the atomiser she was working on with micro-movements. She waited, breathless with hope, but for the first time in several tries, the coil didn't spring back out again.

"Thank Faerie." She slumped back in her chair.

The chair was her favourite thing about the new workshop at the Illusion Court because of the extra-padded back rest, and it had thick arms with compartments for screws and pliers and all sorts of useful things.

As she slid the cap over the coil, she eyed the rest of the workshop. Her enhanced sight gift made the dust dance in the flickering Faelight from the nearby fireplace, and the flames had hues of blue and white in them, sometimes even a beautifully vibrant green.

All this because I had the sheer random luck of being born to someone and not someone else.

Her orb warmed in her pocket and she pulled it out to find a new message.

~Kainen Sucks~

Demi: what time is Reyan going visiting this afternoon?

Molly: I don't know, she had some things to do this morning so I guess after that?

Demi: Kainen?

Molly: Taz kicked him out of the chat again.

Demi: oh for orbs' sake.

Demi has added Kainen to the ~Royal Family~ group chat

Taz: What did you do that for?

Kainen: hello, lover! Great chat title.

Taz: NOPE.

Taz has removed Kainen to the ~Royal Family~ group chat

Molly snickered and pushed her orb into her pocket. The workshop was silent around her but it was fast becoming as familiar as the one in the citadel.

Five days had passed since their visit to the citadel, and while Talie was clearly still fighting out her feelings given the hand-wraps, she was okay. It wasn't enough, but until she had more information, Molly couldn't exactly go charging in.

She pushed herself away from her workbench with a groan and set off to find Reyan. It still unnerved her that nobles would stop in the halls as she passed and bowed their heads in some kind of deference, some with thinly veiled sneers and others with opportunistic smiles.

"Meri!" She walked faster when she saw Kainen and Reyan's second-in-command.

Meri turned around with an armful of clipboards.

"Do you need a hand?" she asked.

Molly nodded. "I'm looking for Reyan."

"Ah." Meri hesitated and cocked her head, as if listening to something inaudible. "Back decks, lower tier. Do you need me to show you?"

"No thanks, I'll find it."

She had to ask maids twice but finally opened a door and got hit by dazzling sunshine.

"Come on out, I'm just picking up some weeds," Reyan said.

Molly shaded her eyes and ventured out onto a semi-circular wooden deck covered with colourful plants in pots. She glanced up to the craggy side of the mountain that the Illusion Court was based in, then a familiar scent wrapped around her and her chest squished tight.

"That smell, what is it?" she asked.

Reyan frowned. "Smell? Oh, you mean the citrus one? That's the lemon balm bushes. These ones."

Molly crossed the wooden decking and peered at the bush Reyan was prodding as the scent that reminded her of Talie clogged her nose. Not the new smell Talie had basically stolen from her that she somehow couldn't find outside the citadel, but the one that reminded her of late night creeping side by side and getting slammed to the mats in the gym.

"I'm going to use this in some of the perfumes we're planning to produce," Reyan said.

Molly sniffed again. "It smells familiar. I'd trade for it if you make like a soap wash or something."

"Consider it done. We could say 'endorsed by the Crown Princess of Faerie."

"Eww, but sure. Oh, Demi said when are you going visiting."

"Orbs, I forgot. I'll go now."

Molly rubbed a couple of the lemon balm leaves between her fingers as Reyan frowned.

"Oh." Reyan's lips twitched. "You have a visitor apparently. We should deal with that first."

"What visitor?"

Wild thoughts of Talie having escaped the citadel filled her head, but the air shivered and a vaguely familiar face that definitely wasn't Talie's appeared.

"Princess." The woman bowed her auburn head to Molly, then to Reyan. "Lady."

"Lady Violetta, right?" Molly asked.

"Vi, please." She smiled. "I'm surprised you

remembered."

"I won't be long," Reyan said, then vanished.

Molly frowned. "Why wouldn't I remember? What brings you to the Illusion Court anyway?"

"There are any number of nobles wafting around courts at any one point, Princess," she teased. "I'm honoured to be one of the memorable few."

"It's Molly. No need to keep calling me by title."

She didn't want to admit that it sounded wrong coming from anyone's lips but Talie's and went for an awkward smile instead. Vi had forgone the dress Molly had seen her in last for a pair of neat dark green overalls and a pale pink t-shirt.

"If you insist." Vi laughed. "As it is, I've been tasked by the ruler of my court to come and befriend you, I believe at the queen's insistence."

"Orbs, she really doesn't give up," Molly muttered. "Are you spying for her now then?"

"Nothing so insidious, Pri- Molly. I mean, if she threatens me I can't very well refuse, but I've no intention of telling tales unless forced."

"Close as I'm going to get to having friends I guess."

"I don't believe it was friendship the queen has in mind. She's touting around for potential suitors. Lady Lolly thought I might be the least objectionable from the Flora Court."

"So how does this work then? I'm supposed to show you favour somehow, but I don't exactly have anything of my own to give yet."

Vi waved a hand elegantly, but Molly noticed she didn't

bother to hide the scuffed nails and calluses under a glamour this time.

"Firstly, you're a princess. Your attention alone is favour enough. The payoff comes from being the go-between. If I'm seen to be part of your inner circle, Fae will be lining up for *my* favour and that will come with trades."

"That sounds exhausting."

Vi nodded. "It can be. It can also be incredibly useful. For example, you might tell me you need a specific type of event or item from my court in passing. I might suggest that we have tea somewhere public so that I can give it to you."

"And be seen giving it."

"Exactly."

"I hate being noble."

"You're not." Vi chuckled. "You're royalty."

"That's worse!"

"Maybe, but I heard you have a crown now?"

"Yeah, a gift from the Oak Court, kind of."

"You should be seen wearing it. The gesture alone might give the queen reason to back off a bit. Give a little and ask for a lot."

Molly wiped a hand over her face with a ragged sigh.

"I'm still getting the hang of all this."

Vi leaned closer. "I'd be more than happy to teach you."

"In public I take it?"

"Or private if you prefer." Vi's voice lowered a note. "I'd have absolutely no objection to private audiences."

"What, now?"

Vi laughed again and shook her head.

"Perhaps not, unless you command it? I only came to re-introduce myself, but I'd be more than happy to be at your disposal should you see fit to invite me."

Molly stared. "Oh! Right. Would you be free then for tea? I'm not sure where'd be best to go but I'm guessing Kainen and Reyan would insist on chaperones and all sorts if it's somewhere public."

"That's so kind of you, I'd *love* to. I'll send you an orb invite and you can let me know if that works for you."

Molly nodded, dazed by Vi's boundless determination. She managed a ridiculous wave as Violetta bowed again and disappeared into the nether with a wink lingering behind her.

There's probably someone I'm snubbing by inviting her to tea outside the bounds of the court first. Why does it always have to be tea?

She rubbed at her forehead again and almost scored her nail through her eyebrow as Reyan re-appeared.

"That was a quick audience," she said.

Molly shrugged. "That was a quick visit to the citadel. What's going on?"

"Nothing catastrophic, but a lot of people are complaining in corners that at least before they had choice, even if there weren't many actual opportunities. I couldn't linger too long, but one woman did mention being 'processed' to get an idea of who they are."

"Processed, like resources," Molly spat.

Reyan nodded. "I know, it sounds like it. I didn't know where to go to find out what 'processing' is. Maybe I should have but I figured you'd want more personal news."

Molly's chest thudded once and seized.

"You mean Talie?"

"Yeah. You want the truth?"

"Always. Is she okay?"

"Physically? Yeah. Bit bashed up around the edges but she had her hands wrapped up so I couldn't see the worst of it."

"She's probably been fighting."

"Maybe. She looked tired though, and she was questioning someone with a bunch of people waiting outside. Guards on the door too. She looks defeated, that's the only way I can put it, but I'm sure it's not that bad."

"Is there any way to get people out sneakily?"

Reyan sighed. "Not through the shadows, no, or I'd offer in an instant. We can't ask Milo either because of he's sworn to Demi. It would take either a strong show of force storming the citadel which Demi wants to avoid while they're not provoking us, or sending someone in to try and establish a realm-skip, assuming we can even build another one now Phoenix has the wards up again."

"Surely we can try?"

Molly pulled her orb out of her pocket.

~Kainen Is BANNED~

Molly: I think we should have tea, or whatever

Demi: Okay, Taz can you cover please.

Taz: I'm not talking to him.

Molly: He's not here

Taz: Okay fine.

Reyan rolled her eyes as she read the exchange over Molly's shoulder and a few seconds later the air shivered and Taz appeared. He cast a suspicious glance around then his shoulders settled and he smiled. Molly fidgeted with the *Akiai* charm on her finger while Reyan related the information again, and Taz sighed.

"We'd need to prove the Fae actually want to leave first, or we're risking breaking our agreement for nothing."

Reyan nodded. "What if we set up a teeny skip-way somewhere inconspicuous? I had the quickest of looks a while back and it doesn't look like the workshop is being watched anymore."

Molly lifted the chain around her neck and undid the clasp so she could slide her workshop key free.

"It's yours still, at least as far as we're assuming, so we'd need your official permission," Reyan said.

"You have it. Whatever you need."

Taz frowned. "Don't promise things like that. Someone else will take 'whatever you need' literally and you could be held to it. We really need to do some proper safety training at some point."

"Fun," Molly retorted. "Kainen's been trying a bit."

"Orbs, that's a horrifying thought."

116

Reyan snickered. "I'll tell him you said that and he'll be even more delightful to you if you're not careful."

"Can you take me with you?" Molly asked.

Reyan glanced at Taz, who shrugged.

"You have to promise me you won't go anywhere, no leaving the workshop, straight in and back."

Molly nodded. "I promise."

"No leaving any hidden notes or anything, no taking or moving anything, just in case."

The thought of the *Akiai* charm currently nestled in her pocket, the one she'd spent late nights trying to get right in case she ever had an opportunity to gift it, flew into her mind.

"I promise," she said grudgingly.

I'll make sure there's another opportunity.

Taz leaned forward and pressed his thumb to Reyan's forehead.

"I gift you with the ability to set down one skip-way inside the citadel boundaries that will allow folk to venture in and out past any wards between."

Molly stared at him with her jaw dropping.

"You can do that?!"

He sighed. "Best you don't dwell on that for now. It only brings trouble. Go on, and I'll go report back to my better half."

He disappeared and Molly took Reyan's hand with her pulse picking up an unhealthy pace. The nether swallowed them and she stared around moments later as the walls of her workshop formed around them.

"I can't take or leave anything at all?" she asked.

Reyan shook her head. "No, and while we're here away from other royal ears, I'm guessing the plan will be to use this skip-way to enquire if there's anyone who wants out, or if there's any justification for us intervening. Right now, we're doing the diplomatic thing and opening up trade routes, but with the well of power down below we can't take any chances."

Molly nodded. "I'll do it if I have to. I know people here."

"Too dangerous."

"I could glamour though and only let it slip with people I trust."

"Maybe." Reyan sighed. "I'm going to unlock the door and keep the key with me. The realm-skip has to be somewhere discreet so I'll be able to go in and out to check on it through the shadows, but we need a physical access as well to be safe."

Molly sank against her workbench as Reyan looked around and ventured behind the screen that hid Molly's bed.

My old bed. She frowned. *Strange this place doesn't feel like home anymore.*

She rubbed her thumb over the *Akiai* charm Talie had given her and fought the urge to leave the one she'd made in return behind.

"There. I've cast an illusion to hide it and it'll be word-protected so that only people who know the safety word will be able to bring it into use."

"And the safety word will be?" Molly asked.

Reyan's lips twitched. "For Demi to issue as she sees

fit. Come on, back we go."

Molly held out her hand and took another look around. *One step closer. One step at a time.*

CHAPTER TEN

TALIE

Talie wiped a hand over her face as the crowd outside the gym storeroom finally emptied. The last wiped mind had wandered out with the guard and she was done. The lists Phoenix gave her seemed to get longer each day, and a couple of people had to come back in a second time for 'tweaks'.

Her mind mapped the patterns endlessly in case there was something she could use, but most of the people Phoenix sent her were either vocal dissenters, witnesses to various quibbles around the tower like the raid on the grain guild's stores, or Fae who simply spent too much time outside the citadel, like those from the Refuse Guild.

She rubbed her hand against the tightness in her chest and stood as Nia appeared in the doorway.

"You look tired," she said.

Talie shrugged. "So? Doubt anyone cares."

"Don't be so prickly. Lots of us care." Nia's expression shadowed. "Anyway, he's summoned you."

"Not even doing his own errands anymore?"

Nia sighed. "Come on, it's got to be better than this. Well, maybe not, but you can call it a day afterward."

Talie grabbed Phoenix's list with a huff.

"Say what you like about the past, but at least that Celeste had a laid-back sort of control," she muttered. "She allowed the nobles to pull rank and the guilds to drain their profits out, but he's going for all-out control, wants us everything except physically tagged."

Nia shushed her and glanced around the tiny room, but the guards were still outside the studio.

"You need to be more careful," Nia warned. "He's fond of you but his emotions are thin and fleeting."

Talie pulled a face. "You still seeing him?"

"What consenting adults to on occasion is nothing to do with you so hush. Go on, before he starts stomping his feet."

Talie let that go, although if Nia was still seeing Phoenix then she couldn't be trusted with any truths, and followed Nia out to the main gym. She walked through the familiar groups sparring and training without stopping and slipped out onto the main lane.

As she walked along with Arrow chasing at her ankles, she focused on settling her mind. She hadn't spoken to Sammy in days beyond the odd sarcastic 'look, I'm still alive' in passing, but Sammy's words hadn't once left her head.

Maybe I have used her as an emotional shield, but if I'm not protecting her any longer then who am I?

She strode into the Menagerie and set off toward the dining hall on the right hand side. It had become Phoenix's more public office since he'd vacated the one at the gym, and she found him shuffling through an endless pile of papers on the long table.

"You summoned?" she said.

He nodded. "Yeah. Forgot you started this morning, but I respect you powering through."

"Nia remembered you mean."

It was out before she could stop herself, but he gave her a rueful smile.

"Alright yes, but it's going to make all the difference in the end."

"Having an entire tower of memory-less Fae is going to make a difference?"

She shifted her stance and winced as her trousers pressed against the new tattoo on her hip.

"I've had to do many things to secure the future of the citadel, and to keep it out of control of the other towers. I take it Sammy told you about your joint pasts by now?"

Talie hesitated. "Yeah."

"Well, that's said and done then."

"I don't get why though."

He frowned. "Well, I knew I'd have to build some loyal foundations and I didn't have much to trade on after Celeste made her move. I decided to bide my time, play nice, and eventually she relied on Marcus for most of the day to day running of the tower."

He shoved at the papers to get them into a neater pile but Talie refused to move forward and help him. She kept her hands at her sides and her stance steady, as relaxed as her stiff muscles would go.

"Birch was my plant," he continued. "I admit that when his true identity was discovered, I had him push into your mind that your needed to protect Sammy, just like Marcus put the suggestion of you into Celeste's mind."

"Why me though? Why Sammy?"

Phoenix sighed. "I did the rounds of a couple of homes in the hope of finding Molly, as you know Celeste took great pains to hide her from me, but then there you were. I don't know, I suppose you reminded me a bit of myself and that gave me the idea to grow some future loyalties."

"So you had Birch pretend to be a kid and put Sammy in the home thinking I'd jump at the chance to protect her, then convinced Celeste to 'adopt' me as one of her future charges to spy on you?"

He rubbed a hand over his face and she noticed the hint of stubble on his jaw. For someone always so strategically clean-cut, it was a tiny sign that he wasn't as unruffled as he wanted everyone to think.

"It does sound a bit convoluted but it's best to have all lanes and alleys covered," he admitted. "That's actually how the Menagerie got its name. I insisted to Celeste we would be the dumping ground for Fae that wanted to prove themselves."

Talie held in her shudder and disguised it as a shake of her head.

"And Birch? Is he really dead or was that some kind of smoke screen to get him out?"

Phoenix shrugged and the air around his body shivered, his height shrinking and his face taking on an achingly childlike familiarity.

"He was- you were him? All that time?" She pressed a hand to her chest as nostalgia fought with revulsion. "That's why he kept saying he had to sneak off on devious tasks for people?"

"Yes, so in that way, he's not actually dead. I haven't mentioned that part to Sammy though. I remember she was extremely fond of him."

Talie fought the urge to drown him and Arrow darted up her leg and onto her shoulder to brush against the droplets of anger brewing on her cheeks.

"I have put great faith and trust in you," Phoenix said, his tone turning grave. "Everything we do is for the good of the citadel. You might think this is just some power-grab on my part, but someone has to run things and it just so happens to be me."

Talie had no words, none that she would feel safe saying out loud. She lifted a hand to Arrow's head instead.

"I could send you further down with the nobility if you're no longer content to work at my side," he added. "But I wouldn't have said society was your favourite place."

Talie bit onto his mocking tone and steeled herself. This was a Fae game like any other, and she had her own goals now to play for.

"No, I'm no good with anything social. It just doesn't seem to be in the good of the people to be wiping their minds like clearing water off a window or to be asking them invasive questions in the name of surveillance."

Phoenix shrugged. "We do what we must to keep things safe. Things are fragile at the moment and the other towers have wealth to press their advantage that we don't. Tying the situation up in paperwork until we can get the upper-hand is a necessary evil."

Talie glanced over her shoulder. She'd spent the previous evening with Finola teaching Arrow how to navigate bits of pipe and she still didn't fully understand it herself, but she wanted to spend her evening practicing with him.

The sooner he's ready, the quicker I can get a message out.

"You do realise it is still an honour to be marked as part of the inner circle, don't you?" Phoenix pulled her attention back. "That tattoo I gave you when you agreed to join isn't just ink and skin."

Talie lifted her hand to show the mark in question on her wrist, moor-grass and *Akiai* stalks under a bright sun. She'd chosen it as a belligerent nod to her wilful intention to find out what Phoenix was up to, her last link to Molly and the realms outside the glass.

"It has certain abilities," he said when she didn't answer. "It will allow you to get through some of the inner-citadel wards."

"It… what? How? Why?"

Maybe I can simply walk out of the citadel, break a bit of the glass and figure out a way down, or keep riding the carts or rubbish chutes and insist one of the nobles takes me to Molly.

"The wards have been put in place for protection, which includes the safeguarding to some extent of the Fae inside the tower. In order for you to be able to wipe their minds without triggering some kind of rebound from the protection, you need to be exempt from some of them."

"Wow." She stared at the tattoo again. "Wait, when you say inner-citadel wards..."

He nodded. "It won't let you get past the glass but likely there are some off-limits parts of the citadel and the Menagerie especially that would be open to you. Celeste's labyrinth for instance. I've had people mapping through to find it, but it's taking a fair while. Once your mind wiping duties slow down, you can join them."

It wasn't a request or even a suggestion, but Talie sucked in a slow breath and clung to her fraying nerves.

"To keep the well safe and the Omens contained, right? Not to use them?"

He smiled, all sharp eyes and wicked astuteness.

"Using the well in any capacity would take a lot of personal resolve. Don't let any of that worry you. For now, focus on your tasks."

She nodded slowly. "There's still a fair few and the list keeps growing, but I'll do what I can."

Can being 'can get away with'. She stalked out of the dining room and up the stairs with her mind swirling. *He'll get me hunting for the well since I've seen it before.*

There was only one thing to do and it would be dangerous to try. The strangely liberating thought that she didn't have to worry about Sammy anymore only made her more determined.

First step, figure out where these maps are being logged. Second step, ruin them.

CHAPTER ELEVEN

MOLLY

"So why this tea-house? Is this the elite of tea-houses in Faerie?"

Molly stared around at the high ceilings trimmed with gold, the tall marble pillars wrapped with exotic vines that smelled a bit like the ones the wine came from back at the Illusion Court. Then she glanced warily at the hushed tables around them, everyone doing their best to gawk and eavesdrop without looking like it.

Violetta smoothed down her immaculate jewel green suit and tapped her lace-trimmed menu on the edge of the table.

"I assumed you wouldn't want to go to the one that has seven different kinds of teacup," she mock-whispered.

Molly pulled a face as the tea-house's proprietress hurried up and ducked into a low bow, so low her elaborate sandy bun threatened to wobble.

"Your highness, this is the highest of honours. My name is Rosemary and I'll be looking after you today, with your permission. Welcome back, Lady Violetta. What can I bring you?"

"The Jasmine tea sampler for me, please," Violetta said. "The full tea service too, for the table."

"Of course, I'll get that started for you right away." Rosemary pivoted to Molly next.

"Um, hot chocolate, please."

A fresh hiss of mutterings did the rounds of the room but Molly waited for Rosemary to leave before hiding her mouth behind her fist.

"What did I do?" she asked.

Violetta grinned. "The crash course? Elbow off the table. Back straight. Don't say please if you can help it either. Those sorts of pleasantries should be beneath you and your right to demand instead."

Molly lifted a hand and poked at the tiara on her head. With a wicked smile that Kainen would have been proud of, she shrugged.

"Some traditions are just begging to be updated."

Another buzz of feverous chatter and she sank into Vi's delighted chuckle with relief.

"As you say, Pri- sorry, *Molly*."

A subtle gasp echoed from somewhere nearby but Molly ignored it as a stream of servers appeared with a towering platter of sandwiches and cakes.

"Etiquette?" Molly prompted wearily.

Vi lifted a napkin and used it to ferry a dainty sandwich quarter with an oak leaf stencilled in the top slice onto her plate, then a tiny cupcake with enough golden frosting to splat an entire face with, along with a sugar acorn. She held out the plate with a bob of her head.

"With your permission?" she asked.

Molly frowned. "Er... yeah."

She reached out to grab her own food but Vi popped her lips and widened her eyes.

"I won't be a moment," she said.

Molly waited, confusion settling uneasily in her gut as Vi cut a tiny bit off the edge of the sandwich and ate it, then a speck of the cupcake.

"Okay, all good."

Molly blinked. "Please tell me you didn't just taste test the food?"

"Of course. *The Golden Pot* is the most established tea-house in all of Faerie, but your rank means some traditions are non-negotiable, at least in society."

Molly swerved the napkin and went for the sandwiches with her bare fingers.

"What if they only poisoned the ones on my side?" she asked, then popped the entire sandwich in.

Vi's eyes widened further and she stifled a laugh behind her hand.

"We usually use knives and forks for the platter, and a spoon for the puddings."

"But you just touched it to get it on the plate."

"Well, yes."

"You can touch it to plate it but not to eat it? How mad is that?" She sighed. "I won't use my fingers for the puddings, how's that as a compromise."

"Royalty doesn't compromise," Vi shot back wickedly.

"Well that sucks. Anyway, it's done now. So, what's new with you?"

"A question that you probably should temper with some prior knowledge," Vi scolded with amusement. "A princess must always retain some small bit of information about those she's affiliated with. It could be as simple as remembering the name of their pet, or the most recent skirmish among their household."

"That's… a lot of people's random stuff to remember."

"Of course, but this is why royals usually travel with entourage to ask those questions. A well-placed noble whose role is to remember so you don't have to."

Molly took a sip of her hot chocolate and closed her eyes for a second.

"Okay that is good. So, this noble would no doubt be extra in favour I take it?"

"Oh absolutely, the highest of accolades is to be top dog of the inner circle."

"How exhausting. Fine, how are your arbor things going? You donated some to Kainen and Reyan's wedding if I remember right?"

"A princess always remembers right," Vi reminded her.

She took another sandwich and speared it on a two-pronged fork with delicate fingers.

Molly smiled. "Perhaps, but a princess might consider that a suitable trap to lure unsuspecting nobles into correcting her with."

Vi chuckled and raised her teacup in salute.

"You're learning. The arbors were custom ordered for the wedding so we have no need to make any more, unless someone decides to order a new set. Right now we're focused on a line of spiralling bookshelves for the Word

Court."

"Spiral bookshelves?"

"No, spiralling. They revolve up and down based on a complex organisation system. Gets you to the book quicker."

Molly reached for a little cake that was mostly a puff of lilac frosting with a golden leaf on top, then wearily stabbed at it with a fork before inhaling it. She ignored Vi's slight grimace.

"Don't tell Milo or he'll want one," she said.

"Oh, well, I did mention it to Tyren to mention to Milo, but he's been extremely busy."

Vi tucked a stray auburn wave behind her ear and sighed loftily, so much so that the hint was glaringly obvious.

"I could have a word with him if you like," Molly offered. "I'm sure there'll come a time where the Revels Court will want to showcase something new."

Vi sat straighter with a subtle brush of her shirt.

"We're always ready to serve the crowns," she said.

"As is everyone else," Molly replied airily. "However does one choose between them?"

Vi grinned. "A wise question, and one I'm sure for much more eloquent minds than mine."

Molly guessed Vi wanted her to press for her opinion, but she only tilted her head and eyed the food platter, now half demolished on her side.

As long as nobody starts saying I'm only allowed one cake, it'll be fine.

Thoughts of Talie filled her head, then of the citadel.

She glanced out of the enormous window and the fair sunshine glowing across the cobbles of the street outside. The bushes were clipped and green, the trees suitably lined with pale blue blossoms, and the finery of Fae walking about could have probably paid for an entire month of food at Butch's shop.

"Percat for them?" Vi prompted.

Molly bit her lip.

Not even a pesana, a whole percat.

"It's strange." She swirled the dregs of her hot chocolate in her cup. "Not even that long ago, I would have worked a few months to earn a percat. The citadel uses pesanas, which I suppose a lot of other realms consider pocket change. But I never went hungry. I always had a warm place to sleep."

Molly kept her voice level, loud enough to be heard clearly. Rumours would do the rounds about her, it was how Fae were no matter their rank or status, but she wanted the nobles around her to know she wasn't going to be an easy one to manipulate or charm.

Vi waved a hand and a waitress hurried over to clear the table, but Molly kept her gaze welded to the window.

"It must be a bit of a shock," Vi said.

Molly shrugged. "I'm one person. Sure, it turns out I've been born to a crown, but I didn't know that until really recently."

She hesitated as a soft foot tapped her knee warningly.

"How interesting. I heard a rumour that the queen herself kept you sheltered under her protection at the royal court until you were due to debut."

"Debut what?"

Vi strangled her horrified squeak and covered it with a laugh as the gawking crowd whispered furiously.

"Society of course, your debut into society to find yourself a suitable marriage."

"Oh. That." Molly fought the urge to be so bluntly honest it would cause the kind of scandal that stopped her getting invited to teas. "Rumours can be such funny things."

Vi's tense shoulders settled. "True indeed. I did hear one recently about a noble who was found singing odes to a barrel of wine, so you never can tell."

"Sounds like Kainen on a good day."

Vi laughed properly. "They certainly do seem very fond of you at the Illusion Court."

"I'm lucky they had space for my workshop. Still, I'm better off gaining my standing and wealth through direct trades and skills rather than favours."

"Favours can be dangerous," Vi agreed. "Still, this was a favour of sorts that I now owe you for, so you're not going too badly."

Molly grinned. "High praise but I doubt the majesty would agree. Are we done?"

"Yes, although it's a shame. I've enjoyed talking shop with you, very much."

Molly nodded, surprised that she could claim the same. In any other situation, the frank smiles and too-long-lingering looks Violetta was giving her might have had her heart fluttering, but it was all pretence for the prying eyes, a part of the social dance and nothing more.

She hesitated as her thoughts twisted instantly to the past, but dwelling wouldn't do her any good in the here and now.

"It's been an education," she agreed.

"Next time, we'll discuss ball etiquette."

"Games have etiquette?"

Vi blinked. "Game- no, balls."

Molly shook her head. "Is that some kind of weird court thing?"

It took all her effort to hide her smile, but Violetta cocked her head with a frown.

"I don't know that balls are a court thing specifically, but you'll need to know how to handle them."

"Oh. Do nobles handle a lot of balls then?"

Vi sighed. "Most won't personally I suppose. They have servants and aides to handle the particulars. Lady Lolly tends to get Lord Tyren to handle most of hers now, to his credit and his endless peril."

Molly's heart sank as Vi winked and stood up.

Talie would never have fallen for that.

As Rosemary hurried over, Molly managed a sincere smile.

"That was delicious." Reyan had at least coached her through the necessities like a clucking mother hen. "Please send me the cost via the Illusion Court."

The crowd noise rose again, but if they were ogling for any information about her, all they would get was the court she'd willingly aligned herself with and a compliment for the tea-house.

"Oh, Your Highness, that is kind but it's on the house,"

Rosemary insisted firmly.

Fighting the urge to argue, Molly settled for the wording Reyan had given her.

"That's very kind. In that case, I offer you my compliments."

Rosemary bowed low and Molly took a step back.

"I'm honoured to have been your guest today," Vi announced loudly. "If I may?"

Molly nodded, guessing some kind of gift might be forthcoming. She lifted her hand ready but squeaked in alarm as Vi bypassed the hand entirely and kissed her straight on her astonished mouth.

It only lasted a few seconds but Molly's insides twisted.

It's not unfaithful, it can't be. Probably just another stupid custom. Orbs, I'm changing that somehow if it is.

As Violetta smiled at her, only half a nose taller and still far too close, Molly saw the abundance of orbs raised around them.

It's fine. The citadel doesn't get many outside channels and Talie doesn't watch them. Orbs, what if she's started to? What if Sammy sees?

"I gift you with a small personal favour from me of your choosing." Violetta winked again. "Use it well."

Molly gulped down the lump in her throat that was quickly turning nauseous.

"I- yeah. I should go."

Violetta nodded. "Of course. Perhaps you can show me around the workshop as discussed?"

Molly couldn't remember that part of the discussion but she nodded numbly.

"Yeah, sure." She held up her orb. "Reyan Hemlock."

Reyan appeared a moment later, but to her credit she took one look at Molly's face and grabbed her hand.

Molly fumbled through a wooden goodbye and sank into the nether that ferried them home and straight into her room at court.

"That bad?" Reyan asked.

"Yeah. She kissed me. I know it was to gift me a thank you, I think, but in the name of Faerie, has she never heard of a hand? Or a cheek?"

Reyan laughed. "She's definitely very taken with you. Lolly said she actually petitioned to be the Flora Court's rep for your company, not that she had much sensible competition."

"Well no more." Molly paced across the shiny floor. "The kissing thing has to go. Actually, where's my orb, I need Taz or Demi to change the rules immediately."

Reyan held up her hands, unable to curb her grin.

"Maybe calm down first. Was it really so bad? She's very pretty, and smart. You have the whole craft thing in common."

Molly hesitated. On paper Violetta was perfection. Even in person it was an ideal match, at least for a few dates to start with.

Even as she considered the possibility, her insides flipped painfully.

"There's nothing wrong with her, but..."

"She's not Talie."

"No." Molly sighed. "Not even close."

The door banged open and Kainen charged in.

"You might want to see this," he chortled, holding up an orb.

As the orb-cast settled on a still of a news-piece, Molly's heart sank.

"Crown Princess Caught Tonguing at Tea-House?!" she shrieked. "That's absurd! It wasn't like that!"

From the picture included, it absolutely looked exactly like that.

"Well of course not," Kainen said. "But these gutter-minds will orb anything as a scandal. More importantly, what do they mean by 'intriguing table manners'?"

CHAPTER TWELVE

TALIE

Talie held the piece of raw meat between finger and thumb and forced herself to smile encouragingly. The main space of the gym was empty of people, enough that she was able to set up a proper multi-junction pipe network for Arrow.

At the other side of the pipes, Finola swiped her hands over her messy brown hair and grimaced.

"You look like you're trying to find a long lost tooth."

Talie slipped into her more familiar scowl and waved the meat irritably toward the open end of the pipes, which were more a complicated bundle of fabrics stretched over aisles of overturned chairs.

"Come on," she muttered.

Arrow blinked back at her, his shiny brown eyes deceptively innocent.

"He did it fine before."

Finola shrugged. "Can't force them. That's half the grain guild's problem."

Talie thought back to the quivering Arrow that had tried to burrow beneath her skin when she found him and her temper softened.

"Okay. I don't want to force him, but I can't rent a bird or use an orb."

Arrow cocked his head and chittered loudly. With a loud thud of his unexpectedly solid tail, the cause of many of Talie's more recent bruises, he scampered through the pretend tunnel and sat expectantly on his haunches to wait for the meat.

"Does he-" Talie frowned. "Can he understand me or something?"

Finola laughed. "Words no. Intentions, maybe. He can probably scent your moods like many other creatures. If you're frustrated, so is he."

"I'm always frustrated though."

"I know." Finola glanced up at the droplets of moisture hanging to the gym ceiling. "Maybe try to work on that."

"Easier said than done."

"I hear that. Work's nicer these days but I sometimes miss the stability of the guild."

Talie stilled. "You were part of a guild?"

"In another life. The guilds have slowly been enthralled to the nobles and I decided a while back that I was better off teaching in the gym than swinging on the ropes of Fae politics."

"Which guild?"

Finola grimaced. "Food production, the ones up on the highest levels above the grain ones. Not many else in this tower nowadays and can you see me as an artificer? No thanks, I'd likely blow stuff up more than create it."

"I heard those were a myth!"

Finola glanced around at the deserted gym.

"It's to protect the flow of production from situations like these. They're guarded of course, and the guards tend to live a few levels beneath before the normal levels start to keep the "rabble" away, but they're there."

Talie noted the sarcastic finger bobs around the word rabble, but Finola swiped a hand over her hair after and looked around again as if to check for listening ears.

"So, you know a fair bit about the different levels then?" Talie asked.

She kept her tone casual and grabbed a bit of treat for Arrow.

"I know enough. You need to if you're dealing with the distribution tunnels and the tunnel-critters." Finola smiled fondly at Arrow. "It's a sight though. The entire levels are full of different produce. Not sure if there'd be much left now though."

"If there is, it'll be in Menagerie keeping no doubt," Talie muttered.

"Yep, or the nobility's. Knowledge of the distribution routes are hard to come by though. Probably why I'm kept close and placated here."

The gym door banged open and Finola uttered a startled curse. Talie flinched as Arrow darted up her side to her shoulder as Nia hurried in.

"Rebels have attacked the production levels, higher up this time," she said, her breath coming in uneven gasps.

"Oh." Finola grimaced. "That's bad. Did they get far?"

"I'm not sure, but news trickled down as Fae were charging up."

"Is it the same people as the grain store before?" Talie asked.

Nia nodded. "Yeah, the white Phoenix with the blood on was painted on the side of one of the carts attacking."

Finola hissed through her teeth and Nia fell silent. Talie lifted a hand to Arrow's back as her mind raced.

How would she know what was on the carts unless she was there?

"I'm thinking you could have seen the cart on its way up?" she suggested.

It was a warning and Nia's eyes widened.

"I could have…"

"Does that mean the food production will be flowing again?"

Finola sighed. "Doubt it. Raiding the production levels will give them enough for a few people, assuming they even distribute it fairly. Taking control might have it last a bit longer, but Phoenix has tripled guards, hired more from the nobility, even traded with other towers for some."

"He fears an uprising," Talie said.

"Exactly. He'll double down and let the boots and the Menagerie get more aggressive, and even if w- *people* do liberate food, the tower still needs to honour our trades that are owed to the others in the citadel, or more shortages will soon follow."

Talie lifted her hand and gave Arrow the treat she was still clinging to. She kept her gaze on him but didn't miss the subtle touch of Nia's hand to Finola's in the pause, or the flash of a small key that passed between them.

"You should get yourself home," Finola said. "Both of

you. I have friends enough to be seen with but it's not good to be moving about alone in these dark times."

Talie snorted. "I can take care of myself."

"Still, good to have someone to be seen with when people come asking if there's anything to be seen. We're probably all under suspicion."

Her voice tailed off almost to nothing as the gym door swung open again and Phoenix strode in. Arrow gave Phoenix a wary grumble, and Phoenix eyed him for a second before he gave Talie a grim nod.

"It's going to be a late one I'm afraid. There are a couple who need to be re-wiped as well."

There was nothing in his tone, but Talie sensed the subtle accusation all the same.

"Fine."

She couldn't see past what Sammy had told her, but she didn't dare bring it up.

"She's worked all day," Nia said gently. "Let the girl have an evening to herself at least."

Phoenix frowned. "We all need to be working. There's been a raid on the production levels. I'm handling it but needless to say the people mustn't hear a word of it."

The people are probably all there helping by now. Talie forced the automatic smile off her face.

Finola managed a suitably horrified curse at the news and Nia gasped softly. Talie couldn't pretend, couldn't pull faces and act upset when she wasn't, so she settled for taking the lead as Phoenix's narrowed gaze passed over all of them.

"Why?" she asked.

"Why what?"

"Why have they raided the production levels? Far as I know, most people thought they were a myth."

"Word must have gotten out," he said. "Some of the borrowed guards aren't under the same oaths so they might be loose-lipped enough to blab in the bars."

"Is borrowing guards wise then?" Talie pressed.

Finola and Nia exchanged a look but Talie held Phoenix's increasingly irritated gaze and kept her posture steady as her pulse raced.

"We have to keep control somehow. You don't seem surprised about the raid."

Talie shrugged. "I thought the food production levels were a myth until now, so how would I have known anyone was planning to raid them? It's not going to solve anything if things are already struggling anyway. You wanted me to lobotomise more people you said?"

Her gut writhed in anxious knots as he stood utterly still for long moments before his expression locked down and he smiled. Slowly. Wickedly. He pulled out his orb.

"How true. I'll show you the lis- oops."

A still image of a newscast from *The Faerie Net* blossomed into vivid detail and Talie sucked in a sharp breath at the photo beneath the ridiculous headline.

She leaned closer, desperation gluing her gaze to Molly's face instead of the random other woman attached to her at the mouth.

She searched for any sign that it wasn't exactly what it looked like, but Phoenix scrolled the image aside to show a list of names instead.

She looked surprised, like she does when she's working and someone doesn't announce themselves quick enough.

Phoenix was punishing her for speaking out, or trying to manipulate her emotions. Either way, even he probably wouldn't have the ability to fake an entire article in *The Faerie Net* just to mess with her.

Arrow tucked his nose behind her ear as her gift splurged out in a sudden gathering of moisture on the ceiling.

"She made her decision," Phoenix said, his tone suspiciously gentle.

"I know."

"I get it's tough and emotions don't turn off like a tap, but we have to focus on the citadel and move on. She clearly has."

Talie caught the unimpressed look on Finola's face and the incredulous fury on Nia's but she didn't look their way.

Everyone's as concerned about his new rule as I am.

She wiped a hand over her face and scratched Arrow's damp head.

"Let's get it done then. Same time again tomorrow, Fi?"

Finola nodded. "Definitely. He'll be pipe-racing in no time."

Talie set off toward the back studio, her tension prickling as Phoenix followed her.

"Pipe-racing?" he asked. "That used to be huge in my day."

She nodded. "Still goes on a bit. The betting's good for morale and it's harmless to the animals. Finola wants to go to one soon, to make sure nobody's hurting them."

Keep it simple, say as little about serious things as possible.

She pushed open the studio door and headed past the two waiting guards straight for the store room.

"Best to keep her on side," Phoenix said. "Or she'll have the entire grain guild pulled down to the rubble and we need all the industry working all hours."

"People are still starving though. Surely we should be focusing on that first?"

Phoenix folded his arms across his chest and she cursed herself for letting her mind slip enough to say what she was thinking.

"We need to focus on security before anything else," he insisted. "The wards keep the immediate flow of power with us, but the other towers will be looking for advantage and you can bet the queens want a way in no matter what the Holly King Consort says."

Talie bit her lip and Phoenix lifted an eyebrow.

"If you've got something to say, spit it out," he demanded.

She sighed. "It's just that I've seen the Menagerie kitchens. We've got plenty there and yet the people, *your* people now, are struggling to feed their kids. How do you think that looks?"

"What would you have me do? Give one a grape and another a pear? What happens when you run out of grapes and pears halfway down the levels? Or do we start with the hungriest first and those not so hungry are still strong enough to start an uprising? You know nothing about ruling."

145

He shook his head slowly and gave her a quirk-lipped, hood-eyed look of pity. She waded through the instinctive burn of shame that seemed to come almost daily lately and clung to the facts.

"I get that, but we can't just let people die."

"You let me worry about the big things. Focus on wiping those memories so that we can ease everyone into the new rules with minimal upheaval, that's all I need from you right now. That and you seem to have charmed some sturdy minds, like Finola's. Keep it that way."

It was as blatant a warning as she would get and she hid a full-body shudder behind the door of the storeroom as the guards let the first few Fae into the studio. Given the worried looks on the vaguely familiar faces, these were the minds that Phoenix wanted re-wiped.

People. She bit her lip. *Not just minds, people with pain and emotions and blood and bone. Forget that, you forget everything that means anything.*

She gave him yet another grim nod.

"I definitely wouldn't get on her bad side unless I had to."

Phoenix's shoulders lowered slightly, a sign that her irritable nature was his idea of 'normal'.

The thought of how easy it would be to simply wipe him instead filled her head but she pushed it out just as fast. If his truth gift let him see intentions or emotions, then she was already kicking dust on the danger line.

As Phoenix stamped out with his usual easy smile, she pulled her orb out to check the list he'd sent across.

Why show me the orb cast though? The knife in her gut

twisted deeper. *It's ruthless even for him. Doesn't achieve anything. I haven't mentioned Molly in ages.*

She closed the store room door and glanced around on instinct before lifting her orb and searching for *The Faerie Net*. The main casts were still there, but several of the actual feeds came up as 'inactive'.

Not the one with Molly though and a fresh ache radiated across her chest as she saw the image again.

Molly's eyebrows were raised and her eyes were wide open but the angle was awful, and Talie snorted as she devoured the words underneath.

Whoever Lady Violetta was, at least Molly didn't look too keen to be kissing her.

I'll train Arrow with every spare second I have. Then 'her highness' has some explaining to do.

CHAPTER THIRTEEN

MOLLY

Molly woke to a gentle shaking.

"Molly?"

She blinked and lifted her head, the scattered pile of books on the library table leaving a stiffness and a line in her cheek. No sign of Reyan in the library, but then a fuzzy memory of Reyan saying she would leave Molly to her researching appeared. It wasn't Reyan looking down at her either.

She sat up and wiped her face as Violetta perched on the edge of the table beside her. She tensed as Violetta reached out and trailed a fingertip along the back of her hand, far too familiar a gesture.

One unexpected kiss and she's touching any bit she likes.

"Who's Talie?" Violetta asked.

Molly flinched. Violently. Her hand caught one of the books and sent it flying.

"W-what?"

"Who's Talie?" Violetta got up and retrieved the book.

"You were saying 'Talie' in your sleep."

Molly's insides crunched as an icy chill swept over her skin.

"Someone from the previous life," she muttered.

Violetta sighed. "Girlfriend?"

"No."

Could have been.

Molly started closing the books and piling them for something to do, and her cheeks burned as Violetta stood watching her fuss.

"I'm not interested in competing with ghosts from the past," Violetta announced. "I like you, but you've never smiled at me the way you were just now while you were sleeping."

"I wasn't-" She grimaced. "Was I?"

"Mmhmm, smiling and glowing gently. Whoever she is, you need to let it go before you're free for someone else."

Molly hesitated. She hadn't actually made any suggestions that she was willing to be free for someone else, or trying to be, but the only way she could see out was through uncomfortable deference.

"Vi, I'm sorry. There's barely any hope I'll even see her again, let alone anything more. But you're right, I shouldn't be looking at others if my head's still jumbled."

Even though I technically wasn't looking, but still.

She bit down the temptation to mention that she hadn't exactly given Violetta any overt encouragement to pursue her in the first place, and tried a weak smile instead.

Violetta shrugged and a sad chuckle bubbled from her

lips.

"If you do find yourself free, let me know. Also, Lady Reyan is looking for you. Something about the queens and a meeting?"

Molly looked at the enormous clock hanging over the fireplace.

"Oh orbs, I'm going to be late!"

It was the coward's way out but she managed another rueful smile of apology in Violetta's direction and dashed from the library.

She was kind and cultured and really good at art. She has her own workshop in an entire court of craftspeople. She tumbled down the chilly spiral staircase, her shoes tapping on the stone. *If I ever see Talie again, I'm going to punch her. A lot.*

She didn't want to dwell on how her heart leapt at even the mere theoretical thought of seeing Talie again.

She dashed through the halls until she spied a familiar figure up ahead and increased her pace.

"You're late," Kainen announced as she drew alongside him.

"I know, but I was- wait, if I'm late, then so are you."

"Ah, but I'm lord of the court. I have my reasons."

"And I'm actually doing work around here," she retorted.

He gasped as they skidded around the corner and into the main hall in perfect unison.

"And I'm not?" He pressed a hand to his heart. "How little faith you have in me your highness."

Molly pulled a face at him as Reyan stalked toward

them.

"You're-"

"Late, we know," Kainen interrupted.

Molly nodded. "No excuse."

"Blame me to the queen."

"No, blame me," Molly sighed. "She's less likely to pulverise me, hopefully."

"Actually yeah, blame her."

"Nice, very lordly."

He grinned. "I thought so."

"Save the double act for the queen," Reyan snapped. "And in the name of Faerie please let Demi do the talking."

"Silent as the grave," Kainen said gravely.

Reyan groaned and waved them away, so Molly took Kainen's outstretched hand and sank into the nether with him.

The throne room materialised around them and Molly pulled her warding around her the moment Kainen dropped her hand.

"You're late," the queen admonished.

"My fault not entirely, your majesty," Kainen said smoothly.

He inclined his head and Molly spasmed a curtsey of sorts as Demi and Taz appeared beside them.

"Are we needed?" Taz asked. "Kainen wants to see the *arunjo* trees in the orchard, and there's a book on giftball official rules in the library. I know those orb-munchers cheated."

"They're said to produce excellent wine," Kainen added. "The trees, not the rules."

The queen waved them away, scarily like Reyan in her dismissal, and Molly watched them scamper off like naughty children.

"You wanted to discuss the situation with the citadel again?" the queen prompted.

She sounded irritable and Molly eyed the height disparity of her seated up on her throne while they stood.

"Is that what this is about?" Demi asked. "I missed a court meeting for this. Not complaining, but you know how Milo gets."

Molly grimaced obediently. She purposely hadn't told Demi the reason for wanting to get them together so Demi could deny all knowledge and any involvement, but she also knew Milo was away so Demi's court meeting couldn't be that important after all.

"I'd have thought you would be more focused on fixing your image," the queen said. "Your first appearance in the Faerie Net leaves a lot to be desired."

Demi snorted. "At least it's not as drastic as mine was."

"Even so. I might be willing to listen to trades for some small measure of input."

"What trade?" Molly asked.

She ignored the warning look flashing icy blue in Demi's eyes and faced her grandmother with her arms folded.

"There's little you can give me that I can't take if I chose to," the Oak Queen said. "If the Holly Queen were to consider returning some measure of value to my lineage however…"

"No deal," Demi scoffed.

152

"Not even for the wider good? Perhaps you're learning. Many of your family are currently in the Holly Queen's keeping under duress, Molinia. I would have them returned to me."

"Well that's-" Molly glanced at Demi. "You kidnapped my family? Really?"

"One aunt who tried to overthrow everything, and I mean literally everything, and your mother. You want them roaming around here at court trading whispers and worse?"

Molly pulled a face. "Yeah that'd be a no."

"Thought so. No freedom for traitors and usurpers I'm afraid."

"I'd advise you to be careful what slander you sling at my family," the Oak Queen said, her tone threateningly soft.

Demi shrugged. "Not slander if it's true."

"Which brings us back to you, Molinia. What trades were you considering for my concession in bringing the citadel to heel?"

"No, no trades." Molly shoved her hands in her pockets. "This is your chance to do the right thing."

The Oak Queen frowned and tapped a finger against her lip.

"Where's the incentive in that?"

"Er... the good of your people?" Molly lost several seconds to incredulous disbelief.

"You'd have us charge in and take control after all? The idea has some merits."

"Not like that!"

"We can't risk it," Demi insisted. "To attack the citadel would be seen as an act of war because they made no move against us first. If they were to attack one of our own, or try to invade outside the glass, that would be different."

The Oak Queen nodded. "For once, I agree. We tried sending nobles in and it made no difference. The citadel is not our conquest to claim, not yet."

Molly slammed her hand down on the desk.

"People are dying! Aren't they Fae too? Fairies? You're queens of Faerie, all of it, and you want to let him sit in his fortress slaughtering in the name of revenge or greed, or progress, I don't even know what!"

Demi grimaced. "I get that, but if queens went around conquering whenever they felt like it, what makes them any different? Oh no offense."

She gave her opponent a fleeting glance. The Oak Queen sniffed and decided not to reply.

"What's the point in being a queen if you can't save people from power?" Molly demanded. "Freedom to choose, that's literally the one thing you were meant to stand for."

She shoved to her feet and stormed out of the throne room. She ignored Marthe scurrying the other way and slammed along the halls toward the kitchens.

I'll go back to the Illusion Court and ask one of the nobles to get me in if they can through the ground level. If I have to trade on my title I'll do it, this once.

She almost collided with Taz and Kainen clustered in the doorway to the kitchens, both wearing identical grins and blocking her rampage.

"I'm going to the citadel, and you can't stop me," she announced.

Taz shrugged. "Nobody's going to. Demi has to be seen to do the right thing, the diplomatic thing. So do I, but we can't control what others do."

He held up a small star-shaped disc. Molly gazed at it, her pulse kicking up.

"Is that..."

"It's for Kainen, not you," he warned. "He's the only one we can trust to- that is still really weird."

Kainen grinned. "You love me, admit it."

"There are some people I hate marginally more than you."

Kainen swiped the wayfinder from Taz's palm and did some complicated wiggle with his free hand until the item disappeared.

"I know he loves me really. Demi can't be seen waging a war, but that doesn't mean the rest of us can't misbehave."

CHAPTER FOURTEEN

TALIE

"You're going to have to talk to me eventually."

Talie kneeled in the gym two days after her last stint of mind-wiping with a bowl of dried meat flakes and the infernal pretend tunnel that now wound around one of the training rings.

Arrow darted around inside in a scrabble of tiny feet and Talie kept her gaze on the entrance as Sammy glowered down at her.

"What do I have to do?" Sammy demanded. "I forgave you when you pretended to be dead!"

Talie bit down the urge to remind her she also punched her in the stomach first as punishment. She wanted to explain, or shout until her lungs ached, that she was doing it to keep everyone safe for all of a couple of weeks, whereas Sammy had lied for most of their lives.

"Do I need to get Molly here to knock some sense into you?"

Talie froze.

She can't, can she? How? Phoenix would have her orb

tracked just like any other.

She firmed her resolve as Arrow darted out of the tunnel and went snout and whiskers first into the treat bowl.

Talie rescued it and threw a piece into the tunnel.

"Tunnel," she commanded.

Arrow shot into the tunnel again and after a brief pause with added chewing, he set off again.

"I could do it," Sammy insisted. "I could say you're missing her. I bet Kainen could find a way-"

"Leave her out of this. I mean it."

"Aha! I knew could break you. Come on, what if I promise to get you an orb call with her? Just to see she's okay."

"She's fine." The news cast image flashed into her mind.

"How do you know?"

"I just do. Leave it."

"Fine. Are you talking to me again now then?"

"No."

"You can't ignore me forever."

Talie said nothing as Arrow reappeared and climbed to her shoulder with a warning grumble. It was the noise he used every time she tensed around Phoenix, a useful alarm that gave her precious seconds to lock her thoughts down tight.

"I've called a meeting of the towers," he announced. "I need you with me."

Talie glanced from him to Sammy and back again. Pointedly.

"Oh, you mean me?" she asked.

Sammy sighed loudly but Phoenix smiled.

"Last I checked, yes. Don't feel obligated but I would have thought you'd like to meet our citadel counterparts. After all, get them on side and who knows? Maybe one day we can even open up trade to the rest of Faerie."

Talie let that shiny carrot slide straight off her back. The other towers would never agree, but it was her best chance of getting the best information out to Molly someday. Arrow's training would take time but given the defeated faces of Fae the passed in the lanes, and the fear lingering in the minds she had to wipe, she had to do something.

She said she might send Aurora with a note though. Maybe it was all talk.

She shook the thought aside and stalked past Sammy.

Forgiveness was still beyond her capability, for the moment at least, but seeing Sammy's defeated face still twisted in her chest.

"You should let the past go," Phoenix said. "She wanted to keep you safe as much as you did her, and I've looked after both of you ever since."

"We are not having this conversation."

It was bad enough he was the cause of all her problems, but now he was lording it over the wreckage.

He honoured her irritable need for silence as they walked the rest of the way down to the Menagerie, but she couldn't ease her stiff limbs. Ever since seeing Reyan in the shadows, she'd kept an eye out but seen nothing.

Maybe I imagined it. Maybe nobody's even thinking about us at all.

She slowed as they walked through the Menagerie's

front doors to a cacophony of fake laughter and excessively loud chatter. Talie eyed the swathes of fine clothing on the gathered Fae and wrinkled her nose. The last time she'd seen that much finery, she'd held a dagger to someone's throat.

"Welcome everyone." Phoenix lifted his voice to quiet the crowd. "Please follow me to our reception hall for discussion and drinks."

He led the way across the hall toward the side-chamber with the enormous table. Talie slouched after him with a wary look at the guests, who gave her equal disdain in return.

The last time I was in here, it was Celeste holding court and Molly was slumped over the table so charmingly intoxicated.

She ignored the swoop her stomach made at the memory and followed Phoenix to the head of the table as the guests took seats around the table. Menagerie staff hurried in with cups and decanters, a collection of tired eyes and for one girl, shaking hands.

Once everyone had taken their seats, Phoenix stood with his hands braced on the table.

"Welcome all. I've met you all in some capacity, but let me introduce Talie, one of my trusted few."

Talie stared around at the gathered lords and ladies of the other towers. She recognised Betula but the rest were a mystery.

"A child, Phoenix? Really?" A man on the far side of the long table scoffed.

Phoenix smiled. "Childhood is an illusion that only

some are afflicted by. Take your seats."

Talie marked out the chair Phoenix took for himself closest to the doorway and counted around the groups. As Sunset Tower, they were seen as the fourth, so Night Tower and the scornful man were on Phoenix's left, with the well-dressed ladies from Day tower on his right, then the deceptively smiley group from Morning tower and some grave-faced men from Sunrise.

Talie hovered at Phoenix's shoulder and built a warding of mental iron around herself.

"I've asked you all here to discuss the unification of the towers. As you all know, we've suffered a great loss due to Celeste's recent treachery. I know she was a friend to many of you, an acquaintance at least, but we're working hard to fix her mistakes and could use aid to achieve it. Thoughts?"

The dismissive man from Night Tower leaned forward.

"We have no way of proving what actually happened in the core of the citadel," he said. "We all know that Celeste managed to seal off all the tunnels and access points, and might I remind everyone that you have done the same since?"

A chorus of nods and affirmative grunts rippled around the group.

"We have no idea what is actually down there, only rumour. Whatever Celeste kept contained, we can't risk releasing it until we're sure it won't bring the entire tower down."

Betula tapped a hand on the table.

"What Argon says is true. Do you really have no idea

where the well of power is yet?"

Phoenix shook his head. "I have the Menagerie hunting and cataloguing the various routes through, but nobody has found the actual location yet. A few have come back whispering to themselves, however, odd things that make no sense."

Talie froze. He hadn't mentioned anything about that to her, or sent her any of those folk to have their minds wiped.

Where would he be keeping them other than here?

He had the whole height of the citadel at his command, so it could be any of the levels up or down.

"I suggest you find this well of power so that we can assess the truth and depth of it first," one of the ladies from Morning tower said.

The entire table nodded and hummed their agreement.

"There are all sorts of tall tales full of possibilities about what lies beneath our foundations," another said. "They belong to the citadel and it is worrying that secrets still seem to be held by one tower alone."

"I am doing everything I can to get closer to the truth," Phoenix insisted.

His face was a mask of utter calm but his shoulders were tense. Talie bit her lip as another wave of muttering passed through the group.

"We can't risk aiding you for you to lock up and lose your senses like Celeste did, Phoenix," Argon said. "You understand."

Phoenix cocked his head. "I can see the merit in being cautious. Remember you run the risk either way, so you can help now and be remembered for it, or you can leave us to fend for ourselves and we may just continue doing so, well or no well."

"That is not a unified approach," Betula warned, her lips twitching.

"Neither is refusing to aid a fellow tower in need, but here we are. If everyone is agreed, then the status quo remains the same for the time being?"

There were a few wary looks passing around, but everyone nodded. Phoenix stood and Talie stepped back to keep clear of him.

"Find the well, then we'll talk," the man from Night Tower said.

Phoenix sighed. "By any means necessarily?"

"If need be. Until the next meet everyone."

The man vanished with the rest of his tower and the others rippled out of the room like a wave. Phoenix leaned both hands on the edge of the table with a sigh.

"Well, as I expected, we'll have to change tactics," he said.

Talie frowned. "You mean the nobles? Not that many have returned yet. Even the guilds are suffering for it."

He shook his head. "Worse. Looks like you might be seeing your royal friends again after all. Argon said as much, 'by any means necessary', which means they've now agreed to me bringing outside help if I decide to."

Talie held her expression as still as she could, not daring to twitch a single muscle as Phoenix cast a narrow-eyed glance at her. Then he sighed and stalked away across the entrance hall toward the labyrinth doors and the unwelcome sight of Mulberry stood in front of them.

Talie slipped behind the doorframe of the reception room and listened.

"Any news?" Phoenix asked.

"Nothing damning," Mulberry said. "The maps have been loaded into the vault."

"The vault? Have you collected all the keys?"

Mulberry's lips thinned at the challenge, even though he kept on smiling like he was Phoenix's best friend in all of Faerie.

"The kitchen staff have keys but we don't need to worry about them. Nobody can get through your famous wards, right?"

Phoenix hummed under his breath and Talie peeked out as the sound of chatter came from elsewhere in the Menagerie. Given the roll of Mulberry's eyes, Phoenix's attention had wandered again.

She strode across the entrance hall and up the stairs before anyone could stop her. The moment she was in the upper halls out of sight, she slipped a hand into her pocket and pulled out a key. She looked from the small piece of metal to the hint of her tattoo peeking out beneath the hem of her sleeve and smiled.

Key from my time as Lia in the kitchens, and a tattoo that gets me through the wards.

She might not have Molly to go creeping around with anymore, but someone seemed to be sending her some luck at last.

CHAPTER FIFTEEN

MOLLY

Molly gripped her orb and took a deep, deep breath as she made the necessary orb call.

"Lady Violetta, um, Revels Court?"

She had no idea what Violetta's family name was, but a few moments of anxious silence later Violetta's surprised face burst into view in front of her, the orb casting across her workshop.

"Mo- Prin- Hi. I'm surprised to be hearing from you." She grimaced as a loud clang echoed out. "One second."

The orb-cast bounced through the air until Violetta reappeared.

"Sorry, forge is really noisy. What can I do for you?"

It was suitably formal and Molly held in the grimace brewing on her face.

"I need to call in that favour, if that's okay."

Violetta nodded. "What do you need?"

Short and to the point, I can't really blame her.

"I need an introduction to the Lady of the Flora Court. I met her briefly but I'd like to do this under the radar if possible."

Violetta's eyebrows rose, no less surprised for the slight singeing at one edge that hadn't been there during the tea-house fiasco, as Kainen was merrily calling it.

"Well, I mean I can certainly ask. Lady Lolly isn't one for meeting much, but if you want to get her on-side for some reason then I'd be ready to talk plants. A lot."

Molly didn't know much about plants, but she had a few ideas of questions she could ask, enough to endear herself before she proposed a trade of sorts.

"She's not too bothered about statuses either," Violetta continued. "But she is trying to get the queens to agree to lift the dangerous imports and exports law temporarily. Something about breeding venom, but the Revel Court affairs are more my area."

And there it was. Lady Lolly wouldn't refuse a royal summons or invitation, no noble would, no matter their views on the monarchies. Violetta's repayment of the favour was the information on how to get on Lolly's good side.

"That's exactly what I need. How quickly can you set up a meeting?"

Violetta frowned. "Well, if she's at court now then whenever you need."

"Now?"

"Let me ask, hang on."

Violetta swiped off and Molly bounced on the balls of her feet as she waited. She expected a call back, but to her surprise an envelope materialised in front of her, the palest pink paper with dark green lettering.

She opened the envelope and pulled out the card, then snorted as she read the invitation, which had clearly been dictated on the spot and sent without review.

The Flora Court cordially invites Princess Molly. She really doesn't have any middle names? Lucky. Elverhill. Wait isn't it Acorn? Anyway. To tea at the Flora Court at her earliest convenience.

Molly pocketed the invitation and bit her lip. She was in jeans and a sweatshirt, hardly royal visiting clothes, but then Lolly was friends with Demi, who needed to be all but physically forced into a crown whenever the situation called for one.

Now she just had to do the unthinkable and ask for another favour.

"Kainen Hemlock." She held her orb up again.

His face appeared a few moments later.

"You orbed?"

She nodded. "Can you take me to the Flora Court?"

"As in Lolly's court?"

"Yeah."

"As in the woman who threatened to take a pair of big gardening scissors to my throat if I stepped on her perennials again?"

"Well-"

"Why can't it be Tyren?" he grumbled. "Hang on."

He vanished in orb-form and materialised in front of her in real form a moment later with a hand outstretched.

"You only need to drop me off," Molly promised. "I can

probably find my own way home."

"Nonsense. Reyan would never forgive me."

He grabbed her hand and whisked them through the nether, right onto a sweeping paved driveway. The sound of fountains trickling filled the air and gentle warmth kissed Molly's face.

"Ah, she's in a good mood." Kainen sagged. "You do the talking."

Molly nodded as the doors to the towering building looming over the drive opened and Lolly swept out. Her tumble of red hair was tied up with a dark green scarf and she had bulky green overalls on with a pale pink t-shirt. Kainen straightened again, waves of relief radiating from him when Tyren followed Lolly out with a weary expression on his face.

"Princess." Lolly curtseyed, then cast a disapproving gaze sideways. "Kainen."

"I'm just the escort," Kainen said cheerfully. "Tyren, didn't you want to show me some kind of new barrel or something?"

Tyren nodded. "Yes please."

Lolly rolled her eyes as both of them hurried off around the side of the house, but before Molly could find her voice, Violetta hurried toward them. She hadn't bothered to change either given the ragged fireproof trousers and the smudge marks all over her arms.

"Come inside, please," Lolly said. "I have to admit I'm intrigued."

Molly followed them toward the court building and through wide double doors into an oasis of plants, high ceilings and airy light. A soft rushing of water echoed all around them off light stone walls, and Molly let it soothe her enough to do what she had to.

"I'm interested to find out if there's a plant that can be atomised to put people to sleep," she announced.

Lolly blinked. "What, permanently?"

"No! Orbs, nothing like that. Call it a matter of academic interest in potential failsafe defence measures."

"Hmm. Well, there's *lavendula* of course, but I've not thought of atomising that and it does have some side effects."

Molly nodded encouragingly. "I did consider gift-use, but I don't want to just rely on gifts all the time when Faerie's got such abundance of its own wonders."

"Exactly! Gifts are great but not everyone has one. What everyone can do is learn to make the most of the natural realms we live in. Flowers for example have been used for so many things."

"Like what?"

"Well, potions of course, decoration, prestige, signifiers. Many a flower has been the symbol of some revolution in some far-flung realm. Petals for dyes, the list goes on. The natural world of Faerie is constant, ebbing and flowing, whereas Fae come and go."

Lolly clicked her fingers and a table arrived in front of them complete with a tea service. As Lolly headed toward it, Violetta gave Molly a nod of approval.

"I have been experimenting with *icalatha* sap recently, and that has similar effects," Lolly continued as they took their seats. "Well, it's more 'knocks you out cold for hours' than *lavendula*, but as long as you catch the person on the way down it's surprisingly side-effect free, but we haven't thought to atomise that either."

Molly waited while Violetta served tea, but she didn't sip it before passing it across like she had done in the tea-house.

"*Icalatha* had some interesting properties actually." Lolly didn't seem willing to stop now she'd started. "Gives the effect of living death, similar to *apanthian* but without the unfortunate skin boils. What do you need it for?"

"As I said, it's more acade-"

"Between you and me as friends of the royals and the rest of the nobles," Lolly prompted. "I understand you came from the citadel before you realised who you really were, and the situation there is said to be fairly dicey still."

Molly nodded. "So we hear. I've not got much to trade on other than my title, so I reckon it's probably safest to make a few minimal-debt alliances so I'm not completely at the whims of the higher powers."

"That's about right." Lolly snorted. "I'm having my own troubles with the Oak Queen at the moment, and she's being utterly intransigent, no offense."

"None taken, and I can absolutely imagine it. Maybe I can help guide her in the right direction? Or try at least, I can't promise anything."

Lolly smiled. "You're learning fast. Alright, can't be bothered with the formal fluff. I'll give you a vial of icalatha sap now in exchange for you doing what you can to persuade the Oak Queen to lift the dangerous exports restrictions. We only need a day."

"When you say dangerous…"

"Once every eighty years or so, we have a growth of sentient speckle-spores near the waterfalls. I'm determined to cross-species this year because they're showing signs of regenerating finally, but to do that we need a different variation of speckle-spores."

Molly let the terminology flow in one ear and out the other, but after a moment of deep thought, Lolly clicked her fingers and placed a vial of pale pearlescent liquid-like goo down on the table.

"It's not atomised so you'll need to find a way to get it ingested. Maybe get Reyan to ask the Fauna court if they know. They make a lot of potions and tinctures so if there's a way to distil or brew it then they'll have the method. Actually, if they do know, I want to know too. Steer clear of citrus drinks though as it tends to mess with the potency."

Molly smiled. "No need."

She took the vial and pocketed it. Then she drew out the item she'd been tinkering with in her workshops ever since Celeste had her go to the queen's court the first time.

"What's that?" Violetta asked.

Molly held it up and tucked a finger under the slim tube attached to the bottle.

"Universal atomiser. The varying internal nozzles took a bit of arranging, but it's worked on every type of liquid and gel and vapour each time I've tested it."

"That is amazing." Violetta leaned close enough to almost press her nose to the glass bottle. "What if it breaks?"

"Impervious glass. That took some doing as well, but the inside is coated and fired with protective gel and the outside with hardening liquid."

She flinched as Violetta's hand landed on her thigh but Violetta didn't seem to notice as she gazed at the bottle.

"I need to know how this works," she breathed in wonder.

Molly tightened her fingers around the bottle and tucked it back into her pocket.

"I'll need to do more rigorous tests first, but it should be enough for what I need the gel for."

Lolly smiled. "I won't ask. Next time you visit, I want to know how much I'd have to pay for some of those atomisers. I also forgot to put a deadline on our deal, but if I can ask for some help with the Oak Queen in the next few weeks, that'd be great."

"No problem."

Molly twisted around mid-smile as Kainen strode into the hall alone.

"We've had a summons," he announced.

"Oak Queen?" she asked wearily.

"Nope. The citadel has requested another meeting."

Molly stood immediately, which dislodged Violetta's lingering hand, and Lolly did the same with a tiny curtsey.

"Thank you for honouring us with your presence, Princess."

"Call me Molly, and no curtsey if you can help it."

Lolly grinned. "Phew. I can't ask you to excuse me and neither can anyone else, so maybe lead with that next time."

Molly smiled her goodbyes as she took Kainen's hand, barely able to suck in a breath before he whisked them away again. The space in front of the Menagerie formed around them and she bit her lip at the sight of the wide open doors.

"Do I need to be in the meeting?" she asked.

Kainen shrugged. "I said I'd meet Taz inside. He didn't actually mention bringing you, so I'm assuming not. I'm likely to get so absorbed in watching him be pompous that I'll quite forget you're here at all, so don't be gone long if you're planning on being gone."

Molly grinned and slipped into stealth.

"Oh, and if I see her, I'll send her out to play, yeah?" he called.

She didn't need to ask who he meant and decided it was best not to respond. Thoughts of the scenes the Oak Queen had shown her in the orb filled her head and her heart sank as she crept up the lanes. There weren't any people destitute on the lanes as she passed, but there weren't signs of people anywhere. Doors were shut, some shuttered. Windows were curtained over. Holes in the lane were still patched over or fenced off.

The other towers won't help, that's probably why Phoenix has called Taz in, although how he'll get them to be okay with outsiders I have no idea.

She needed better information, and where better than from people she knew.

She slipped out of stealth as she passed through the door to Butch's shop but it was empty and the shelves all but bare. Butch lifted his head, then his shaggy eyebrows.

172

"Miss Molly, or is it Princess now?"

"Molly's fine, Butch, please."

He smiled. "As you wish. I doubt I have much left to interest you though."

"How bad is it?"

"Honestly? Bad. Everyone's struggling and the food runs have all but dried up. We see grain going down but there's nothing coming back up. Some who've been growing their own had to move their stuff inside to avoid it being stolen. Thieves are running further up and down and there have been raids on the grain levels."

Molly grimaced. "And what's being done about it?"

"What else can anyone do when anarchy takes hold? The thieves are left to do what they want but any who speak out appear a day later with no memory of the previous day. Some have disappeared and it's the artificers all over again."

"But we still have trades, don't we? Why has the food stopped coming?"

"I'd imagine it's not so much stopped as being stockpiled on its way up. By time it reaches this far in the clouds, it's nothing but crumbs."

"And Phoenix is doing nothing?" She folded her arms.

"Who knows? I've been here even longer than his father's father, and I've not seen anything to redeem him yet. He may have taken over Celeste's domain, but she at least knew how to keep things functioning."

"She was the one who pulled it down during a tantrum," Molly muttered.

"I'd imagine so. Phoenix is right that his family ruled

before she did, but it's more likely because it's situated over the core of power."

Molly hesitated. "Everyone knows about that?"

"Of course. Rumours run the lanes faster than the Arumpii do. Rumour has it he's hunting for it and spending all the man-power on navigating whatever is standing in his way. Rumour has it the other towers won't help until he gives them access. Of course, rumours can be wrong."

"Rumours often have a grain of truth," Molly said. "If I can do anything, I will. I'm not sure what, or how, but I will."

Butch patted her hand and her mind ached with all the possibilities she didn't have. She couldn't give him finery because he wouldn't be able to use it for anything useful, and she couldn't promise any of the food-growth bags that the Illusion Court were producing because they weren't hers to give. She had nothing Kainen and Reyan would want from her as a trade either.

She pulled out the atomiser and the vial. Butch watched with intrigue in his eyes as she removed the stopper from the vial and tipped it into the atomiser. After making sure she had screwed the top back on tight, she held it out.

"You know Talie, right? She has a sister, Sammy, and knocks around at Phoenix's gym?"

He nodded. "I know Young Talie of course. She hasn't been by in a while but I see her walk back and forth."

"Can you give her that for me? Say it's a gift from a friend, no obligation. If she's in danger from anyone, just give them a spray with that and be ready to catch them on the way down."

His lips twitched and he took the vial.

"Consider it done. If you are able to contribute a few edible morsels sometime for the wider good, I think we're beyond pride now."

Molly nodded and strode to the door.

"*When* I'm able to contribute, I will be straight back, or I'll be feeding you him instead."

Butch wrinkled his nose. "That would be disgusting indeed."

"True, but one day I'll be back to fight."

"If you do, there'll no doubt be people ready to follow you in."

Molly let that thought settle as she gave him a rueful smile. She slipped back into stealth the moment she was out of the shop and hurried back down the levels toward the Menagerie.

She hesitated at the entrance to the park. The grass was still green but the space was deserted, and her heart sank as she saw the closed shutter on Merry's kiosk. She ducked her head against the chilly air and hurried toward the only person in the park, his shoulders hunched as he swept a broom idly back and forth.

"Wick?" she called out.

He lifted his head and gave her a wan smile that didn't reach his eyes.

"Molly. Didn't expect to see you around again."

"This is bad," she announced, then grimaced.

He nodded. "It is. You can see Merry had to shut up shop. Not enough supplies to keep serving, let alone people to buy what she could make."

"How is it happening?" she asked. "Where are the stops?"

"Where aren't there stops? We've had reduced industry for a while now but the guilds have fled further down to bow for the nobles, so we have fewer people to sell our wares and services to and can't afford to run them further down."

Molly glanced around at the park, then up at the vents. The core functions would keep running and the Menagerie would be paying them to keep doing it, but the rest of the tower were left to suffer.

"Has anything been done though? What about sharing schemes?"

"Fern's been championing up and down the levels but people are scared. We've had a few who spoke out when they came back from outside the glass, but then they reappear a day or so later with no memory of it."

Molly tensed. "How many?"

"Now? Probably over a hundred. A couple even seemed to be getting memories back, then they disappeared. People are too frightened to speak out now."

He's got Talie wiping over a hundred minds for simply having their say.

She wiped a hand over her face, lost in the mire of all the things she couldn't do to help.

"Word has it he's traded forty percent of our grain production to another tower for very little in return," Wick muttered under his breath. "The grain goes out but nothing new comes in. Rumour floats up of thieves in the middle levels jumping distribution carts and selling things on at inflated prices."

"And he's doing nothing?"

"We've not seen him. They marched us all in to declare ourselves then we've not seen any of them since."

"Declare yourselves?"

"We had to give our names, where we lived and what we do to contribute to the tower. We also had to state that we have no issue with the new governance taking over. Back then we thought it was a new start. Then they disappeared and everything dried up."

His gaze focused and he eyed her up and down warily.

"I'm Molly," she said. "I'm not glamouring or anything. I want to help."

She cringed at how hopeless it sounded but he only sighed.

"That would take a complete overhaul. I only keep my job because the wage helps ease what I can for those around me, but no point having a pocket full of pesanas if nobody's got anything useful for me to buy with them."

"There's still the organic food sites though, right?"

She knew the answer before she'd even finished the sentence and both their heads tilted back.

"In this environment?" He shook his head. "The vents haven't changed in a month. The food sites have all but died off. A few think the vents are probably just stuck, but I reckon its deliberate. People get obedient when they have nothing."

"Or they fight."

Molly swallowed down the promises bubbling on her tongue.

She had promised not to tell a single soul about the skip-way in the workshop, but that didn't mean she couldn't tell someone to keep an eye on the workshop for her, then accidentally find a way to throw stuff through it.

I just have to convince Kainen to convince Taz to find out from Demi where exactly the entrance point is.

"I can't promise anything, but anything I can find to help, I'll do what I can."

Wick smiled. "Many of the young ones say the same, but the less I say about that the better."

He lifted his head and his expression thinned.

"You'd better go on your way. The boots are more than happy to continue doing the Menagerie's bidding. Not subtle about it, but I'd imagine they've got subtle ones lurking around too."

Molly nodded and shoved her hands in her pockets. She vaguely recognised the man lingering at the edge of the park but he didn't stop her as she strode past and continued down to the Menagerie. The doors were still open so she made herself visible again and swept through.

Forehead to chin right into Talie.

CHAPTER SIXTEEN

TALIE

Talie stumbled back as Molly walked straight into her and the infuriating waft of citrus filled her nose.

I should have known Kainen wouldn't come without her.

She wrapped one arm around her middle and rubbed her shoulder with the other hand as her insides somersaulted. Wild thoughts of demanding to know who the random woman at the tea-house was filled her head, but she shoved them aside as Arrow chittered loudly and took a flying leap from the top of the stairs. Whether he was feeding off her emotions or just sensed Molly was no threat, he skittered down the length of the banister and darted across the floor to Molly.

"Hello," she said with a startled laugh. "Arrow, right?"

Talie stared as Arrow climbed up Molly's leg and clung to her upper arm with his whiskers on auto-twitch.

Traitor. She bit down the sudden urge to laugh. *He knows somehow, he must do.*

All humour fled as Phoenix approached with Taz and

Kainen flanking him warily.

"You have a habit of disappearing around here lately," Phoenix said.

Talie stiffened and even Arrow went still with his back paws wedged firmly in the crook of Molly's arm.

Molly tilted her head, her gaze full of fire as she stared back at him.

"The Menagerie trained me well," she said. "Place looks a bit torn through still."

Talie held in her groan with great effort.

A few months and she's striding around like she's invincible.

"I'm sure it's nothing as grand as your great palaces." Phoenix shrugged. "Too lowly for a princess, I'm sure. Still, we do what we can."

"Careful," Taz warned.

Phoenix smiled. "It is what it is."

He flinched, visibly, as the doors to the labyrinth swung open and Mulberry strode out. The moment he noticed them all assembled, he twisted around to hurriedly shut the doors and stand in front of them.

"Still digging?" Taz asked.

Phoenix folded his arms across his chest, his shoulders tense as he gave Mulberry a quick glower.

"Securing safety, but I doubt that's the crown's issue. We're here to talk trade, but perhaps the girls would prefer to catch up on their own."

It was an order veiled in fake kindness and a desperate attempt to distract attention from talk of the labyrinth, but Talie knew the only way she was getting out of anything without being made to tattle on Molly and the others was to play dumb.

"I doubt we have anything left to talk about," she said coldly.

Molly's face shivered with pain, enough for the same feeling to crash through Talie's chest. She clenched her muscles tight to keep from backtracking.

"Well, at least he's glad to see me," Molly said and looked down at Arrow.

Talie steeled herself to do the worst of it, to chase Molly back into safety for good.

"We don't need royalty swanning in if it's just going to be as bad as your mother."

Molly went still. She dropped into a crouch and guided Arrow gently to the floor, then stood up again. Her cheeks were flushed as she held her hand out.

"Here."

Talie stared at the small *Akiai* charm lying on Molly's palm. It wasn't the heart-shaped one she'd given her but a new one, the strands intricately woven to form a small, multi-coloured rainbow with a hole for a necklace to fit through. Molly had even put a thin silver chain on it ready, and Talie's heart shattered.

She can't be here. If Phoenix realises she mapped the core, even part of it, he'll never let her leave again.

"Don't want it." Talie folded her arms and forced a sneer onto her face. "Give it to your girlfriend maybe, now you're all fancy kissing in tea-houses."

Molly veered back as if she'd been slapped and her fingers curled around the charm tight enough to whiten her knuckles.

"It's not- it wasn't…"

Talie shrugged. "Not my business."

She stalked away, half-expecting Phoenix to call her back. Perhaps even he realised she was perilously close to the edge as the silence clouded the air behind her.

Talie stared into the freezing air gusting down from the vents and willed it to dry the tears away.

The words weren't lies exactly, but they burned like the realm's worst headache on her tongue.

I need to get out of here. I need somewhere safe to think.

She slowed her pace and stared at the entry to the workshop alley, as if instinct had led her there.

"Hello, Young Talie." Butch eased himself away from the stretch of wall he was leaning against.

"Hi Butch." She hesitated when he continued eying her. "You need something?"

"We all need something, now more than ever."

"True."

She wanted to say she was doing everything she could, but she was afraid it would be closer to a lie than the truth.

"I hear you're climbing the levels socially," he continued. "Inner circle of the establishment, some say."

She shrugged. "Everyone's trying to survive, protect stuff."

"True," he echoed. "I remember when the citadel was a rambling hive of draughty stone tunnels and walkways, but the distribution of power and wealth was fair as Fae can get. It was long before your time, before even Phoenix's father took control of this tower, but things have grown up and degraded down ever since."

"Was he a good man?"

"His father? No, not especially. He did achieve many trades with other towers, but that sort of affluence comes with lingering debt."

"Not a spade for a fork then."

"Exactly. Custodians became guild members, then nobles, then Menagerie assassins. The reason the citadel was built was sullied and all but forgotten."

"The well." She glanced around but the lane was empty.

"Yes. The last time the horrors that lurk under all this glass and greed were free, awful things happened."

"How awful?"

"The dead rose without living, nightmares became real, and it took all the effort of so many to trick them into stone chains. Then they built the citadel on top as a defence."

Talie tensed as a wave of icy revulsion sluiced over her skin. The whole dead rising thing could be what Ru was talking about on his orb notes, and then she had to consider the man from the Refuse Guild and his claim of missing bodies.

"Many would say that's an unlikely story," she said carefully.

"Many don't want to see past their own nose and pockets. Faerie and the nether are locked in a timeless dance, a symbiotic romance of opposing strengths. Faerie has her own ways of holding balance but the nether is its own master, and there are places it dwells and gathers."

"I've heard that before, that the well is like a pool of the nether."

"You have well-informed informants then. Most drift up and down without a single thought for what lurks beneath their feet."

"Or outside the glass."

"Or that. We've been contained for so long, I'd imagine only true desperation bordering on mania would make anyone look outside the glass."

"Mania sounds about right," she muttered.

"I'd also assume that with pressure from other towers, tempers will be running high and caution should be taken."

"I think I'm beyond caution now. I've made the failsafes I can for others."

"Not for yourself?"

"Not much point."

"There's always a point, even if the past or the present looks murky."

"The veiled truths are cute, but I'm no hero as it is."

"Then I'll tell you this with no veil whatever. When he was a child, he fell into the waterways. Almost didn't make it out. Still avoids the waterworks levels even now. He's taken great pains over the years to hide it, but I don't think he's faced it. Two very different things."

A kaleidoscope of memories filled her head of every snap and microscopic flinch Phoenix had made about her rain gift.

She caught Butch's eye.

"Thank you."

He nodded. "No debt, just an old man grateful for those willing to listen to his old stories. Now, before I forget, Someone asked me to pass on a gift to you."

"Who?"

He smiled. "A friend, she said. Perhaps she thought it safest to trust those of us beneath notice."

He lifted his hand out, a small bottle with a delicate tube and pump bubble.

"Perfume?" She wrinkled her nose. "Who is 'she' then?"

She couldn't rule out other towers trying to target Phoenix through her, although she was close to considering letting them.

"Not perfume for you, as I understand it. She said to spray it on others in emergency situations, and be quick to catch them on the way down."

He proffered the bottle again.

"But who is she? I'm not touching it until I know."

Butch laughed. "So suspicious for one so young. Youth is wasted on the wise. Take it, she of all Fae means you no harm."

When she took a step back, he sighed and set it down on the lane between them.

"Interesting girl, Miss Molly," he added. "I've not seen impervious glass for near an age, but I can easily believe she made that one herself."

Talie's heart squeezed as Butch walked away up the lane. She gave it all of a second, then seized the bottle and hurried into the alley to get a better look.

It was delicate and small enough to fit into a coat pocket, but a quick squish between finger and thumb and it wasn't breaking any time soon.

She came to leave this for me so Phoenix wouldn't

know, like I tried to do with the liquin when Celeste held her hostage.

Talie pocketed the bottle and wiped a hand over her face. Butch had no reason to trick her either, unless someone was glamouring as him.

She eyed the barrels that would lead her up to Molly's special place on the beams. She hadn't taken the *Akiai* charm either, and her outburst would likely be enough to chase Molly off for good.

She inhaled a sharp gust of chilly air to force the burning tears back.

If only there was some kind of random skip-way. I'd jump into it and never come back.

A warning chitter from near her shoes had her swinging around, but Arrow's attention was fixed on the deserted far end of the alley where Molly's workshop and the little house were.

Not deserted.

Shadowed.

CHAPTER SEVENTEEN

MOLLY

Molly dropped Kainen's hand the second they arrived back in his office at the Illusion Court.

"Of all the ungrateful- I couldn't help the thing with Violetta!" she seethed.

Kainen and Taz exchanged a glance before Taz sank into one of the chairs and Kainen perched against the desk.

"She did seem a little bit volatile about it," Kainen offered.

"I never thought she could be that vindictive. It was downright mean!"

Taz frowned. "Maybe it wasn't as mean as it seemed."

"Didn't you hear what she said to me?"

"Yeah, every word in great clarity, and yet she doesn't strike me as the vindictive type somehow."

Molly scowled. "Neither did I, but she was- wait, do you think she was being compelled?"

Taz leaned forward in his seat, his expression irritatingly amused.

"I don't think so, but Talie has spent her whole life

looking after others, right? Why can't she be doing the same now?"

"You mean chased me off to keep me safe?"

She frowned. If Talie had spoken to her like Phoenix had suggested, she could have simply said as much.

Then again, I wouldn't have listened if she did.

"A wise man once said, 'we are the moment between joy and despair, between laughter and tears, between always and never have been. All that matters is the truth before us in the moment'," Kainen quoted.

Molly frowned. "Who said that?"

"Me, just now." He grinned. "I do feel sorry for Talie though, when I think about it."

"Why?"

"Well, she's doing the noble thing."

"What do you mean 'doing the noble thing'?"

"She's not dim." Kainen frowned. "She clearly sensed something wasn't right and decided to stay close to him, maybe even because she wanted you safe out here with us. She's defensive and snappy and suspicious, but she's not cruel. Comparing you to your mother? Classic ploy to chase you off. Something's going down and I'll bet she's planning to sacrifice herself and keep you out here safe while she's at it. You're the only person I've ever seen her smile properly at. She cares."

"And you knew this?!"

He shrugged. "Well, it's sort of obvious."

"She told you this?"

"She didn't have to." He gave her a withering look. "The girl is clearly in love with you, and what other reason would you reject someone you lov-"

"WHY DIDN'T YOU TELL ME?!"

She stormed out, Kainen's doleful voice echoing behind her.

"Sometimes I don't think anyone appreciates me."

Molly made it all of half a hallway before seething through her teeth and turning back. To his credit, Kainen had left the study door open for her to slink back through.

"Sorry," she muttered.

"No harm done, except to my ego but Reyan insists it needs denting a bit."

"I'm worried about her," Molly admitted. "What if she is still on his side? What if she's not who we thought she was?"

Kainen's expression turned soft. "What if she's all you thought she was and more besides?"

"I'm... still worried." She couldn't quite bring herself to say 'scared'.

"Think about it this way then. You can achieve all the accolades and travel to the furthest reaches of Faerie, but it's all hollow without people. Respect is earned, and you can love several people over a lifetime, but sometimes there's that one person and you just know. Go find out if she's yours or not."

"You're lucky you found yours already."

He laughed. "I am, and that she puts up with me. It's easy to mistake respect for that though. I once thought grudging respect for Demi meant I had to make her mine."

"Orbs, and she didn't decapitate you?"

"She should have done," Taz muttered.

"She was afraid of me for a long time." Kainen's face turned grave. "She'll have my respect for the rest of my life, and hopefully I'll earn hers in return, but it wasn't the same."

Molly sighed. "I only hope I can be as lucky as you then one day. Redemption and finding the other half of your soul, some don't even get one let alone both."

"Don't expect it to be simple, that's all I'll say. It's rarely like the stories. It'll come quietly when you're least expecting it, in someone who pushes all your buttons and challenges you."

"...Yay. But what if life gets in the way, or you keep missing each other?"

Kainen stood and walked to the door. Only once he was halfway through it did he glance back.

"She risked going into the Menagerie with only a slim hope of getting you out. She went into the core to get the fairies out with no real gifts to defend herself with. She faced the core to stay beside you rather than let you go alone. From what I hear, she's had a careful eye on you from the beginning. Maybe it's not life that's getting in your way."

As Kainen left the room, Taz leaned forward with his forearms braced on his knees. Even with the casual clothing and the youth in his face, it was a king looking back from behind the stormy turquoise eyes.

"When you go into a relationship, any relationship whether it's friends or romantic or any other, you have to approach it with the other person in mind."

"Well, obviously-"

"We think we do a lot of the time, but often we're either thinking in terms of what we can take or what we can give."

Molly frowned. "Giving is good though, helpful."

"Is it?" Taz lifted an eyebrow. "Did you ever stop to think that what you're wanting to give isn't what they need?"

"I... I want her to be happy, but she won't let herself."

"Maybe Talie doesn't want to be happy. You can't force her. You can only give her what she wants. Don't be so arrogant to assume you know what she needs better than she does."

"But if she's self-destructing, I can't just sit around and watch."

"No, and you shouldn't, but she has to make the journey for herself. All you can do is be there for her while she makes it. If she forgets to eat, take her food. If she's tired, do something relaxing with her."

Molly's heart sank.

She did that for me countless times, bringing food or checking on me, training me to fight, freeing the Fairies when I couldn't.

"What does she want?" Taz asked gently. "Not what you think she needs, what does she want?"

"Sammy safe. Me safe. The citadel safe." Molly groaned. "But she never once thinks about keeping herself safe, and who else is going to look out for her? I need to get inside."

Taz shook his head. "No, you don't. We managed to agree to discuss the situation again with Phoenix and we'll be arranging for some further supplies to be sent in via complex nobility trades, but she made her choice."

"So you just expect me to leave her there after all that?"

"For now, yes."

Kainen rolled back in with Reyan before Molly could explode.

"You can get me back into the citadel, can't you?" she demanded. "I need to try and convince her to see sense."

Kainen grinned. "Action, I love it. But no, we can't, not yet."

"Never thought I'd see you talking sense," Taz said.

"Oh, we're absolutely going in to get Talie out, just not right now."

"We can't."

"We can."

"No, we can't."

"Absolutely can."

"Why are you so determined about this?" Taz demanded. "Talie made her choice."

"It was the wrong choice then." Kainen snapped back, barely able to hide his grin as Taz glowered at him. "Talie's practically family once she and Molly sort out the lovers' tiff. She's a sarcastic pain from what I've seen but good where it counts."

"She's too much like you, you mean."

"Exactly! She's basically me in a skirt. Except I doubt she's ever worn a skirt, but still, who wouldn't want any variation of me in a-"

"Don't finish that, I beg you," Reyan groaned.

Taz huffed. "It's not the same."

"Kind of similar though. I'm sure I have better legs."

"Not the skirt bit! Molly's young-"

"No younger than you were when you and Demi were running around blowing up country clubs and assassinating kings."

"That was different!"

"Kind of not different though."

"BAUBLES!" Molly winced as the word ricocheted out of her mouth at an earth-shattering volume, but it worked as the entire office fell silent. "I'm capable of deciding this for myself. Slightly put off by the skirt part, no offense, but I'm going in and nobody's stopping me."

Kainen lifted a hand and his expression turned serious.

"How about I go? I can travel through the shadows and see what the options are, how far down toward the core they are. It could buy us some time if they're nowhere near it."

"Yeah, you we can spare," Taz retorted.

Kainen stuck his tongue out.

Reyan sighed. "Faerie give me strength."

CHAPTER EIGHTEEN

TALIE

Talie eyed the alley outside Molly's workshop, then surged forward past the door as the shadows twitched at the far end.

"How is she?" she demanded.

No body formed, but she thought she heard a sigh, like a distant wind through a gap in the glass.

"Stung," Kainen's bodiless voice answered, although there was a faint air of amusement lingering in the gloom.

"Oh."

"She can't see the truth in front of her face," he added. "So I had the tiresome task of explaining the obvious to her."

"The obvious?"

"Well, that performance in the Menagerie was clearly to push her away. It might have worked but she'd have figured it out eventually either way."

Talie looked over her shoulder. "I had to."

"I know. Could have softened it a tiny bit though. That

dig about her mother was unnecessary."

"Maybe, but she wouldn't have gone otherwise, she's too stubborn."

"That makes two of you. It was pointless too, because he asked Taz for extortionate deals he's in no position to be demanding."

"You think the meeting was likely just to rattle the other towers?" She bit her lip, unsure how much of Phoenix's plan to reveal.

"Or glean information about how much we know. The towers all want access to the well and we can easily imagine what they'd want to use it for. We can't risk letting the Omens loose either."

Talie shuddered. "No, we can't, but I'm working on it. Is she... is she happy otherwise?"

"Happy isn't the word I'd use. She barely sleeps, tinkering away in that workshop at court late into the night. Keeps storming about threatening royalty for not intervening. That bit's brilliant, but anyone would think she's avoiding facing something. Or someone. You want me to tell her anything from you?"

"Tell her..." *What can I possibly say?* "Tell her we're fine."

A gentle snort. "That would be a lie."

"Maybe. Then don't tell her anything."

Kainen was silent so long that Talie thought he'd gone.

"She won't stop, you know," he said gently. "Are you sure you wouldn't rather be on the outside fighting in?"

Talie folded her arms over her middle and clenched her muscles tight. Temptation warred with the sinking realisation that Butch had given her the one thing she needed in order to take Phoenix down, his fear of water, but she was the only person she knew who had the gift to do it with.

"I can't. There's something I might be able to do to stop him, and I have to take that chance. He's had me wipe a lot of minds as it is and it's only going to get worse if I don't. He's been controlling the whole thing from the beginning, Celeste, me, Sammy, all of it, and if he finds the well there'll be no stopping him, with or without the other towers involved. They want it too."

The swoop of relief seesawed with the unnerving realisation that if Phoenix could somehow divine her treachery, or had ways of listening in, she would be done for.

"Noted. Keep yourself safe. Oh and be prepared. I think Molly's planning to yell at you a lot the next time she sees you."

The shadow dissipated into normal gloom and Talie dropped her head back. It took a moment of confusion about the state of her face before she realised it was her lips lifting.

The others wouldn't let Molly come in now they knew the depth of the danger, but she was out there trying. It was enough.

She slouched back to the Menagerie, reassured that Kainen's bodiless appearance meant Molly was already safe outside the citadel.

The entrance hall was empty and even Mulberry had removed his awful presence from outside the labyrinth doors, which meant Phoenix was probably somewhere else entirely.

Talie walked toward the stairs, her mind full of what she'd heard about the vault being the location of the mysterious maps Phoenix was having made. From what little she'd heard, there were a set of storage rooms near the back of the Menagerie and the vault was a securely locked room for keeping valuables in.

Halfway across the entrance hall, a loud rumble filled the air. Shouting echoed and several guards shot past her toward the kitchens.

People cascaded out of rooms as the doors leading to the kitchens slammed off their hinges and a wave of something beige burst past.

Talie stared at the explosion of what looked like corn as two people slipped in it and others tried to wade through.

Her gaze drifted sideways, toward the open doorway leading to the storage rooms. She sidestepped around the edge of the corn and sidled through the doorway that led into the storage, and the Menagerie's vault.

The shouting continued but she pressed on past piled furniture and old tapestries dumped in corners to reach the deceptively boring wooden door in the far corner.

She pulled out the key she'd kept from her time masquerading as a maid in the kitchens. She'd managed to work out exactly where everything was in her previous attempts to free Molly months ago, something she was grateful for now.

Her heart pounded as she slid the key into the lock, and she glanced over her shoulder as the mechanism clicked.

The shouting was getting quieter and less frantic as she slipped inside and eyed the room. Square and full of stuff in glass cases or wooden lockboxes nailed to the wall, she remembered the trunks in the library full of maps, but there were no trunks to be seen.

Maps would be on an orb maybe.

She looked around for an orb reader, but even though the room was neat and heavy with dust, she couldn't see anything remotely resembling an orb.

A small glass cabinet caught her eye, along with the fingerprints haloing the dusty lock. She squinted through the gloomy beam of light coming from the open doorway.

Last known recipe for enervation. What the hell is enervation?

She pulled her orb from her pocket but couldn't risk Phoenix having secret access to it. There were far too many steps and ingredients, scribbled in a barely legible scrawl on aging paper, but it was the line at the end that had her frozen.

Three days' infusion and shock and enervation is complete. Ensure the body has no decomposition and check on resurrecting that inner decay is minimal.

She pressed a hand to her mouth. It was beyond old, but it was also the only thing in the recently opened cabinet. Phoenix's wards kept everyone else out, if what Mulberry had said was correct, so he might be the one opening it. Reading it.

He might be the one using it, or planning to.

She shuddered as chills raced over her skin while her insides bubbled, but the slightest hint of precipitation beading on her skin had her walking fast out of the room. If there were any maps, they were either concealed or Phoenix had hidden them elsewhere.

She pulled the door shut behind her, locked it and pocketed the key.

He isn't worried about replicating gifts. He's resurrecting people to wield them.

She had no proof but given his weird behaviour recently, and some of the methods familiar to the potion Celeste had been using for gift extraction like coalbane and channelling through the nether, she'd have bet on it.

She eyed the corn already being swept away in the entrance hall and lifted her head in alarm as Sammy skidded to a frantic halt in front of her.

"Phoenix is looking for you."

Her insides cramped with panic, but unless he saw her poking around she was still safe for a while longer.

"What else is new?" She shrugged, the movement jerky.

"Just listen. He made me pack a bag for you."

Talie shrank into her coat.

If he found me...

"What for?" she asked.

"A delegation from the towers arrived pretty much the moment everyone left after your ridiculous diva performance, and what was that about? Molly looked heartbroken."

Talie grimaced as her chest twisted tight.

"What did the delegation want?" she prompted.

"They said if Phoenix doesn't produce access to the well in the next seven days, the other towers are going to assume command."

Talie's jaw dropped. "That's never happened before."

"I know. I'm worried, but he wants you down in the labyrinth with him."

Talie bit her lip and stared at the double doors closed at the front edge of the hall.

Choices danced before her, to find a way out, or to a hiding place for her and Sammy until she could.

Or to use what Butch had told her and take Phoenix down

I could always delay things until the other towers come in. Can they really be any worse? Can I take that risk?

"Talie."

She jumped at the rough bark of her name and looked up as Phoenix strode down the stairs toward them. Sammy held out a bag, bulky and full of what Talie assumed would be clothes.

"Sammy's told you what happened?" Phoenix demanded.

"About the delegation, yes, but-"

"No, about the kitchens."

Talie blinked slowly. "The kitchens?"

"Yes. The Menagerie kitchens have been raided. Would you happen to know anything about it?"

"Me? Why would I?"

His head tilted and he smiled dangerously.

"Well, you were so concerned before about feeding the tower. Rebels are targeting the grain stores, the food production levels, and now our kitchens have been pilfered from with no sign of forced entry."

"And you think I had something to do with it?"

Don't mention maps, please don't ask about the maps.

"Did you?"

The memory of a small key passing from Nia's hand to Finola's filled her head, and their veiled conversations about caution.

She lifted her chin and settled her weight steady over both feet as she faced him down.

"No. I didn't. I didn't have anything to do with the grain store, or the production levels, or the kitchens. I haven't even been near the kitchens for ages. I don't even *know* anyone from the kitchens, not since you replaced the ones I worked with when I was in here last time."

She wouldn't wilt under his fierce gaze, no doubt digging with his truth gift to divine the depths of her soul. Droplets launched from her skin into the air, enough to bring Phoenix's gaze away from her face and upward. He grimaced at the sight of the water hanging in midair and sighed.

"Fine. Let's go."

He set off toward the far end of the hall and Talie grabbed Sammy's hand.

"Be safe," she murmured. "If all else fails, workshop."

She had to hope Kainen would reappear at some point and take care of Sammy.

"You too. I'm sorry about everything. I wish I told you everything years ago, but you don't under-"

"TALIE."

"Orbs, I'd better go."

She squeezed Sammy's hand and swung the bag over her shoulder. Phoenix stood with Mulberry, who looked her up and down with the usual sneer as she approached.

"Remember, remove dissent by any means necessary," Phoenix said.

Mulberry smiled and Talie's skin crawled.

"Extermination?" he asked hopefully.

"I expect to find calm when I return," Phoenix said. "Whatever way that needs to be achieved is up to you to decide."

As he stalked ahead through the double doors, Mulberry gave her one last scathing look and strode away toward the door to the kitchens. Talie peered after Phoenix with her heart pounding and her skin damp then bent down to Arrow waiting by her feet.

He turned his little face up expectantly and she hoped he would understand her.

"Stay out here, okay?"

He snuffled his whiskers and chittered a sharp note she'd come to recognise as irritation. As he scampered through the doors ahead of her, she took a deep breath and followed him into the gloom.

CHAPTER NINETEEN

MOLLY

Molly wiped a hand over her sweaty forehead, then grabbed one of the many charcoal grey towels lying around the workshop as the door swung open. She tensed as Glennoria Featherdown swept in, then managed a smile as Glennoria bobbed her head in acknowledgement.

"It's… a serviceable work station, I take it?" Glennoria asked.

Molly gulped down the snort brewing. In a sweeping maroon dress of crushed velvet, complete with an ostentatious matching hat full of feathers, Glennoria didn't look like she patronised workshops often.

"It's got everything I need and more," Molly agreed. "You want something fixing?"

Glennoria grimaced. "No, and I will ignore the fact that as Crown Princess of Faerie, you shouldn't be grubbing around with dirt all over your forehead."

Molly scrubbed her face with the towel in her hands and let it drop onto the worktop.

"It's oil and it comes off thankfully. How can I help?"

"A princess doesn't ask how she can help."

"Well it's a lot nicer than saying 'what do you want' or throwing something at your head."

Glennoria's lips twitched. "I suppose so. I thought you might like the latest news from the citadel."

Molly sat up then caught herself.

"What trade do you want for it?"

Her insides pounded at the thought of anything from the citadel, but nothing came for free in Faerie.

Glennoria sighed. "Straight to business, that I can appreciate, although it wouldn't hurt you to be seen around court a little more in the company of someone other than the lady or lord."

Molly cocked her head. "I see. I'll bear that in mind."

"Good. It's infinitely sensible to be establishing your own connections in Faerie's elite circle."

"Not my grandmother's?"

Glennoria's lips thinned and she glanced around before approaching the workbench.

"That would be the easiest route to power. She'd give it willingly at first of course, as long as you're amenable."

"I'm not well-known for being amenable apparently."

Glennoria chuckled. "No, I've heard rumblings in a similar vein. But court connections can be extremely useful, especially considering the citadel is said to be about to fall."

"Literally?" She bit her lip.

"I'd say in more of a social and economical sense. The nobles are talking about moving their holdings again and wagging tongues say even the boots are grumbling because they're doing overtime in the core tunnels."

Molly grabbed the towel again and wiped vigorously at her hands, smearing the oil as much as she was wiping it.

"The boots often grumble," she said, clinging to a last hope.

"I wouldn't know, but rumour has it they're ingratiating themselves with the nobility as private guards against the upturn in thievery running amok among the levels."

In a way, she couldn't blame them. The boots were people like any other with families to feed and protect, but with the food not even making its way up anymore, she couldn't rely on the establishment to help her take on Phoenix.

"The artificers are also worried because they're detecting unhappy levels of the nether," Glennoria added. "Everyone knows the citadel was built there for a reason, but if the power is excessive and the artificers are blabbing about it, then soon everyone is going to want a piece."

"Which is why Celeste wanted it kept secret," Molly muttered.

"Quite. The queens will no doubt want to pull rank, the nobles will want a piece and the people will be the ones used to obtain it, at any cost."

"You almost sound like a fan of the moral side."

"I never said that. I simply know how these things work and align myself accordingly at the time."

"Hmm." Molly frowned. "Well Demi won't be questing to use it, I know that much."

"You believe that much."

"Not a fan of the queen?"

"She's young."

"Is that why you're so against Reyan too?"

Glennoria watched her but Molly held herself firm. If people were going to keep insisting she was a princess, she would take the safety that came with it. Glennoria was very unlikely to blast her off the face of the planet and risk angering the court and the queens. She only hoped her shaking hands were hidden by the towel.

"The lady is young too. Many nobles weren't pleased with her promotion to rank and title. She used to be a mere laundry girl and suddenly she's advanced herself to ruler. It doesn't go down well with those who have fought and machinated their stations through effort rather than something as simple as love."

"Love is anything but simple."

Glennoria smiled. "Perhaps, but it can be worth it."

Molly let that slide, mainly because she didn't want to push her luck by asking about Glennoria's personal life, and also because she couldn't exactly answer the question if it was returned.

"Well, court politics aside," she sighed. "Let's hope something can be done to bring the citadel back to calm and fairness, even if that means getting rid of another despotic leader."

"I'd advise that it's unwise to be so open about the causes you support. It can make you an easy target for those who intend to charm."

"You sound like Kainen."

"The young lord plays the fool often, but he's not entirely dim."

Molly grinned. "Careful, that almost sounded like grudging admiration."

"I wouldn't go that far," Glennoria said sniffily. "I'll take my leave, Princess, with your permission. But a word of warning, even if they get rid of Phoenix, it'll leave the other towers at the advantage to swoop in, unless someone else steps in to take over from him."

Molly frowned at Glennoria's back as she swept to the door and out. She was still frowning when Kainen ducked in a minute later.

"I saw Glennoria storming out with a smile on her face. Offered her another tea, did you?"

Molly shrugged. "She wanted to trade citadel information for being seen with me around court more, nothing I'd labour to give in return. Was singing your praises though, even turned her nose up slightly less when I mentioned Reyan."

"Miracles will never cease."

"Well, we could do with a miracle. I still don't know what to do for the best. All this power I'm supposed to have as a princess and I can't even sweep in to fix anything. It's all obligations and tea-houses and favours. When do I get to start using this power for the better?"

"Honestly?" He grinned. "When you stop whining about it."

Molly stilled. "What?"

"Okay, crash course. A title isn't power. It means nothing. All a title is, is *influence*. The power comes from what you do with it. You don't like the court games and the favours and the intrigues? Abdicate."

"Demi never has to do any of this."

"Yes she does, but remember that Demi essentially started a court and got to choose her own people. Joining an established court is different. Look at Reyan. She came into this court where the alliances and vendettas are already firmly bedded, and she earned her title through fighting for it."

"She says she had to because you skipped off somewhere."

"Exaggeration, I didn't skip. But she did have to, and she did earn it. Now's your chance. You either learn to navigate the current game, or you be prepared to smash through it and risk a war. Would you cause a war for a few people, or perhaps for just one?"

"I don't want to cause a war! I just want to do the right thing."

He picked up one of the pendulums she was fixing and swung it back and forth with one finger.

"And those that don't want to do the right thing? You going to stomp on them because their idea of 'right' isn't the same as yours? Who decides? As it is, if you want to save the citadel, what are you willing to do to save it? Work that out, then we can talk."

Molly frowned. "The royals can't go in without invitation though, not without breaking the covenant thing."

"True. So how do you get around that? Or do you just go through it? You know the-"

A subtle shiver in the air had them both jumping back. Molly threw up a protection warding before Kainen could dodge around to her side, but she almost dropped it again as Sammy staggered into being and slammed hands first into the workbench.

"Sammy! What are you doing here?"

"Need-" Sammy gasped a ragged breath, her dark eyes wild. "Help."

CHAPTER TWENTY

TALIE

"Hurry up."

Talie ignored the snap in Phoenix's tone as he stalked ahead of her through the labyrinthine tunnels. They had abandoned the fixed lighting a while ago in favour of lanterns, but Talie still didn't dare make any rude gestures or pull any faces behind his back.

"How do we know where we're going?" she asked.

Phoenix flicked an irritable glare over his shoulder. Long gone were the smooth smiles and calm sentences, his control unravelling even faster than his brief rule.

"I could ask you the same thing. You've been down here before, yet you haven't given me a single suggestion."

She tensed at the warning in his tone and firmed a protection warding around herself. It wouldn't last long against him so diplomacy was still her safest bet, or as diplomatic as someone like her could manage.

"We weren't exactly following a path before either," she muttered. "Just wandering in the dark. We got lucky- actually, we got led."

Phoenix halted and she stumbled sideways to keep distance between them before he could find the edge of her warding.

"Led how?"

"There was a voice, weird one, inside my head." She couldn't exactly lie or refuse to answer. "It kept going on about power and then we found Celeste."

"And yet you never mentioned it."

She shrugged. "You never asked."

"Oh, but I did. Not the exact question perhaps but I asked you to tell me what happened and you never mentioned hearing them."

Them. Of course he would know the Omens aren't just one voice, one entity.

Talie shoved her hands in her pockets to hide them shaking.

"It was chaos."

He cocked his head and she held his gaze with her heart pounding. Rain beaded over her skin and she focused on keeping her breathing steady to avoid it evaporating into clouds above them.

Her fingers skimmed over the tiny perfume bottle, apparently a gift from Molly although she still had her doubts.

"I know you don't agree with my ideals," he said. "You're hopeless at hiding your expressions. You've been extremely useful to the cause over the years though, and I don't want to have to lose you."

Icy revulsion rippled over her skin and the moisture leaked upwards.

"But you will?"

He nodded. "If you force my hand I'll have to. My family ruled this tower before Celeste arrived, and the entire citadel before that. It's my birthright and I will reclaim it."

"By any means necessary? Is that why you're so desperate to get into the core? You can't do it without the extra power?"

She had no chance of achieving anything by keeping him talking, but she had to know. Even if she had two seconds free to run, she would orb Molly and tell her, consequences or not.

"The core has many resources, and I need access to those to continue my family's great work."

Talie shuffled a tiny step back.

"Butch said there used to be loads of weird things being done when the power was unleashed before, and now there are rumours of resurrections and all sorts."

Phoenix smiled, the movement slow and monstrous.

"Imagine if we could? What an asset it would be to resurrect long-lost gifts that have gone extinct, or even reunite people with their loved ones? For a cost of course, but how much would people pay for that? It could fund the citadel six times over, I'm sure."

Talie kept the revulsion off her face even as her lips fought to curl.

"So it's about money?"

"Everything needs money, Talie. You should know that by now. Besides, considering your lofty views about death, I'd have thought you'd see this as a positive thing."

"Exploiting people and their dead loved ones for money is never going to be a positive thing." She caught the flicker of irritation on his face and panicked. "How are you even going to get that past the other towers?"

"The other towers will concede when they see I hold all the cards. I've learned the most power comes from wielding the best trade in all of Faerie, the same as always." He flicked a hand in her direction and she flinched. "Leverage."

She turned enough to look back over her shoulder without losing sight of him. The thoughts of drowning him in one of the bat pits, assuming she could find them again, swept out of her mind as two women appeared.

"What's going on?" she demanded. "Why is she here?"

Sammy pulled a face. "Nice, hello to you too."

Talie grimaced but the look on Finola's face was equally grim.

"Is this really necessary?" Finola asked.

Phoenix nodded. "Oh yes, I think so. I'll make you a deal, both of you."

Talie opened her mouth to refuse, to insist she wasn't going anywhere until Sammy was safe, but Phoenix snapped his fingers and a bunch of papers landed in his hand.

"These are records from the kids' home you both came from. All I need is your compliance, and I'll give them to you."

Sammy gasped but Talie twisted to put herself between them.

"Say it then. Say both our parents are named in them."

Phoenix laughed. "So suspicious, I'd be wounded if I weren't so impressed. I have trained you well. These papers contain not only Sammy's parentage but yours too. Do you want to know your real name?"

"No."

She didn't, but it surprised her that Sammy didn't say a word.

"It's a pretty one. They named you after a flower before abandoning you."

"So? Tons of Fae are named after flowers. Doesn't make a difference now. Are we walking on or what?"

"Not before you tell me absolutely everything about your previous visit here."

She shrugged. "How far weren't you following us for then? That rockfall you so happily caused almost did me in. Assuming there's only one way to the core, you might have even sealed it off for good with that."

"That was a regrettable oversight."

Talie snorted. "Don't lie."

"Talie." Sammy tugged on her sleeve like she used to as a child. "Don't."

Talie bit her lip. Phoenix wanted answers and she needed to stall enough to get Sammy out somehow.

"Fine. We wandered for a long time, no way of knowing how long. After Celeste's torture rooms, there were long tunnels and not much else. One cavern had a load of bats, but they didn't do anything. After that, we started hearing the voices. Oh, and the bat room had loads of pits in the floor. That could be the other side of the core though for all I know."

Phoenix hummed under his breath and looked at the tunnel behind him. He vanished the papers in exchange for a small scrap that he cupped in one hand, and Talie tensed as Finola dragged Sammy close by the shoulder.

"*Count of three,*" she mouthed.

Talie didn't even have time to wonder how Finola was planning to tackle him, but there were two of them against one now.

"*One.*"

She didn't drop her bag, not wanting to draw attention as Phoenix eyed the small piece of paper in his hand.

"*Two.*"

Finola lifted a hand and Talie eased her weight over softened knees, ready to spring. A subtle glow flickered in front of them, a ghost of purple grey light clouding over the wall as Phoenix turned around.

"Three!"

Phoenix roared as the skip-way flared to life in a swirl of purple and grey. Finola shoved Sammy toward it with her hand still on her shoulder, but Talie dodged behind her to help push as Sammy struggled to stay behind.

Talie shunted herself sideways as Phoenix lifted a hand to grab Sammy. He almost caught a chunk of her braids as she stumbled forward, but Talie smacked his hand down and forced her entire body weight against him. They tumbled to the floor as Finola reached for her next, but she twisted away as Phoenix leapt to his feet and tackled Finola instead.

The skip-way wavered and the second of hesitation between helping Finola or charging after Sammy sealed her fate. The swirl of nether dissipated into nothing, and Talie winced as Phoenix caught Finola by the throat and slammed her against the wall so hard her head knocked against it.

"Let her go!" she shouted.

"No. There's nothing worse than a traitor."

"Proud of it," Finola seethed. "The moment you put the wards up again, I knew we'd lost any hint of who you once were."

"So you've been plotting against me, sending those pathetic reject kids you call students to carry messages to people who want me gone. Do you really think they're all loyal to you?"

His hand clamped around Finola's throat but her eyes blazed as she stared back at him with laboured breaths.

"Yes. Unlike you, I can trust mine."

Talie had nothing except rain and glamour to help Finola with, neither of which would make any dent in Phoenix's rage.

Except the water.

She sucked in a breath and focused on pulling as much moisture from the air as she could.

"Trust? What do you know about trust?" Phoenix spat. "You think I didn't know you had something to do with the raid on the kitchens?"

Finola pushed her chin as far forward as she could manage with his hand clamped around her throat and her dark eyes flashed with malice.

"So worth it." Her voice dripped with venom. "You only care about yourself, your legacy."

Talie froze with a cloud forming above her head as a small shadow moving fast zipped across the ground and launched upward for Phoenix's face.

"Arrow, no!"

He heard her mid-leap and used Phoenix's shoulder as a springboard to change direction with such astonishing speed that she gasped. He chittered angrily as he landed on the ground and shot off back into the gloom of the tunnel before Phoenix could get at him.

I should have spent more time training him. If only I could have gotten him out to Molly with a message.

"Where did you send her?" she asked, if only to get Phoenix's mind distracted.

Finola coughed. "Somewhere safe."

"I don't know how you managed that, and to get through my wards of all things, but no more." Phoenix's hand tightened and Finola's eyes widened before she closed them tight.

"Just get it over with," she hissed.

Talie realised what that meant and ran forward, right into Phoenix's impenetrable warding. She bounced off and crashed into the opposite wall, but she didn't even have any of that fancy iron that had worked so well on Celeste before because she'd handed them all back when she decided to return to the citadel, to Phoenix's control.

"Stop it!"

She had nothing except words left. Even her gift seemed to be beyond reach now and Phoenix wasn't listening. Scattered clouds formed above them in her desperation but it wouldn't be anywhere near enough rain to scare him off, and she couldn't focus enough to draw it together.

Finola's face contorted and Talie couldn't look away as her features went slack and her body dangled. She winced as Phoenix dropped Finola's body to the ground like a discarded sparring glove and stalked past her.

"We can't leave her," she insisted.

"Carry her then. You try to stop me or undermine me, or cross me in any way, and you'll get the same."

Talie crouched beside Finola as the clouds unleashed a torrent overhead, drowning her cheeks like gigantic tears.

"I will come back for you, I promise," she whispered. "One day, if I survive, I'll take you home."

She had to stand, to steel herself and firm her warding afresh as she walked after Phoenix. She had no idea where 'somewhere safe' would be for Sammy, but she trusted Finola. Even if it was simply somewhere else in the tower, it was better than down in the core.

Without any idea which route they were taking she couldn't guarantee what lay ahead, but as she ventured further into the endless gloom, she promised herself that she'd torment Phoenix any way she could.

Hopefully right into the nearest pit to drown.

CHAPTER TWENTY ONE

MOLLY

Molly ran for Sammy then staggered to a halt a few steps away.

"What are you doing here? Is it really you?"

Sammy huffed a laboured breath and waved a hand, still doubled over the workshop bench.

"Yes, Sammy, I'm me."

Molly flinched as Kainen bodily guided her aside, court lord and protector in an instant.

"One more time to be safe, please."

"I'm definitely Sammy- eww is that what compulsion tastes like? Talie wasn't exaggerating. Orbs, Talie! You have to help us!"

Molly jostled forward again but another shiver of air dumped Meri, Kainen's second-in-command, between them.

"There's been an unauthorised realm-skip," she announced, then eyed Sammy with disapproval. "That one."

Kainen huffed. "Do you not think I'm aware of that?

I'm literally standing right here looking at her. If I was Reyan you wouldn't be fussing."

"Hmm. What does she want then? Do I need to prepare a room or are there other events you've neglected to warn me about?"

"I am perfectly capable-"

Molly rolled her eyes and barged through both of them to grab Sammy's shaking hands.

"What's happened? Is she okay?"

"No. Phoenix dragged her into the core and he made Finola bring me too, leverage he said, and why would he need that if he's not going to hurt her?"

"Orb muncher!" Molly swore.

"Finola threw me through a skip, I think, or Talie did, and he tried to stop us but she hasn't made it through. He even said he kept records of our parents and never gave them to us, and he wants Talie to do something for him but I don't know what and last time you went down there she almost died and I can't lose her! This is all my fault."

Molly managed to make out the tail end of Sammy's speed-babbling, enough that her insides squeezed tight with fear.

"I'm going in," she said. "Don't care how or what."

"Are you sure?" he asked.

She nodded. "Go round or go through? I'm finding a way through. If I do it, then the queens go on not knowing it happened until it does. If need be, I'll give up my title. I just need that map I made from Milo."

Kainen pulled an orb from his pocket.

"You won't get that easily."

"It's my map! I made it, or charted it or whatever."

"Yeah, and handed it over to another court without even making them trade something for it. It's like I haven't taught you anything. Oh for Faerie's sake. Orb the group chat and tell Taz the doughnuts need more sugar."

"What?!"

"Just do it."

Molly grabbed her own orb with a feral glare.

~NO Kainen~

Molly: Kainen says "the doughnuts need more sugar" apparently.

Demi: Er... what?

Reyan: Huh?

Taz: Ah. It's meant to be more jam, not sugar. I'm on my way.

Demi: Do I want to know?

Reyan: I've learned not to even ask that

Demi: Fair.

Molly barely even got her orb back in her pocket when Taz appeared.

"What's the plan?" he asked.

"Talie's in trouble, which means the citadel is probably in trouble, which means you get a chance to defy both queen and wife in spectacular fashion," Kainen announced.

"Yay me." Taz groaned. "Wait, so we don't have an actual plan?"

"Do we ever?"

"Fair."

"We can't get through the Menagerie without a fight," Molly warned.

"We can't bring in FDPs again either, not this time," Kainen said.

Molly shook her head and grabbed the bag she kept ready under the workbench.

"No need." She slung the bag over her shoulder. "I asked around last time and Butch said there might be a few in the citadel willing to stand."

Sammy nodded. "Nia and Finola have been training some of the kids. I can tell them all."

"No going back to the Menagerie yourself," Molly insisted. "She'd never forgive me."

"Oh, she would. It's me she's angry at, and she'd probably forgive mass murder if it was you doing it."

"How are we going to find them though?" Taz asked.

Molly tapped a hand on her bag.

"I dropped off a gift last time as well. Put a tracker in it. Are we going or what?"

Taz and Kainen eyed each other.

"Are you sure she's related to you and not Demi?" Kainen asked doubtfully.

"Hey!"

Taz pulled out a familiar looking door key and swiped his thumb over it. A skip-way bloomed like an orb-cast in front of them and Molly grabbed Sammy's hand to lead her through.

Her citadel workshop was still caked in dust, but she pushed aside the swell in the pit of her stomach as she released Sammy's hand and strode across to open the door to the lane. She peered out but saw nobody.

"Right, promise me you won't go into the core or the Menagerie," she muttered to Sammy.

"Yes, yes, I promise I won't go into the core or the Menagerie unless forced. I can raise more than enough trouble for him outside."

Molly gave her a tight hug. "Don't I know it. Okay, go. Don't run, don't draw attention."

Sammy nodded and slipped into the lane out of sight.

"How are we doing this then?" Kainen asked. "This is your mission and your arena, Molly."

"Can you buy me some time. I need to get up a couple of levels and spread the word. Maybe go cause some confusion at the Menagerie? Distract them?"

Kainen grinned. "That is my favourite bit. What's our cue?"

"When you see me, we make a run for the core and hope nobody notices. We'll just have to style out the rest."

Taz sighed but Kainen threw his arms out wide.

"Actually, I think she takes after me the most since I honorarily adopted her."

"Stop saying you've adopted everybody."

"Aww, jealous? I can adopt you too if you like. We can have matching leather jackets."

Molly slipped into her stealth gift and into the alley with the sound of their bickering echoing behind her.

"I'd rather never eat doughnuts again."

"Okay that was uncalled for!"

Molly hurried up the levels with grim looks at the shuttered windows and empty alleys she passed.

Butch was almost done shutting up for the evening when she stepped beside him and dropped her stealth gift.

"Hello there, Miss Molly. Is it time?"

"Yeah. Anyone who wants to stand, do it now while Phoenix is deep in the core."

Butch lifted his eyebrows, then bent down to pick up an old tin can. He weighed it in his hands and sighed.

"Hoped I'd never need this again, but sometimes hopes are for fools and knowing better is for those that endure."

He breathed in deep, raised the can to his lips and whistled.

Molly took a step back and wondered if she had time to go and find someone else who might be able to help, although with Talie in the core already, she wasn't entirely sure who.

Butch pressed a hand to the wall of the shop and bent down to drop the can. With a swift kick, he sent it spiralling down the lane. A soft whistle of undulating pitch echoed out and faded as it disappeared around the bend and out of sight.

"Right, well..." Molly took another step back.

A head popped out from the window above the shop

next door.

"Time?" the woman asked.

Butch nodded. "It is. Round up on the way down and I'll start heading upward for a second wave. Orbs, I'm getting too old for this."

The woman disappeared but doors were opening elsewhere and people filtered out into the deepening evening gloom.

"Molly." Rowan from the tailor's shop approached first. "We'll follow your lead. Not because you're all royal or anything, but Butch said you're on our side."

Molly clenched her fist inside her jacket pocket and swallowed the lump in her throat.

"Um, okay? I'm not really leading, it's just we need cover and distraction to get us inside-"

"Say no more. Time we show those Menagerie orb-munchers whose tower this really is!"

The gathering crowd cheered and Molly didn't bother to mention she used to be one of the enemy.

With a gaggle of charged-up Fae behind her, she set off back down the levels. More joined as they passed but the Menagerie doors were still open when she breezed right through into the main hall.

Several of the boots and Menagerie members were gathered, but none of them were doing anything about the two man show currently dying a death in the middle of the hall.

"I'm sure he said something about a meeting though?" Taz asked, making a big show of scratching his head.

"He did?" Kainen frowned and tapped his chin.

"When?"

"You know. I can't remember."

"Crown digging a bit tight these days?"

"No more than your ego is strangling your brain cells."

Molly cleared her throat and they twisted to face her. The gathered guards saw the massing crowd and silence fell. When nobody spoke, Molly decided to make it up as she went along.

"We're taking over," she announced. "You can fight, or just accept it." Still nobody moved. "So, yeah. A couple of us are going down. The rest are staying here to get a handle on things- wait, do you lot have a new leader in mind? Can someone manage this until Butch gets here?"

High-strung chuckles echoed out among the crowd but the guards were still too stunned to react. A couple started muttering to each other, but no signs of charging.

This is going way easier than I thought. Perhaps there's hope yet.

"We'll be fine." Fern ambled forward. "Off you pop."

Molly hesitated, but Crown Princess of Faerie or not, there were some people you weren't dim enough to get on the wrong side of and Fern was one of them.

I need to get to Talie.

She headed past the guards toward the core entrance doors with Taz and Kainen flanking either side of her.

"Now, let's put this silliness aside," Fern announced. "Pre-Phoenix rules to be reinstated. We call a meeting of the towers, rescind any offers he's not bound already and get the grain going out and the food moving up."

Molly pulled out her orb as they entered the core

tunnels.

"Will we get to keep the non-uniform policy?" a hopeful voice asked.

"And the on-shift biscuits?"

"We have more important matters to sort at the moment than uniforms and biscuits, but-"

"That's what they all say."

The sound of discontented grumbling rumbled after them and as the crowd noise grew, a loud bang bounced off the walls and a man strode through the enemy ranks.

Molly recognised the broad-shouldered guard and her heart sank. Mulberry had been the class of cruelty that everyone kept at arm's length, even Celeste.

Everyone except Phoenix apparently.

"Princess," he sneered.

Those gathered behind her weren't enough to break the line of guards, but given the ferocity of many faces they were ready to try.

"Are we asking them to disperse, Sir?" someone prompted.

"There isn't a due process in the new handbook for riots," another said.

"There are a lot of them."

"That'd be a lot of processing."

"Enough!" Mulberry snapped. "Our job is to keep control. So keep it. Anyone steps out, or speaks out, detain them by force."

The guards glanced at each other and a ripple of unease passed between them in a wave of winces.

"Well then, at your leisure," Fern said. "We're not

standing down."

She unearthed a ball from the insides of her cloak, wound her arm back and threw.

Mulberry lifted an arm on instinct instead of warding, and a huge splatter of something sour-smelling exploded over his head.

"Was that your last batch of *Bulbur* berries?" Butch asked.

She nodded. "If we don't make it out of this, nobody's going to be buying any more *Beast* anyway."

Molly didn't say that *Beast* tasted so different outside the citadel, or that *Bulbur* berries weren't mentioned on the official ingredients. She joined in the collective roar instead as several people grabbed whatever they could and launched forward.

Taz threw out a hand to catch her but she dodged.

"We need to get Phoenix, remember?" he said.

Molly lifted a hand and let her sunshine flow into her hand until it was a ray of heat beaming at the enemy line.

"I know, this won't take long."

"Yeah, don't fuss." Kainen joined in. "You've grown so *ceremonial* lately."

Taz squawked with outrage. "I have not!"

Molly left them to it but a few of the guards were fighting with gifts behind their wardings and everyone else was left to throw things.

Molly angled her sunlight to keep the line.

"You know we can't intervene without crossing the royal restriction," Taz insisted.

"Absolutely." Kainen kicked a stray piece of what

looked like a wooden plant bucket that bounced off their warding back into the fray. "Oops, my foot slipped. Ah, and my hand flinched."

Molly choked over a laugh as a passing chair 'accidentally' bounced off his outstretched fingers.

A loud rumbling shook the ceiling and the chaos wobbled, a still point as both sides looked toward the stairs.

A feral battle cry tore through the momentary silence.

Molly's jaw dropped as a wave of people tumbled into view at the top of the stairs, mostly her age or younger. At the front, Sammy and a kid Molly vaguely recognised from the gym had a length of rope between them.

The boy darted down the stairs, followed by most of the youth of the tower given the sea of them, but Sammy vaulted one-handed onto the banister.

"Orbs no!"

Molly ran forward seconds too late as Sammy leapt off the edge toward the battle. She twisted in mid-air and her shoes tapped the warding, rebounding her away again. With the rope still in one hand, she landed on the floor and set off as her friend reached the bottom of the stairs and went the other way.

Molly flinched as a hand landed on her shoulder.

"They're tying them in," Kainen said with an impressed laugh. "Even when they drop the warding they'll have to wade or cut through."

It wasn't even a tie, more complicated weaving of a net, but Sammy moved like she'd been born to fly off wardings.

"Stay and gift her with something safe," Molly begged

as Sammy skidded to a halt beside her.

"More useful skills than waving a gift about." Sammy heaved breathlessly over the words. "You think Talie's the only one that trains herself for the worst? You think she's the only one who can see trouble coming a mile off and plans accordingly? There's a way through, look. Trust me to handle this and go get her."

Molly's chest twisted. In the few moments of chaos she'd almost forgotten.

She gave Sammy's shoulder a squeeze and left her doubled over panting as she hurried past the fading battle.

"You can keep trying but you've nowhere to go," Fern crowed.

Mulberry turned in their direction as they strode past but Molly ignored him and headed for the labyrinth doors. Sammy had asked for trust and she had more than earned it.

"You'll regret this!" Mulberry shouted.

Molly rolled her eyes as she grabbed her orb from her pocket and swiped through to the tiny tracker she'd hidden in the cap of Talie's atomiser bottle. It had cost her an extremely long tea with one of the artificers at the Nether Court to obtain, but it was worth every meandering tale.

"Orbing Fae," Kainen muttered.

Taz nodded sagely. "Same in every realm."

A soft flutter brushed Molly's hair and she gulped down a shriek as Aurora sailed ahead like a spectre into the dark.

"Did you know she was here?" Taz asked.

"No, I thought she was back at court."

"Very loyal birds those are," Kainen said. "I bet she's

scouting ahead."

"What do you know about birds?"

"I know those are loyal ones. Oh, and there's a giant sea bird somewhere that can essentially reproduce on its own."

Molly took the lead as the tracker illuminated a small ball of green light that skewed toward the left-hand tunnel ahead of them and the sound of Faerie's elite echoed behind her.

"Oh well." Taz sighed. "Into the chaos we go again."

"It could be worse, at least you have me."

"Faerie save me."

CHAPTER TWENTY TWO

TALIE

"Which way?" Phoenix demanded.

They stood at a junction with the erratic tapping of his foot echoing off the walls, and Talie tensed as she surveyed the three turnings ahead.

"I don't know. All these tunnels look the same."

"Then how did you make it through do quickly last time?" he demanded.

"You followed us, why don't you know where you're going?"

"I mapped to the cave-in but we're past that now on another branch."

Talie sighed and rubbed her exhausted head with a grimy hand.

"You mean when your cave-in almost came down on my head? That might have been the only way in, and Molly stopped mapping around then anyway."

"Molly had a map?"

Talie grimaced and firmed her warding tighter around her.

"She was taking basic notes I think."

"Another thing you didn't tell me."

"What does it matter? It wasn't a full map of the entire core, and she's not here to give it to you anyway!"

"You'd pick her over me wouldn't you?"

She hesitated at the almost crazed gleam in his eyes.

"That's not-"

"Answer me, or you're of no further use and I'll finish you like I did Finola."

The image of Finola's body circled in Talie's head and the air dampened inside her warding.

I can't take him down, but I'll take as much of him as I can on my way out.

She dropped her hands loose at her sides and let the moisture build in the air, the pressure crowding against the edge of her warding as she thought of Molly and took a deep breath.

"Yeah, I would, because she's not some power-crazy psycho."

Phoenix lashed out a hand and Talie released her warding to focus all her energy and effort on the torrent of water she'd been slowly gathering to her as they walked. The surge splashed Phoenix square in the face and he reeled back with a scream.

Talie darted away and turned to run, to find another endless tunnel, anything was better than facing him.

Fingers snagged in her hair and she yelped as Phoenix dragged her back and smashed her face first into the nearest wall.

"You could have been such an asset," he snarled. "You

could have wielded such power with me. Now you're nothing but a liability, a traitor. Even your precious princess has abandoned you. Where is she now?"

She tried to say something but her cheek was jammed too hard against the rock and his hand on her throat too firmly for more than garbled sound and a feral screech.

The screech that wasn't coming from her own mouth.

The fingers around her throat disappeared and she staggered around as a flash of pearlescent white tore a stream of red from Phoenix's face.

Aurora.

Talie choked over a sob as Phoenix waved his arms and grabbed Aurora off him. Arrow darted up his arm before he could throw her, or worse, and Talie gasped as Phoenix lost part of his finger.

He staggered free of the assault and pointed his bleeding hand at her, the other clamped to the side of his face.

"You'll find the core, and me," he shouted.

"If I do, I'll find a way to finish you," she yelled back.

Arrow scampered up one arm looking like one of the late night budget scare-reels that the orb-waves kept running on a loop with blood dripping from his mouth, and Aurora settled on her other shoulder.

She wrapped a shaky warding around all three of them.

"You do that, and she's dead," Phoenix insisted. "The royals can't draw first blood. If you're on her side, and you attack me, I can demand her crown and her life."

He staggered off into the darkness of the leftmost tunnel and Talie let a frustrated sob bubble out. Arrow shot up her arm to nudge her soaked cheek and Aurora settled on the opposite shoulder.

She took a couple of staggering steps after Phoenix this stopped with a hand against the rock. They likely wouldn't pass the pits and the bats again, but if she was going to stop Phoenix before he reached the core without drawing first blood, then she'd have to think of something and fast.

Footsteps thudded off the walls, the sound of people moving with purpose.

I don't even have energy left to fight anyone.

She slid her fingers over the slim dagger wrapped against her wrist anyway as Arrow hurried down from her shoulder, but Aurora remained with her as three faces came into view.

"Talie!"

Talie bubbled out another sob as Molly hurried forward, only to get stopped by Kainen's arm around her waist.

"Wait until we know it's her," he warned.

"Of course it's her. Let go!"

Molly kicked his ankle hard enough to make him hiss and let go of her.

"Ouch! Not fair, no kicking!"

Talie stumbled forward as Molly threw her arms around her neck and a hysterical laugh burst from her lips.

"You smell really bad," Molly muttered.

Talie let the tears flow and tightened her arms around Molly's waist.

"And you smell like a fancy parlour."

"What do you know about fancy parlours? What's going on? Are you okay?"

A thud echoed down the tunnel and Talie flinched

away.

"He planned the whole t-thing," she choked.

Molly grabbed her by the forearms as Talie sagged against her.

"What? Who? Phoenix?"

She nodded. "He killed Finola, but Sammy-"

"She's safe outside, that's why we're here. Come back with us now."

"I can't."

She clung on for one last aching moment, breathing in Molly's smell. Then she wriggled free.

Molly shook her head. "Whatever madness he's convinced you of-"

"He's been pulling the strings all along, even had Sammy lying to me. He used you to target Celeste, and he'll use me to target you, and the other way round. He's been looking into old recipes for bringing people and gifts back from the dead."

"We'll stop him," Molly insisted.

"You can't! He knows I'm on your side now. If any of us attack him, we break the anti-royal rule."

Molly shook her head. "Come back with me. We can take this back to Demi-"

Talie grabbed Molly's blissfully warm hands with ice-cold filthy ones.

"You are sunshine and brightness and everything good," she insisted. "I'm gloom and misery and all things bad. He gave me rain, remember? I'll ruin your shine if I hang around long enough. All the minds I w-wiped for him, everything I've done."

She yanked her hands free. Molly reached out for her, but Talie twisted into the gloom and set off at a lurching run after Phoenix.

As she ran on, tiny flickers of purple light streaked the walls, the same that Phoenix had been using to mark their progress.

Molly would be right behind her, and she had no idea what way Phoenix even went, but she had to find him before they did, and before he found the well.

"Welcome back, little warrior."

She groaned as the familiar voice echoed insidiously in her head. She hadn't even considered she would need to keep the Omens at bay, whispering and bribing inside her head.

"So soon too. He's almost with us, and you won't best him without our help."

"Doesn't need gift magic to drive a blade into someone's chest," she muttered. "I can renounce any link to royalty before I do it. It's not like I'm blood or married to any of them."

Her chest heaved with effort and her footsteps felt like falling every time they hit the ground but she tumbled on.

"Talie!"

She swore under her breath. The others sounded right behind her. She didn't dare turn around even though every instinct screamed at her to stop, to let Molly and the others in, to let them help her.

If I don't do this, if he harnesses the Omens, they'll never be able to stop him.

They would insist on going back, discussing it over and

over, and then it would be too late.

"There is always a choice," the Omens urged. *"You can take it, if only you let us in."*

She ignored the seductive promises as the tunnel opened out ahead and a puff of white light curled out. With her sleeve back ready to pull her dagger out, she slowed her pace but couldn't do anything about the frantic seesawing of her breath.

Phoenix stood at the edge of the well that tumbled downward with the white smoke teasing around him.

"I wouldn't listen to them, it's a trap to lure you in," she called out.

He glanced over his shoulder and she sagged. No white eyes yet, but she couldn't hesitate once she took her shot.

"I have a bloodline raised over this well for generations," he said. "This is my birthright. Where Celeste used products of the well, I'll siphon it directly."

"She tried that, eyes went white and everything, and we still beat her. Give it up!"

He ignored her and the others as they jogged to a stop beside her. She dodged when Molly reached out and kept distance between them, even though the torment on Molly's face tore at her insides.

"Ah, welcome. Perhaps it's fitting you're all here." Phoenix turned around as the smoke billowed thicker around him, gathering strength. "You'll be able to witness my ascension, and no doubt with you all here it'll go into the fabled Book of Faerie, a tale to be immortalised for future generations."

"Can you hear yourself?" Molly shouted.

"Yeah, sounding a bit mad mate," Taz added.

Talie grimaced as Phoenix laughed and the smoke curled against his face to obscure it from view.

Got to pick my moment. She shuffled a step forward.

"I'll make you a deal Talie, for old times' sake." Phoenix's voice boomed from inside the white haze. "Wipe their minds and convince them to leave the citadel, and I'll let them go. It's too much hassle to deal with a diplomatic incident."

A cloud of glittering black shadow domed around them and Talie bit her lip. She hadn't even considered that the others would be warding her as well, but a few more shuffling steps and she could feel the zing of power thrumming between her and Phoenix.

"Talie." Molly's tone was soft, almost begging. "You don't have to keep doing this for him. You can choose a different side, even now."

She didn't understand.

Even now she still thinks I'm on his side. Perhaps it's for the best that way.

"You and Sammy can still come to court."

Talie shook her head. "You don't get it. Someone needs to end this."

"But it doesn't have to be you!"

After all I've done? Yeah, it does.

As the white smoke channelled itself into Phoenix's eyes, his nose, mouth and ears, she charged forward. The warding between them bounced her back and she noticed Kingkiller, the fancy iron sword, hanging at Taz's side. With his attention on Phoenix, and Kainen's, she ducked past Molly and hauled the sword free.

Shouts echoed behind her as she slashed through the warding and ran. They would seal it behind her because Molly was so much more important to protect, she trusted that much.

Phoenix threw out an arm as the white smoke consumed him and she screamed as it blasted right through her pitiful warding and launched her off her feet.

She closed her eyes and endured the inevitable smack against the hard ground. Her limbs jolted and she had the faintest sensation of something softer under her head.

Get up. Get up before it's too late.

Her body wouldn't obey. All she could do was open her eyes to a hazy carousel of gold.

"Why didn't you ward?" Molly seethed.

The softness under her head was Molly's hand, and the pressure banding around her upper body was Molly's arms hauling her up to sitting.

"Anything broken?"

Talie winced. "I don't think so, but I need to stop him."

"Why do you have to be so... so... arrogant! He's beyond powerful already, what were you planning to do? Stab him and hope the Omens let you skip off?"

"Wasn't planning to skip off."

"But you were planning to stab him?!"

"Maybe."

"Urgh. I can't with you. This is not how I wanted to spend my day."

Talie grinned through the pain, she couldn't help it.

"Worse places to be than with you, Princess."

She twisted her head to see Phoenix domed in roiling white smoke that raged against a glittering cloud of black shadow and blazing ice-blue fire.

Taz and Kainen were holding firm, but over the crackle of the flames and the distant roar of the white smoke, a set of footsteps thudded closer.

"Sorry I'm late." A female voice said cheerfully. "Got lost."

CHAPTER TWENTY THREE

MOLLY

Molly dragged Talie to her feet and hauled her further behind the line of Taz and Kainen as Demi sauntered past with her hands in her pockets like she was out for a casual stroll. The fire and shadow receded, and even the white smoke seemed to hesitate.

"Come to reason with me, little queen?" Phoenix taunted. "What can you do now I'm here?"

"Duh, queen." She jabbed her thumb to her chest.

"A crown to rule over some nature and a bunch of useless nobles, so what? The Omens are raw power and with them I will be able to take on you and the Oak Queen, to the very fabric of Faerie."

Demi smiled, and in the depths of her electric blue eyes danced ice and Fae malice.

"You made a mistake in all this fanciful planning."

"Pure power doesn't make mistakes," he scoffed.

Demi lifted a hand. "No? This should be fun then."

With a flick of her fingers, a wave of darkness cascaded around the circle. The walls of the cavern groaned under the weight and Molly stood, torn between hauling Talie out while she still could and helping Kainen, who was fighting to hold Taz back from charging after Demi.

The darkness ebbed enough to see through. Phoenix stood crunched over, his head raised and his face snarling.

"A party trick, but the citadel is mine. I'll tear it to the ground before I allow more royal scum to fill it."

"Nice." Demi snorted loudly. "But you overlooked one thing. You might have been chosen by the Omens, but I was crowned by the nether they spawned from. Kind of makes it a family affair, don't you think? Ever played chess?"

"What?"

"Chess. It's a human game of strategy. You have these pieces and a board, and the-"

"No I haven't orbing played chess!"

Molly snuffled a laugh.

"Nobody can infuriate people like she can," Taz said proudly, then gave Kainen a dismissive look. "Except maybe you."

It was almost worth all the chaos to see the look of utter delight on Kainen's face as Demi faced Phoenix and stared nonchalantly at her fingernails.

"Shame." She shrugged. "See, with chess, even the queen is just another piece to be used. We all go into a box at the end, and I forgot that, too busy being proper instead of doing what's right."

Molly pressed a hand to Talie's shoulder as she lurched forward.

"Don't even think about it," she hissed. "Unless you

think you can do what a queen won't be able to?"

Talie scowled. "No."

Phoenix stood with both hands raised in front of his chest, but his eyes were darting back and forth.

Demi sent a whip of ice one way and a lash of fire the other, her hands lazily stretched out to the sides, palms up.

She's distracting him to confuse the Omens, freedom, power and entitlement all fighting inside his head.

"What are we doing then?" Taz asked.

Demi shrugged as she kept Phoenix in view.

"I'm here to keep the family in check entity-wise. As for him, that's not my fight."

"Scared to face me?" Phoenix sneered.

"Bored. I'm getting so orbing bored of despots and elitist psychos. Come on then, Omens, leave him be and come have a chat with me instead."

"That part of the grand plan?" Kainen asked warily.

Taz ducked past him as the white smoke left Phoenix and unfurled in great plumes toward Demi. It hit her warding and she smiled.

"Never said I'd let you in easy, but keep talking."

Phoenix lunged toward her, but Taz had Kingkiller to pierce his warding and transmutation to crumble the rock under Phoenix's shoes. He stumbled back and Molly hauled Talie aside with Kainen just in time.

Demi had a hand outstretched, completely absorbed in her own battle with the Omens, but Taz wouldn't do more than keep Phoenix away from her.

"He's still a threat," Talie muttered. "Always will be."

"Stay with me," Kainen warned.

Molly could feel his warding solid outside hers, and as Talie managed a shaky one, hers merged automatically.

"I'm fine," she grumbled, even though Molly still had an arm around her waist.

"Never said you weren't, Sunshine. Once we're out if this though, out of the citadel, you and I are going to have words."

"We need to stop him," Talie insisted. "*I* need to stop him. Even if he doesn't win today, your lot still can't interfere or take him captive unless he kills one of yours first. He'll just be straight back down here and with endless immunity."

"We'll figure that out, but-"

"No buts. I can stop him if I can get close."

"How? No sacrifices, promise me."

Talie hesitated. "It's the only way. Unless he draws first blood on any of you, you can't kill him, but I can."

"No, not happening. I need you to trust me when I say I have a plan."

"What plan?" Kainen asked, one hand raised to strengthen his warding as Phoenix prowled around the outside.

"One I need trust for. Something I've been working on in the workshop."

She held his gaze even though her insides writhed with adrenalin and doubt.

"A weapon? You've been building a weapon in my court?"

"I- in a way you could call it that. I just need to get close to him."

"I don't know whether to be horrified or impressed." He grimaced. "Both maybe. You have thirty seconds or I'm pulling you back behind the warding."

"A minute." She definitely wouldn't need any more than that.

"You're not going along with it?!" Talie hauled herself free of Molly and glared at Kainen. "She's far too valuable to risk going out there."

Molly grabbed her hands and held tight when she tried to pull away.

"Remember what you said about being the rain and me being the sunshine?" she asked. Talie nodded. "Together they make a rainbow. My turn to shine now, okay? And when I'm done, you can rain away the dust and grit, and we'll be all the colours together."

She slid her arms tight around Talie's waist and clung on before pulling back slowly.

"You truly don't believe you deserve good things, do you? You've convinced yourself that you're expendable."

Talie's breath caught in her throat but Molly forged on, aware of Demi and Taz mostly obscured by the Omens and Kainen holding Phoenix back with glittering black shadow.

"So many people have used you," Molly murmured. "Celeste. Him. Friends probably when they saw how well you could fight and protect them at school. That wasn't love, so you convinced yourself you're unlovable. Only to be used."

Talie winced and closed her eyes tight, like the words were a punch to her gut.

"How could they love someone like me?" she whispered.

Molly heard the veiled question running beneath; *how could you?*

"Because you got dealt a cruddy hand." Molly smoothed a straggle of hair back from Talie's face, forcing her panic as deep down as she could manage on feeling the gritty skin crusted with dried tears. "You got chosen for something awful, and it changed you, but you didn't choose it. You can't blame yourself for what others have done with you, only try not to do the same."

"I'm broken."

Molly smiled, her own tears leaking free as she forced Talie's chin up with her fingers.

"Maybe, but we both are. We can be broken together. Family is what you make it and I want you in mine, but it has to be your choice."

"Princess?" Her voice cracked. "Why me?"

"Because it doesn't make sense with anyone else."

Molly dropped her hands to her sides and shuffled backward as Talie watched her. Before she could doubt, Molly shoved Talie to the side with all the strength she could muster. Kainen caught her arm and hauled her behind him, gave Molly a nod.

"Molly!"

She ignored Talie's scream and stepped out of Kainen's protection to find it an impenetrable shield of black shadow on the outside. The Omens were roaring like distant air through a tunnel but Molly faced Phoenix.

"They sacrificed you in the end, did they?" he scoffed.

"I'm surprised at Talie but the others not so much."

"Keep her name out if your mouth and your soiled excuse for a self away from her. Consider that your only warning."

"Oh please. You're a child. Who are you to threaten anyone? I may not have the Omens, yet, and we may both have breeding, but I have the experience."

"Maybe, but you did make one mistake." She sketched a path through the dust with her foot. "You can't see the truth of someone if they're lying to themselves so deeply they're convinced it's real."

"What's that supposed to mean?"

"People as things, that's where it falls down," she insisted. "Instant fail. You can't track them like cattle, you can't tell them what to think or feel. All you have are lies and manipulations, and pretty Fae trickery that never lasts. What's important is down to the bone, and the bones will always be the hardest to burn away."

"And when I resurrect the bone?" he sneered. "Over and over to serve the legacy my family built?"

"So that is your plan. You're one man against an arsenal of ancient power already honed, against families that run so much deeper than mere bloodline. You won't win."

Phoenix hunkered into a ready stance, a shimmer of power curling in translucent prisms behind him.

I have no idea what gifts he has, not that it matters now.

It was beautiful in an ethereal way, a wonderland of colour you could dive into and never need to surface from.

Molly sucked in a sharp breath, forcing her focus onto the dust beneath her boots.

Dust and grime wasn't beautiful.

It wasn't wonderous.

But it was real.

She glanced back at Talie dodging to get through the shadow even as it curled to hold her back.

We choose our own beautiful.

Kainen had given her more than a minute. She faced the enemy with a smile on her face.

With all the beauty in her world standing behind her, the warmth burst inside her chest as she radiated blinding light. Taz would know to get Talie out safe. Kainen would know to shield her sunlight from the others with shadow. It would be enough time and power to distract the Omens, and then the others could deal with Phoenix.

She closed her eyes and rubbed her thumb over the *Akiai* charm as she shoved her hand in her pocket, feeling the power raging against the light, the push and pull of it fracturing every essence inside her.

The Omens danced in her head, cajoling her to join them in a distant carousel of whispers. She let them latch onto her, let them distract themselves enough that Demi could start working on containing them again. They hadn't discussed any kind of plan, but she trusted the queen of Faerie to do the right thing.

Molly kept the memory of Talie's face laughing on top of her secret spot above the workshop alive in her head. She remembered barely there kisses in tents, and laughter, and smiles that hardly anyone else got to see.

She let those thoughts fill her entire being and drive the light to pierce through the power and its depths.

She thought of Celeste in that split second as realisation took hold, deathly calm warming the last fragments of her consciousness.

CHAPTER TWENTY FOUR

Talie burst past Kainen's warding as he yelled even louder than she had. The moment she was out of his protection, a whip of white smoke snared her and yanked her to Phoenix's side.

He clamped a hand against her shoulder but it was an absentminded hold as his attention stayed on Molly.

Talie could see every flicker, every move Molly made, like tiny sparkles of light against the endless roiling pit of horror the well had produced to fight Demi.

She clung to the words Molly had given her, wanting nothing more than to believe them and knowing she couldn't.

Molly was everything good and beautiful, of course she would say kind things. Hadn't she said herself that truth didn't see through lies buried so deeply? Molly wanted so badly to believe the best of everyone. She didn't even consider killing Phoenix before turning to face the darkness with the others, something Talie would have done in her place.

She recognised the slight extending of Molly's arms at her sides and realisation flared a second too late. Her lips stretched open to scream, the anguish tearing at the corners

251

of her mouth, even as the glow of Molly's gift burst through the chamber.

Talie ducked with one arm over her face and squinted underneath as Kainen held shadows between them and the shine.

Terror tore at her insides, ancient claws of innate emotion deeper than Faerie, the well or even the nether itself shredding Phoenix's hold on her like cheap fabric.

She shot forward straight into the end of a flaming wing. King consort or not, if Molly was sacrificing herself...

She ducked again and landed a savage punch to his side, her hand bouncing off his waist as she shoved past him into the shadows.

Plumes of smoke wrapped around her before she could reach the edge of the glow, leaving her sightless in a wall of darkness.

She dodged from side to side but either the smoke of the Omens had turned dark or Kainen was keeping her safe.

Molly will have told him to.

Talie opened her mouth and screamed again, the sound shattering the quiet hum of the power vibrating. Except it wasn't the same tone as the power, there was a calm to it, almost lyrical without any distinguishable notes, a lullaby that burrowed right into her heart and left the softest of bittersweet kisses for all the real ones she would never have.

She hit the ground with a thud that jarred her knees, noticeable only through her pain because she could actually see the stone now, the smoke receding until she could see her hands, grotty with dirt, nails chipped and skin marred with tiny nicks and scratches.

Somehow she found the strength to push up to her feet and stand, teetering off balance and staggering a few steps sideways.

Taz was already at Molly's side, his body not wide enough to block the open, unseeing eyes or the pallor of death in her skin. Kainen's face was a picture of heartbreak, but it was directed at Phoenix, who stood chest heaving, no sign of darkness gathering around him.

He's still strong here.

Talie couldn't contain her shaking, unable to coordinate her movements smoothly. She struggled to keep her aching head straight, muscles pounding with unkempt fury.

"Talie, with me, now," Phoenix snapped.

Kainen snarled in reply. "Don't even think about it. You've killed Molly through all this, you're not taking Talie as well."

Furious, as if he actually cares.

Phoenix wiped a hand over his face, no sign of his previous confidence left. They were all going down fighting raw.

No more.

Talie dug deep inside, forcing her limbs to steady as best she could. There was a certain calm that came with finality, and she hoped Molly had been blessed by it when she went.

She dropped any hint of control over her face and let the utter devastation shine in her eyes.

Make it believable, make it work.

She approached Phoenix steadily and turned to stand at

his side.

His shoulders lifted a little taller, a hint of previous swagger returning. He stepped forward as Kainen lifted Molly into his arms and stood beside Taz and Demi. Taz had his hands on Demi's shoulders as she stood with her eyes closed and her hands pulsating grey and purple swirls of smoke toward the stone pillars. Fixing the circle of protection to keep the Omens in.

"I can rebuild the citadel in time, but you and your family will not take the legacy of mine away from me," Phoenix announced.

Talie could only see half of Kainen's shoulder and arm with Phoenix now standing in front of her.

And the tiniest hint of Molly's lolling hand, the angle making it look like she was giving Talie a thumbs up sign.

As if she knows. Talie almost choked over a grief-stricken laugh. *As if she's telling me it's okay.*

"Leave the citadel immediately," Phoenix folded his arms. "Sign over any claim the royal family had, or will ever have, to me. Otherwise I will obliterate you both."

Taz bristled even as Kainen's hand landed on his shoulder to hold him back. Phoenix managed a strained laugh.

"Don't even try it. Molly made her choice and look how she ended up. That's what this is all about, right? Choices? Well now you get to make yours."

Talie lifted her arm. Molly had said much the same, and she was done letting others make her choices for her.

With every residue of strength she had, Talie angled the short blade she'd stolen from Taz's belt on her way into the shadows. The split second of decision hung between the metal tip and the flash of exposed skin, a choice to be made. Phoenix hadn't even noticed her move, too absorbed in facing his more adequate opponents.

"I've been using the well all along to add gifts to my own bank of power," he crowed. "I will take on the other tower leaders and all will be ruled in fairness."

"Fairness dictated by you," Kainen snapped. "I've seen it play out and your side never wins."

Phoenix shrugged and Talie's hand shook around the blade.

As Demi finished containing the roiling white smoke, Phoenix shuddered. He staggered back and Talie almost impaled him in the neck. Stumbling to the side, she lowered her hand. The urge to kill him chanted inside her head, but it sounded muted, as though echoing through a veil.

Or a circle of powerful protection.

The rage swelled in her chest and stabbed over her skin. Phoenix lunged forward and made a swipe for her with an outstretched hand, but she opened her mouth and screamed, a wild, raw echo. Rain washed over her skin and shot upward, but it wasn't the subtle dissipating into a wispy barely there cloud.

A loud crack echoed overhead, rumbling enough to shake the walls. Demi froze, Taz twisting around beside her. Kainen's black shadow pulsed warily. A torrent of water dashed down toward Phoenix, a maelstrom of pure grief-driven fury whirling in mid-air toward him.

He ducked his head and reached out for her again but

she danced back. Kainen roared something she couldn't make out, but she was already halfway across the ground toward them by time the glittering black shadow reached her. The cloud was spent and the thunder had rumbled away, but Phoenix was still there.

"You?" Demi eyed Kainen.

He shook his head. "I don't have a weather gift."

All eyes turned to Talie but her gaze was fixed on Phoenix, and he was still lingering, his eyes wide like he had realised where the thunder and rain had come from.

"We can work through this," he said.

Talie flinched back, moving in an arc to keep herself between him and the others.

"Get away from me!" A strangled sob tumbled out of her mouth. "You killed her!"

"She did that herself."

His face twisted with irritation and he lunged for her, but a wall of power blasted him back. Talie stared at Demi, but it was Kainen that approached, his eyes roiling with fury.

"I will hunt you down, slowly and painfully, if you go for her again."

"You think this changes anything?" Phoenix spat.

"You're outnumbered and the Omens are contained," Demi said. "So, yeah."

"The tower will never accept royal rule." He staggered backwards.

"It doesn't have to. We're not against the tower, or the citadel."

"Only you," Kainen added, his tone the lethal slice of

sharpened blades. "Go while you still can and be grateful we're letting you keep your head."

Phoenix eyed them all and Talie gripped the blade still in her hand.

I could make it. He doesn't deserve to live after what he's done.

Only the thought of Molly, still limp in Kainen's arms, kept her from throwing the blade straight into his chest. As Phoenix turned and ran toward one of the other tunnel openings, Talie sagged.

"He'll go to one of the other towers maybe," Taz said.

"Maybe, but we shore up security of this one for now either way." Demi sighed. "Go. I still have the nether to handle yet."

"I'm not leaving you."

Demi rolled her eyes but she didn't fight the hold he had on her, his arms wrapped tight around her waist.

Vaguely aware of Kainen reaching for the dagger still in her hand, Talie let him take it. He now had Molly bundled awkwardly over his shoulder and her heart shattered to irretrievable shards. She gulped against the urge to be sick as her eyes burned and the air above them turned soggy again.

"Come home," he said, his tone utterly broken. "Let's take Molly home."

Talie couldn't speak but when he put a hand awkwardly on her shoulder, she didn't fight it off. She couldn't even bring herself to spare more than a habitual thought for Sammy. She'd made her choice, and Talie guessed Nia would keep an eye out for her in Phoenix's absence.

I should have gone with Molly all along.

Kainen called for Milo but Talie stared at Molly. Her eyes were closed now but Talie knew she would have nightmares for the rest of her life about the wide-open vacant stare.

"You don't think she's…" Taz hesitated.

Demi shook her head. "I wouldn't get your hopes up. Take her back to the house and wait there for me. Then we can take her through the skip-way. Phoenix drew first blood, so now we're within our rights to hunt him."

"He did." Kainen frowned. "But I still don't understand how."

"I'll explain later."

"He needs to die," Talie said, her voice faint in her throat.

"We will sort him out," Demi promised. "But we need to make sure we do it properly."

Talie let Kainen keep hold of her as Milo appeared. His eyes widened at the sight of Molly but he didn't even say a word, simply placed a tentative hand on Talie's forearm and the other on Kainen's shoulder with Molly.

Demi talked about doing things 'properly', no doubt because she had rules to follow as queen.

I don't.

She would see Sammy right, make sure she was set up for life somehow, then she'd take herself off and be done with it. She couldn't trust anyone else to bring Phoenix down now, and Kainen couldn't force her to leave the citadel.

CHAPTER TWENTY FIVE

Talie lifted her head, aware Kainen was talking to her, or more accurately at her. They were still in the little house beside Molly's workshop with Molly on the bed covered in a sheet, but Talie couldn't shake the memory of the deathly pale face and vacant eyes.

"We'll give you and Sammy a place at court of course, Molly insisted on that more than once," Kainen said gently.

Talie cleared her throat and took a deep breath. Every time she even tried to speak, the tears leapt from her eyes to the air above them and everything around the room was damp.

"Sammy should."

There. They couldn't make her go, but with Phoenix still lurking she wanted all links he could use against her out of the way.

"Oh orbs, Finola." She covered her face with both hands. "I promised I'd bring her back."

"Is she…"

"No, she's gone, but I promised."

"Alright, we'll have her found, I promise you that."

He would as well, Talie knew she could trust that much.

They still had to find Sammy, but she would know to check the house and the workshop. Then they would try to convince her to go with them as well, but as soon as she saw a chance she would slip away.

"I know you're not planning on coming with us," Kainen said. "There are things that need to be done first, and done right, but after that we won't stop you."

Talie shrugged. She had nothing left in her to argue with.

"Is there anyone you need to call? Someone who you can rely on?"

She glanced at Molly, pale and still.

"No."

"Well, at least consider leaving the citadel. We have no idea who will take over, but we've done our best to block off the Omens, at least for now. Whether Phoenix has escaped to another tower or not we can't be sure yet. It might not be safe for you here."

"It's not safe anywhere. It never has been."

Kainen sighed. "Not one of the cheery childhood bunch then?"

"I learned early that you punch first, even if you've no chance of stopping them anyway. You wouldn't understand."

She couldn't even find a single twitch or shudder as the memories roiled up, of hands and harsh voices and laughter as she did everything she could not to cry.

"You think you're the only one in Faerie who needed to learn that?" Kainen scoffed. "You think because I was born to a title that I didn't have to suffer in other ways? There are more currencies than coin out there, and I was used to pay several of them over younger years."

Talie heard the darkness in his voice, a truth that ran beyond shadows and illusions, something unyielding and real. She recognised it.

"You didn't take- I don't know, saved up some pocket money or something and just leave? Why not?"

"You think you're the only one with a sister you had to protect? Everyone's got a sob story of some kind. The only choice we have is whether we choose to do good or bad with it."

"There's nothing good about what I can do, or what I've done. Never has been."

Kainen sighed. "You sacrificed your life to raise a sister who I believe isn't even yours by blood. Even if everything else you say is true, Molly saw good things in you."

"She saw the good in everything." Talie closed her eyes against the next onslaught of tears, her eyes so badly burnt by them that she was surprised she still had anything left to cry out.

"Perhaps that's your rose-tinted glasses talking, because she was always more of a problems that need fixing kind of person."

"She sees the ideal potential then, not the reality."

"I guess you could say that, but as far as I can work out she's never been wrong yet. Your gift is removing memories, right?"

Talie nodded. "Yeah, and plenty have made great use of it."

"Did you know Molly didn't use her compulsion gift

until recently because she was scared of what it might do, or how easily she might be seduced into using it for bad things?"

"No, I didn't know she even had compulsion for a long time. She used it on me once though."

"She thought it was too powerful, too easily used for bad things. But when it came down to it, she used it for good things. I used to use my compulsion for really awful things. Thought it was just what everyone did. Until I learned I had a choice. We have that choice every day."

"What would I even do with it other than wipe memories?" she asked.

"Imagine if you could use it to remove painful memories from people who need relief. What if you could help people near the end of their life find peace?"

"And then eventually there'll be 'just a tiny favour' and I'll be back working for queens or people like Phoenix. No thanks."

Kainen smiled sadly. "None of us would insist on it. Can't say we won't ask if we need to, but several people have been asked for their gifts and had no penalty for refusing. There's a reason the courts of Faerie are united for the first time in over an age."

"Yeah, bloodlines, everyone knows that."

"Family. Not bloodline family, but the one we build. Demi made sure of that. She's building a Faerie where everyone gets a fair shot. Can't say it won't take a long time, nothing's easy, but it's what I put my trust in."

Molly would tell me to live.

She nodded, as much concession as she'd give Kainen

for the moment. He eased to his feet and padded toward the door, leaving her alone with Molly.

Talie wiped both hands over her face with a groan. If she accepted Kainen's offer, truly accepted it, she would need help. The darkness in her head would ruin any chance of the future, even though she was too exhausted and broken to fully acknowledge it yet.

A soft rustle poked through her attention and she looked up, a strangled scream creaking out of her mouth as a frighteningly familiar voice filled her ears.

"Talie? Why are you on the floor?"

CHAPTER TWENTY SIX

"You're not one of mine."

The strange echo of a voice filled Molly's head and she opened her eyes, or experienced the sensation of opening her eyes, to utter darkness.

"It didn't work," she muttered. "Oh orbs. Where am I?"

"You're *definitely* not one of mine." The voice sounded almost irritated.

"Um… I don't know what that means, and thanks for the snarky tone about it, but whoever you are, or whatever, no offense, can you just tell me if the people I left behind made it? Is there any way to ensure they are okay? I mean, I'm talking, or thinking at least because I don't seem to have a mouth or a body, just a thoughts, so is this some kind of Fae 'beyond'?"

"The Holly Queen is no weakling, Princess. She was chosen by the nether and has more than earned her reputation."

Molly hesitated. "I'm guessing that's the only reassurance I'm going to get. Is this some kind of Fae beyond then? I'm guessing my plan didn't work and I died."

"Someone has already claimed you, or you would be."

"Who? Wait, is that where I am? Am I in the nether?"

"In a manner of speaking, yes. The balance of Faerie and the nether has ebbed and flowed since beyond time, but Fae do tend to make things interesting."

"So, if I'm not 'yours', then whose am I?"

For a long moment, nobody answered and she wondered if perhaps being demanding with the fabric of reality was pushing it a bit.

"Perhaps I will add a tilt to the balance," the nether said, echoing like the embodiment of all things wicked. "I'll send a little gift to one of my own, to rumble things in their favour. That should please you, little royal."

"Wha-ahh!"

The sensation of a rough shove knocked her awareness sideways, the feel of tumbling through the dark that made her snap her eyes shut on instinct. Awareness of her limbs danced in her mind moments before they thudded painfully onto something warm and soft. Light tinged behind her eyelids and she opened them to blissful warm sunshine, fragrant natural air and the awareness of an awful lot of green.

"Now then, how many of you are going to end up tumbling to me in this way, hmm?"

The voice was feminine, motherly and with the essence of ancient permanence.

Molly eyed the lazily waving branches of a willow tree amid the endless grass under a hazy summer sky.

"Over here, dear."

She squinted as the branches of the willow tree parted to reveal a face on the trunk, a combination of knots forming alarmingly expressive eyes and a moving mouth.

"Hello." Molly hesitated. "I'm Molly."

The sound of chuckling rustled through the branches.

"Of course you are. You may call me Tara."

"Okay. Where am I? I was in the nether, I think, and then it taunted me and shoved me and now I'm here."

She bit her lip as her tone hitched and the exhaustion caught up with her.

"Are they okay? Talie, Kainen and the others?"

"One thing at a time now. Oh, yes, she's sprouted her first acorn look."

Molly glanced over at a small oak plant sprouting nearby within the protective boundary of Tara's bountiful branches.

"You're lucky the Holly Queen is unfailingly kind, or she might not have been able to save you."

Molly frowned. "What happened, do you know?"

"Patience, dearest. Honestly, Fae get faster and faster. You're not here because you died. Well, you almost did. That trick you pulled was risky at best."

Molly tucked a hand into her pocket and sagged.

"It worked?"

"It did."

"Then how did I end up in the nether?"

Tara sighed. "The nether likes to have its fun as much as anyone. You are one of mine, but the nether has claimed others since. Perhaps it wanted to meet you by acquaintance, or to see what the future might hold. Luckily, the young queen thought to ask for a tether to that baby oak there, and I was able to pull you back."

"From the nether?"

"Well, yes. It shouldn't be taking those that are mine, but no doubt you would have had to barter or trade a debt or more otherwise. You must be more careful about walking that line between life and death, even in imitation."

Molly shuddered. "I don't think I even fully understand it yet."

"Good. Those that can admit they don't know everything are those that will at least eventually learn something."

"I don't want to be rude, but can you tell me if Talie's okay? And the others?"

"Dear dear, always in a rush. Would you like something to eat first, or drink?"

Molly shook her head. "No, thank you. It's kind but if I can get back then I need to. I'm guessing this isn't the kind of place where people can just pop in for a visit, or I'd offer."

"Oh that would be lovely! Demi or Taz can bring you any time you feel like visiting of course. I always like to see my little family."

"Family?" Realisation dawned. "Oh orbs. I'm sorry, I didn't even realise. You're Faerie aren't you, as in the embodiment of it, or… emtreement isn't a word I don't think."

Tara rustled her branches and Molly decided it sounded affectionate rather than irritated.

"No, it isn't, but perhaps it should be. Fae can achieve whatever they want really, with a bit of perseverance and social skills."

"I'm not that great with people."

"That's what Demi said and now look at her."

"She still doesn't have any people skills though. She gets Milo and Ace to do most of it. Or Kainen."

"Well, yes, but she's queen. And you're a princess. Anyway, think of it like this, if the young queen hadn't thought to gift me the acorn that plant grew from, would I have had anything to tether you to? Faerie can do many things, but Fae don't often remember to gift back these days."

Molly frowned. "That's really sad. You know most kind of think you're not sentient though, right?"

"I suppose that's my penance for many things, and my protection. Fae would probably start asking me for things then. Either way, true kindness will always be the most powerful form of currency."

"Not love?"

Molly hadn't ever heard a tree snort in derision before, but it was an oddly liberating experience.

"Love is many things, and it can be wonderful, but it can also be possessive, consuming and soul-destroying. Respect? Kindness? Even trust? Those are true gifts. Anyone can love, but not everyone can earn respect or risk trust."

Molly rubbed a hand over her forehead.

"Talie will be impossible if she thinks I'm dead. Kainen and the others have Phoenix to deal with still, even if Demi sorts the Omens out. But at least they can go after him now. Will this stand though if I didn't actually die? Can they hunt him now he's at least tried to murder me?"

She shuddered again and a branch came down in front of her face to tap the side of her cheek softly.

"He would have killed many of you and nobody can argue that, not even I or the nether. It was a test, as many things are, but you're here and you're safe."

"I don't understand then." Molly frowned. "What did a test even achieve? I almost killed myself, so if we can't even hunt him after this-"

"Did you ever consider that perhaps you weren't the one being tested?" The responding woody smile was wide, knowing and utterly unnerving. "We are all the main characters of our own story, from the unsung heroes to the mightiest myths and told tales. Learn to know things exactly as they are, not how you see it, or wish it was. Then, you'll begin to understand."

"Taz said something similar, and Kainen. They said I should give people what they want, not what I think they need."

The branches rustled with delighted laughter.

"Ah yes, the young Lord of Illusions. I can't claim to have any control over the whims and decisions of Fae, but if I could, his redemption might even be one of the greatest triumphs to be talked of. But the less said to him about that the better, hmm?"

Molly smiled. "It would do wonders for his ego so yeah, probably better not to say anything. Can Faerie lie?"

"Oh child, what a question. Faerie is much like a tree. Leaves fall but new leaves are born. Sometimes entire branches die out. But sometimes they're cut off, removed completely by design."

"Didn't answer the question but okay."

"Humans can lie, and there is power in that. Power in so many things Fae take for granted. If you could, would you lie to save a friend? Yourself? Or would you lie for security, or the validation that power can bring?"

"Do you ask Demi these questions?"

"The queen of winter asks herself these questions every day, I have no need to mind her. Yet. She has a good heart. The summer queen's power will wane however, and the nether will choose her successor."

Molly's skin chilled, the memory of roiling darkness and a knowing deep in her bones, a claiming.

"It doesn't automatically go to May?" she asked, still half hoping the whole thing was a hallucination.

"It might, it might not. The nether crowns kings and queens in its own mysterious way, but it also listens to the ebb and flow of power."

"So the powerful always win? Somehow that's really bleak."

"Power comes in so many more forms than mere dominion. Ask the queens to tell you their stories. Watch, listen and learn. Who knows? Maybe one day you will be queen of summer."

Molly shuddered. "No thanks."

"Well, there's time yet. Now, back you go. Lots to do and to mend."

"No more words of advice?"

Tara chuckled. "If I simply told you all the secrets there would be nothing to discover, and where's the fun in that?"

Molly sighed as another branch tapped her nose gently.

"I will give you something for the future, though, for your trouble:

'She will be the first of a new age, tawny of hair with gold in the eyes, and a circle of royal statues to surround her. But she will always hear the call of the wild, of Faerie and the nether, until the blood revives a heart of stone.'

Molly shivered. "Um… that's…"

"It'll be noted down in the Book of Faerie, dear, don't worry about remembering it. You can claim it as your first royal prophecy."

"Do royals get them a lot then?" she asked, bewildered.

"No. Now, close your eyes. Might want to lie down as well."

After all the information and stress she'd experienced, Molly flopped back without a shred of hesitation and did exactly as she was told.

CHAPTER TWENTY SEVEN

MOLLY

Molly opened her eyes a second later and winced. The light was dim by any standards, especially after the warm glow of Tara's home, but it burned all the same. She shuffled a tiny bit until she could look around at the rest of the living room she still thought of as Beryl's, but even that hurt. Her body felt like it had been crushed by an entire citadel and doused in ice, her skin scraped raw and her insides groaning with enough hunger to make her queasy.

As she looked down and saw the startled hazel eyes ringed with gold blinking up at her, she tried to smile.

At least Talie looks a thousand times worse.

"Talie?" She winced at the scrape in her throat. "Why are you on the floor?"

Talie's first sound was a squeak of pure horror. The second was more like a foghorn. Molly tried to get up but her muscles were still rubbery and she fell back onto her shoulder with a pained 'oof'.

The door slammed open and startled faces peered in. Then Sammy appeared, and she had a brief moment of relief until Sammy started screaming too fast for any normal person to understand. Reyan slapped a hand over Sammy's mouth and turned her head.

"Oi, you might want to come and see this," she yelled.

Molly grimaced. "Everyone stop shouting, please."

Taz and Kainen appeared in the doorway as Reyan hustled Sammy through with a hand still over her mouth, the sound of burbled words still leaking through Reyan's fingers.

"What the f-" Taz threw his hands in the air. "I'm going to kill- She never said a word of this to me!"

Kainen eyed the absolute chaos and crossed the floor, dropping to sit beside Talie as a cloak of smoke drifted around them and muffled most of the noise.

"Let them fight it out a while," he suggested. "I take it you had a plan? Otherwise a lot of people are going to be seriously mad at you, me included."

Molly nodded. "I'm still not sure what happened, but I ended up with the nether, I think? It didn't seem to like me much. Then I went to a tree called Tara and she said a lot of confusing things. I did have a plan though. I thought... well, I wasn't planning on, you know."

She glanced quickly at Talie sitting entirely still, snared by shock.

Kainen sighed. "Then you're braver or madder than most of us. You realise if Demi knew about this Taz is going to slaughter her. He's been kicking himself for hours because you went and sacrificed yourself like an idiot."

"I had to."

"They might not understand it, but I do. Demi will as

well probably." He frowned. "We could have handled it ourselves you know. Phoenix drew first blood."

"He did?"

"Yeah, otherwise how would Taz and I have been able to go down into the labyrinth past all his wards?"

Molly grimaced. "I didn't even think of that."

Talie cleared her throat, but even as her lips moved, she didn't seem capable of words.

"It's strange." Kainen's lips lifted and his expression turned wickedly innocent. "It means he must have attacked something at least one of us cares about before we even left the entrance hall."

"It was me," Talie muttered.

"You?"

"I said I'd renounce any link to knowing anyone royal so I could finish him."

Kainen tapped a forefinger against his lip slowly.

"You chose a side through sacrifice then. Interesting. And the nether recognised it too, given that sudden storm that chased Phoenix off. Even more interesting."

Molly shook her head, the complexity and constant clawing pain clouding around her ability to understand.

"You fit enough to stand?" Kainen asked.

"Don't think so. I'm starving though."

"I-" Talie stumbled to her feet. "I'll…" She pointed in the vague direction of the door, still lost in the haze of smoke.

Molly held her hand out. Talie reached for it, her fingers brushing Molly's as though she expected her to snap or disappear.

"It's okay," Molly promised. "We're okay. Keep everyone away from me for another hour or so while I get my head back on right."

She choked over a laugh as Talie only clung onto her fingers, reluctant to look away even for a moment.

Kainen grinned. "*I'll* go sort out the food. You two get some rest. Oh orbs, don't let Taz kill his wife if you can."

The smoke dissipated to reveal Sammy grinning while trying her hardest not to, and Reyan trying to calm Taz who was glaring at Demi.

"You could have told me!"

Demi sighed. "There wasn't time. Besides, you didn't tell me about that ridiculous deal of yours when you abdicated. I wasn't even sure if the acorn would work. I didn't want to get anyone's hopes up in case it didn't happen."

"Not happy," Taz muttered. "Seriously not happy."

"I love it when it's not me in trouble," Kainen said happily, heading for the door and snagging Reyan's hand as he passed.

Taz turned to Molly next, his arms still folded.

"If you're going to yell, please wait until tomorrow," she said.

"I'm not going to yell."

Demi rolled her eyes. "No, he's just going to sulk and make you feel guilty for an age. The acorn worked?"

"I think so. Tara said it did anyway. Not sure how. My plan worked too though."

"Ah yes, Kainen mentioned something about a plan. Care to fill us in?"

Kainen came back in and gave them a nod, but since he didn't have any food immediately available on him, Molly wriggled around with a grimace as aches blossomed across her body. She slid her hand into her pocket and yanked it out again with the small item nestled on her palm.

"That's…" Talie's mouth dropped open.

Molly nodded. "This is the atomiser I asked Butch to give you. I figured you'd keep it on you if you thought it was from me. Worst case, you'd trust what I told him to tell you, that it could help you in an emergency by putting someone to sleep, or you wouldn't and I could get it from your pocket next time I saw you in here."

"That's…"

"I grabbed it from your pocket just before I faced him."

"How…"

Molly held up the bottle to reveal a tiny magnet on the bottom that she'd fashioned as an attachment.

"I only did a couple of test runs so I wasn't sure it'd be strong enough, but it worked."

"That's…"

"I think you've broken her," Kainen teased.

Talie glared at him almost without realising but she didn't argue back.

"I figured if I distract the Omens, Demi could contain them, then there'd only be Phoenix left. The plan was to just play dead, but it kind of worked a little bit too well."

"Tha- I-" Talie scrunched her face up. "Why didn't you tell me this?!"

"There wasn't time. I would have, but I also didn't want you insisting you should do it. I needed him to attack me so that he drew first blood and we could remove him completely from the citadel. I didn't know it had already been done though, did I?"

"So, you did die or you didn't?" Demi asked. Taz gave her a look. "What? She's obviously back now."

"I was on the line apparently. Ended up with the nether first, and it kept insisting I didn't belong to it. Then it said something about sending a rumble to shake things up, whatever that means, and punted me to Tara."

Demi nodded. "I thought it would be wise to give her something to tether you to, just in case. You have a habit of doing your own thing."

"Right, outside *now*." Taz launched to his feet and jabbed a finger at the door.

Demi rolled her eyes and ambled outside with him right behind her, his shoulders rigid and shaking as his wings flared with fire.

Kainen stood too with a gleeful grin, but he only made it two steps before Reyan shook her head.

"Nope."

"Oh come on. How often do you see a queen getting yelled at?"

"Leave them be."

"Fine." He threw himself into the nearest chair, legs sprawled and arms folded. "Demi will likely need to sort out what's happening here now."

Molly frowned. "We can't force royal rule or anything though."

"No, but I imagine most will at least be glad to see the back of him?"

"We haven't though, have we?" Talie said quietly. "He's still out there, and I'll bet one of those tunnels will lead to another tower, or he'll find a way to go hide out in one."

"Maybe, but once things are established here, he won't be able to get in easily. We'll help whoever takes over establish safeguards."

"More wards?" Molly asked.

"Not if people don't want them. One step at a time. Food should be here soon, then you two need to rest up."

Reyan nodded. "Demi will likely want you both in the discussions with the citadel Fae and whoever they choose to take over. At least we're on the progress side of things now."

"Oh, there's a new prophecy in the Book of Faerie apparently," Molly added. "Tara gave me one but I can't remember it. Any chance that food's coming any time soon?"

Kainen smiled. "Spoken like a true princess. We'll go see if we can hurry it along."

He got up and swept an arm around Reyan's waist as he passed, even when she gave him a weary look as he peered outside hopefully for the sound of arguing.

Sammy was missing, but Molly couldn't help being glad to have the privacy as she bit her lip and eyed Talie.

"I really would have told you if there was time," she said.

Talie nodded as her gaze darted over Molly's face and a subtle roll of thunder echoed overhead.

"I get it. I need you to know that I've been on your side

though, even when it didn't seem like it. What I said last time-"

"Doesn't matter." Molly held up a hand. "Took me a few minutes or more but I know you were just trying to chase me off to keep me safe. That's becoming a really bad habit of yours."

Talie's lips twitched and a gentle patter of drizzle started up above them.

"You're one to talk."

"Match made in disaster."

Talie's eyes widened and the drizzle froze in mid-air.

"Do you-"

"It's ridiculous." Kainen's voice bounced into the room ahead of him. "I don't see why they can't argue in public like normal people."

Molly glowered at the door, but then she saw the wicker basket in his arms and decided she could have 'the conversation' with Talie once she'd eaten most of whatever he had to offer.

He dropped the basket on the bed with a flourish, then snapped his fingers to produce two small glasses full of purple liquid.

"Drink up, then eat up, Marthe's orders."

"You went to Marthe? Does the Oak Queen know?"

Kainen snorted. "Your *grandmother* is furious with everyone except you, apparently, for dragging you into this, even though you started it."

"I'm sure Taz and May are delighted by that," Molly muttered.

"I haven't asked them, but I absolutely will at the first

opportunity. Anyway, Marthe managed to smuggle those tonics out when she wasn't looking."

Molly eyed the tonic then downed it. Talie hesitated but once Molly had taken hers, she followed. Then Molly grabbed a meat pocket from the basket and sank into it.

"Still not a hundred percent right," she muttered to an accompaniment of crumbs. "Talie, eat, come on. We'll sort everything out tomorrow but you're no good to us passed out from hunger."

Talie took a meat pocket when Molly handed it to her, but she only nibbled around the edges.

"You were dead," she huffed. "Forgive me for taking some time to recover. I guess we're even now."

"Not even slightly. I did all of an hour. You did it for weeks."

"Technicality."

"Fact."

"Factual technicality."

"Actual technical- wait, no."

Talie smiled, and it was worth everything. Molly smiled wide and finished Talie's food as Reyan hovered in the doorway.

"Sorry, and Demi's sorry too, but the tower representatives are calling for a meeting now and Demi wants to know if you're fit enough to go and be a go-between of sorts."

Molly groaned. "I reckon I can."

"Are you sure?" Talie stumbled to her feet and loomed over her. "You don't have to do anything yet. You've done more than enough already."

"I'm okay. Actually, I'm not, but I'll survive."

Molly eased the covers back and managed to stand unaided. When Talie slipped an arm around her waist she didn't argue, but she freed herself when they got to the door.

"Tonic's kicking in," she said. "Let's do this while we still can."

Kainen shook his head. "You lot scare me."

CHAPTER TWENTY EIGHT

MOLLY

Molly could barely coordinate her feet despite the tonic. She slipped and slithered along the lane as they wound down toward the Menagerie, but she didn't fight or argue when Talie slipped a little finger around hers.

They walked through the Menagerie entrance to find a cluster of faces, several familiar, lingering in fractured groups. The nobles in their varied finery dropped their chins in deference to Demi, but Fern and Butch and the others she recognised from the citadel stayed one step short of hostile.

"You'll forgive if most don't bow, queen," Butch said. "We don't recognise royalty here."

He'd put on a bowtie for some reason over his shirt, but apart from that there were no other concessions for the occasion. Fern hadn't even bothered to remove her cart-pulling gloves.

Among the muttering nobles, Glennoria stepped forward, a vision in scarlet velvet complete with a feathery hat.

"You recognise their nobility quickly enough when you've need of us," she said.

"Stand down on both accounts." Demi lifted her hands for calm. "I'm here to referee, if that. Molly's family, so consider me here in a personal capacity."

Another round of discussion whispered through the different clusters, but nobody made any move to get anything started.

"We should go sit down," Molly suggested. "Maybe we should nominate a chair."

"I'll chair," Butch offered.

Talie walked toward the side-hall and Molly followed with her limbs aching. As everyone cascaded into seats around the long table, she balanced her elbows on the top and focused on keeping her eyes open as Talie took a seat on her right and Reyan on her left.

"Welcome all. We'll need to nominate spokespeople first from each group. Are the nobility speaking as one?"

Wary glances passed around the half of the table nearest the doorway and Demi turned a tiny snort into a cough with great performance. While they deliberated, a woman stood from her chair and swept a hand through her short brown hair.

"I'll speak for the grain and production levels," she said. "We're not guilded, but they've trusted me to speak on our behalf."

"Trusted you to massacre innocent creatures that can't work, you mean," Talie muttered.

Molly nudged her elbow. "What?"

"Where do you think Arrow came from, Princess?"

The others hadn't overheard so Molly missed the woman's name, but she didn't look like the animal-rescuing type.

Then again I reckon a lot of people would say Talie doesn't either.

"I'll speak for the nobles," Glennoria announced.

"Why is she doing this and not you?" Molly asked Reyan quietly. "Or Kainen?"

Reyan leaned closer. "She has holdings here. We don't. This is about Demi refereeing a new rule that harms the least, not courts or crowns taking over."

"I'm surprised Kainen isn't here though. He usually loves this kind of drama."

"He has his reasons."

Molly let the mystery of that pass and turned her attention back to the table as the various guilds named their speaker. Once the guilds and nobles had done the rounds, Fern announced herself as speaker for "the decent and hardworking people who have actually worked and lived on the levels".

Butch sighed and steepled his hands in front of him on the table.

"Welcome all. We all cohabit here and it's time we decided what is best for our home. That said, I think we can all agree we need to tread carefully and avoid alienating anyone who still wants to make this tower profitable so that everyone can live here safely and happily."

"And who would that be?" One of the guilds piped up. "Someone you've chosen from your own meagre ranks no doubt. Look how well that worked with Phoenix in charge."

"What even happened to him anyway?" someone else asked.

Molly slid her hands under the table and clenched them on her thighs.

"He tried to take the tower by force," she said. "From what I've heard, in the short time he ran things, everything fell apart. Is anyone here willing to vouch for missing him, or wanting him back?"

She laid down the challenge with far more strength in her voice than she had in her muscles, but nobody disagreed.

"Nobody can say Phoenix's rule benefitted anyone much," Fern said.

The man from the Artificer's Guild nodded with a rueful sigh.

"We agree at least on that. Who ever heard of a guild being *taxed*? We earn the taxes, not pay them."

Butch gave Fern a sharp look as her mouth swung open, and she rolled her eyes before closing it again.

"Phoenix has fled. He may return at some point," Demi said smoothly. "If he does, he's violated the covenant between the citadel and the crown, and as such his fate belongs to me and mine."

Looks passed around the table and Molly would have bet her fancy new crown from Marthe that some of them already knew where he fled to.

"We know very little about the tunnels under the citadel," she said.

Demi nodded. "Again, not really my affair right now, but if anyone knows where he is and decides to pitch in on his side, then just know you'll be against me and mine. Until then, I'll continue to honour the previous terms of the covenant and leave the citadel be."

The nobles glanced uneasily around at each other but the guilds were showing signs of interest, and Fern was eying Demi with renewed curiosity.

"Then what happens?" someone else asked.

Glennoria smiled. "We could establish a co-rule of different factions, but I don't think anyone would ever agree."

"Don't think we want nobility rule either," Fern snapped. Butch laid a calming hand on her shoulder. "What? We don't."

"The nobility and the guilds have the funds and resources to rebuild," one of the guild leaders said.

"So why haven't they?"

Molly heard the words coming out of her mouth, loudly, instead of echoing in her mind as they were supposed to.

"Exactly what I'd like to know," Fern said. "Now there's a chance of power, suddenly everyone's got deep pockets and a heart. No thanks."

"We still have our trades with the other towers to consider," The woman from the grain production level warned.

"Oh they can go hang, Hostia," Fern muttered. "What help have they ever offered us?"

"Still, we need that trade to function."

"We can't do without trade with the other towers!" The

man from the Artificer's guild gasped.

The clamour of voices rose and Molly waited for someone to calm it down again. Butch sat back in his chair with a groan and Fern had joined in just as loudly as the others. Demi and Reyan rolled eyes at each other.

Molly slammed a hand on the desk and winced as the sound bounced off the walls. Several pairs of eyes swung in her direction as she sank back in her seat.

"We choose a figurehead," she said. "We all nominate someone, then vote on it. Everyone around this table has an interest in the citadel and a stake in its future. We all have families here, or most of us. Everyone at this table gets a say."

"Even outside royalty?" The man from the guild piped up.

"We abstain ours," Demi said. "I'm fine letting the citadel plough on without me as long as the Fae inside get fair living."

A wave of wary glances fluttered around.

"Mine too," Reyan added. "Until we trade here we won't earn a voice here."

"A vote then," Hostia agreed. "No voting for ourselves either."

"Wait, do we get a chance to discuss first?" A woman from the Chartist's Guild asked.

"No. If you can't name someone other than yourself, then you don't know enough to vote," Fern said.

Amid the nods, Reyan summoned paper slips and pencils. Once everyone had one, everyone scribbled frantically. Molly stared at her slip.

Butch won't want it. Fern maybe? Not the guilds, and Glennoria won't put the Fae first I don't think.

She let her gaze drift around as people started throwing their slips into the middle. She didn't know Hostia, but the woman understood the tower's trade, and she had been among those ready to fight the guards in the Menagerie.

She scribbled hers and threw it in, then sank back in her chair.

Butch eased to his feet and kept one hand braced on the table as he reached for the first slip.

"Primrose - Artificers Guild."

He handed it to Fern, who smoothed it out in front of her.

"Arbor Fennelseed the Third - nobility."

"That'll be Glennoria's I bet," Reyan whispered. "She's often seen about court with him."

Molly held her tongue where both Fern and Talie didn't, Fern rolling her eyes at the title and Talie covering a snort with her hand.

"Who did you vote for?" she asked quietly. "Butch? Or Fern?"

Talie stared at Butch as he rolled out the third slip and his lips lifted.

"Molly - part-time Princess, part-time spy."

Molly's insides tumbled and her face burned as mutters circled the table.

She clenched her fists on her knees in horror.

"What the-"

CHAPTER TWENTY NINE

TALIE

Talie bit her lip to stifle a bubble of laughter. She wasn't sure she could blame her reactions on hysteria anymore now that Molly was very much alive, but Molly was glaring at her like she'd had something to do with it.

"Don't look at me, Princess," she said. "I didn't vote for you, but now I wish I'd thought of it. I assumed the voting didn't extend to me."

Molly eyed the faces around the table but Talie couldn't see who she hesitated on. She couldn't think who would have voted for her either considering Reyan and Demi also abstained.

It might mean she has to stay though. Talie's heart lifted. *She could agree to keep the wards down. Tiny matter of her probably never wanting to see the place ever again, but she can refuse it if they ask her.*

Butch grabbed another few slips and read out names, but each person had voted for someone different.

"You promise it wasn't you?" Molly muttered.

"I promise it wasn't me. But why not? You've always

championed the citadel, fought for it, left what is no doubt a lavish court more than once to be the heroine. Why not you?"

She waited for the inevitable reminder that Molly wanted out, but Butch read out Hostia's name twice and Molly huffed with relief.

"That awful to be here is it?" Talie muttered.

Molly scowled. "No of course not, but I know nothing about ruling anything."

"Neither does anyone else, clearly. You can't be any worse."

"Oh wow, thanks for that."

Talie grinned. "Anytime."

"Molly."

"Yes?" Molly squeaked.

Butch waved a slip at her.

"That's two votes for Molly, two for Hostia."

"I don't have time for the social crud of ruling anything," Hostia muttered. "What now?"

Butch eased himself back into his seat with a suspiciously serene smile.

"Talie hasn't voted yet," he said.

Talie tensed. "I'm fine."

"You're sat at this table. Everyone else has voted. You live here and know many of the dealings of the past rule too. You vote."

"Can't I abstain?"

He shook his head. "I wouldn't. You either vote for someone with one vote and take us into a triple tie, or you choose."

Talie thought of Hostia across the table, obviously with no desire to rule, and the memory of Arrow darting into her arms filled her head. She glanced at Molly wide-eyed beside her.

"I'm only sixteen," Molly hissed. "This is madness!"

"Is it? You could use this to set up a council of people you trust to act in the tower's best interest, then step down."

"Shared power you mean?"

"Exactly."

"Similar to how the Courts are functioning now."

"How come they get to confer?!" someone shouted.

A round of disgruntled agreement circulated and Talie rolled her eyes, but Molly only frowned at the table instead. A hue of consideration crinkled over her brow as she worked out potential strategy like a giant puzzle.

No point dragging it out. Talie sighed. *I'm sure she'll forgive me. Eventually.*

"I don't need a paper," she announced. "I vote for Molly."

She cringed as a bunch of clamouring tore through the air, the nobles and guilds alike all talking over each other.

"The vote stands." Butch's voice silenced the table. "Molly will take the role of our tower's figurehead, represent us to the other towers and rule in our *collective* best interests."

Amid the renewed voices, Talie slid her hand over Molly's.

"Tell them business starts tomorrow. Actually-" She stood up. "Molly will be out of action until tomorrow.

Hero's day off or whatever. Anyone who violates her space goes to the bottom of the queue for a meet and greet."

"It's called an audience," Reyan whispered.

"Yeah, that."

Molly bit her lip, her frightened gaze darting back and forth around the table. One of the nobles, a tall black woman in an abundance of maroon velvet, had summoned a fancy goblet from somewhere and raised it at Molly with a smirk.

As Molly nodded weakly back, Talie got her to her feet and steered her away from the table.

"We'll check in tomorrow," Demi said with amusement. "If you need any advice, just orb, but Taz will have left some food at the house for you by now."

Reyan nodded. "Go and rest. You don't have to do anything today, or tomorrow. We'll visit very soon."

Talie led Molly out of the room and the Menagerie.

"I had to," she said the moment they were walking up the lane.

Molly sighed. "I know. I never wanted any of this."

"Nobody does, but it doesn't have to be forever. It's your chance to finish what you started."

"Our chance you mean." Molly bumped her shoulder, then grimaced. "You're not getting out of this either."

Talie grinned. "Nowhere else I'd rather be. Oh, by the way I think my rain gift is evolving."

"Evolving how?"

"When you did your ridiculously stupid sacrifice, I somehow made thunder and a storm happen. Not sure if I can do it again though."

"Ah. That might be my fault." Molly smiled as they turned into the alley and passed the workshop. "I taunted the nether."

"How does that cause me making storms?"

"Well, it said it was sending a rumble to shake things up, but I'm still fuzzy on a lot of it."

Talie blinked. "So, you taunted the fabric of our reality and it targeted me instead?"

"Kind of, yeah. I didn't ask it to or anything."

"You have that kind of power?"

"I definitely do not have that kind of power," Molly huffed. "I was frazzled and confused and it was being rude."

"The nether was being rude."

"Yes! So I might have backchatted it a bit and it sent you a storm gift, I'm guessing, then kicked me across to Tara, who's like the embodiment of Faerie."

Talie pinched the bridge of her nose as they passed the workshop and stopped outside the door to the house.

"Remind me never to get on the wrong side of you," she said.

Molly smiled, and something sharp removed some of its claws from Talie's chest.

"Why change the habit of a lifetime?"

Talie snorted. "Nice, Princess, really nice."

CHAPTER THIRTY

MOLLY

Molly ignored Talie smirking beside her and dug out the key to the house. The sound of stillness swelled out as she pushed the door open and stepped inside, but finding Taz and Kainen lounging on the sofa wasn't what she expected somehow.

"Well?" Taz asked expectantly. Kainen kicked him. "What?"

Molly rolled her eyes. "I'm... I don't even know what I am, but they want me to be the new figurehead I think."

"Well of course they do," Taz said.

Kainen nodded. "Best choice for the job. You know the citadel, you know the people, you've got links outside that you can trade on to build back up."

"We've got very little to offer though," Molly reminded them. "I have no idea where to start either. Do I find someone who can ward the tower first? Not to stop people going in and out, but to keep it safe. But then, what if everyone leaves now they can?"

Talie laid a calming hand on her shoulder. "It doesn't

have to be sorted right now. People will find some way to celebrate tonight."

"Exactly." Kainen grinned. "Never underestimate the need to celebrate a win. My advice would be to speak to everyone first. Let them know what to expect from you, little things that you can stick to that will build trust."

Taz snorted. "Says the one who lets his wife run things for him."

"Says the one whose wife literally runs everything without him."

"Hey! I do plenty."

Molly bit her lip on a small smile flickering, but Talie groaned loudly.

"If you two are going to fight, get out."

Amused that Talie was essentially backchatting the King Consort of Faerie and the lord of one of the most favoured courts, Molly let herself relax. It would take time and she had so much work to do now, but she would do her best for everyone.

"Sorry Mum," Kainen said cheerfully.

Taz scowled. "I am still technically King you know."

Talie ignored both of them and headed toward the little kitchen at the back of the room.

"We'll keep the lines of communication open," Kainen insisted. "Rest tonight. Tomorrow be seen out and about, talk to people, reassure them. Food and safety come first, so if the other towers start throwing their weight about, say you're taking a short time to get things in order before you start on the wider issues, but they're welcome to send requests and reports if absolutely necessary."

Taz grimaced. "Do you want us to loan you a secretary of sorts? We can't spare Milo, and Ace is out of commission with him, but maybe Cheryl could be spared."

"No thanks." Molly shook her head. "No gifts or trades or favours or loans until I'm settled and know exactly what I'm doing. If I need advice on who to trust here, Talie knows anyone I don't."

Talie lifted her head. "I'd say get Nia on side first. Fern. Butch. You can't meet everyone but they know people who will."

"Good point," Taz said. "Be seen with the people more than the guilds and the nobles. Make them wait and stress a bit. Make them work for your favour."

"You sound like Violetta," Molly replied wearily.

She grimaced as the name tumbled off her lips and Talie's entire back stiffened.

She knows. Orbs, how do I even explain it?

Kainen glanced between them and a devilish grin danced across his face.

"Ah yes, the agonising darts of unrequited love. Lolly said she was quite put out you weren't interested."

Molly's cheeks burned but the slight lowering of Talie's hunched shoulders was reward enough.

Sometimes gifts are simply just kindnesses when you need them most.

She smiled. "She'll recover soon enough. I'll take a few days to see people and ask them what they think needs to be fixed, then the nobles and guilds. After that, maybe you can bring all the courts for a visit. We won't be in any fit state by then, but I reckon it's important the nobles know there's others that might be willing to come and take their place once we rebuild."

"Oh orbs." Taz grinned. "She's taken to it already."

"Are you sure she's related to you?" Kainen countered.

"Don't start."

"You started it."

"I did not."

"Did."

"Didn't."

"OUT."

Talie's voice bounced off the walls and made all three of them wince. Aurora clicked her beak in disapproval and Arrow chittered irritably where he had his paws up already on the kitchen counter.

Taz and Kainen exchanged a glance and burst out laughing.

"We're going don't worry," Taz said.

He headed toward the door but Kainen stayed to set a glass bottle with a pale pink and sunshine yellow label onto the table.

"Reyan told me to give you this, perfume from the lemon balm bushes. Your endorsement apparently caused an order surge, so we should probably discuss a commission."

Molly opened the bottle and smiled at the whiff of lemon balm that curled out.

"I'll take a favour owed from your court to my... whatever this is."

She waved a hand in the air to indicate the tower, amused when Kainen pressed a hand to his chest.

"Finally, she learns," he teased.

Taz rolled his eyes. "Come on. Leave them be. The group chat is non-negotiable, Molly. If we lose that, we'll worry."

Molly nodded and wiped a hand over her face as they stood up.

"That I can handle, just about."

"I need to be re-added," Kainen said.

Taz shook his head. "Absolutely not."

"I promise to- consider the possibility of behaving myself."

"No."

"I'll buy you a doughnut."

"…No."

"I'll name my first-born child after you."

"No."

"Okay, I'll name my first-born *boy* after you, assuming Reyan agrees."

"No."

"I'll tell Demi you were the one that submitted her singing to that season of *Siren-Sing-Along* a few years ago."

"How do you know about that?!"

"I have my ways."

"FINE. I will re-add you to the group chat, as long as you promise never to tell her."

"No."

"Oh come on!"

The sound of their bickering disappeared as they both realm-skipped out in a swirl of purple and grey, leaving silence behind them.

"Here." Molly held out the bottle to Talie.

"What's that for?"

Molly shrugged. "You don't smell right using mine, that's all."

Talie didn't smile, just took the bottle and sniffed the contents before setting it down with a nod.

"You know you don't own the other smell, right? Or has all this power gone to your head?"

Molly smiled. "Yes, and no. Just take it."

"Okay. Are you going to move into the Menagerie do you think then? Bring in outsiders to help?"

"What outsiders?"

"Well, you must have made friends, like *Violetta,*" Talie said, her tone scathing.

Molly bit back a smile. "Nobody that would want to come here I'm sure, and I'm going to stay right here. If I need to stay at the Menagerie for meetings or something then fine, but until then I'm going to keep my independence and live here."

"You'll have to use the Menagerie as an office probably if nothing else. It'll be expected. He made me take your old room there as well, so…"

Molly shrugged. "You can keep it if you want."

"Too big. Too full of memories. Assuming you've no objections."

"Why would I?"

"Well, this is yours now. The tower is yours to lead, so I guess if you tell me where to stay I can't say no."

Molly stalked across the short space of floor and leaned

into Talie's face with her arms folded.

"You can always say no, always."

Talie hesitated, searching her face. "Okay. Then I should stay wherever you are."

Her lip twitched before she snared it between her teeth and she looked away. Molly smiled and that not so tiny skip in her chest that had been absent outside of the tower returned with great force.

"Because I need protecting?" she asked. "You said that before."

Talie nodded, her gaze still fixed to the floor.

"You can't fight," she muttered.

"I can actually."

"If you say so. You need someone to guard you and watch your back either way, so it makes sense for me to stay here as well."

"It does, or you could stay because you want to."

Talie lifted her gaze warily. "Or that. It has two rooms I suppose, and we've shared closer spaces before."

"I guess so." Molly sighed. "I'm not going to get any peace now, am I?"

Talie's smile appeared, tiny and hesitant but still there.

"Nope, but I'm on your side," she said.

"On my side?"

"On it, at it." Talie rolled her eyes and the lingering awkwardness between them died away. "You need minding, Princess. Or should that be Lady now you've your own court essentially? Would it be Lady Princess or Princess Lady? Should I be bowing?"

"Do it and you're banis-" Molly sensed the subtle

warning as the words slithered across her tongue. "I really need to start being careful what I threaten, don't I?"

"Probably. Where do we start first?"

"Sleep and food."

"I'll take the bed out here." Talie moved past her into the room with a cursory glance around. "Safer that way."

Molly eyed the bed that still had one of Sammy's hair wraps on it and nodded. She locked the door behind her and stared at the room. Tomorrow she would need to stock the kitchenette, be seen visiting people, and probably at least arrange meetings with the nobles and guilds for the near future.

"Not tonight," Talie said.

Molly frowned. "Huh?"

"Leave the deep thought until tomorrow. I'll go out and get some food from the kiosk. I'm actually surprised Marthe or more of your mad family haven't busted in yet."

It was said with all the familiar snark Molly had missed for months, but she heard the softness underneath. Thoughts of the past months filled her head, including the brief not-exactly-a-flirtation with Vi, along with a tirade of Kainenly advice.

As Talie trudged past to go out again, Molly reached for her hand. Talie stared down at their fingers entwining and her throat bobbed.

"I'm not going to have to swear fealty or anything, am I?"

Molly shook her head, her pulse thundering as she moved so they were standing face to face.

"No, probably not."

"I will if I have to."

Molly smiled. "No deep thought, remember?"

"Then what, you don't want kiosk food? Am I forgetting something?"

"Yeah."

Talie flinched as Molly closed the space between them. The kiss landed featherlight, a question more than anything else.

Talie pressed her forehead to Molly's, her eyes firmly shut.

"Are you sure?" she asked, doubt lacing her voice. "There are hundreds of eligible nobles out there with fancy fortunes-"

"I'm sure." Molly tapped a finger on Talie's lips with far more boldness giggling through her limbs than she felt possible. "Don't forget that next time."

Molly turned toward the bedroom, her mind still jangling with the potential perils that the coming days of ruling would inevitably bring, but Talie scoffed softly.

"As you wish, Princess. All eyes will be on us now, so we should probably make the most of the good stuff in between the bad."

Molly groaned. "I thought you said no serious stuff until tomorrow. Having second thoughts?"

She glanced over her shoulder as Talie turned in the doorway with a soft smile.

"Wouldn't be anywhere else."

She ducked out and shut the door behind her, but Molly stayed staring at it for a long while after.

The future wasn't in any way bright yet. She still had

the other towers to handle, and the never-ending feuds between the people and the guilds and nobility to handle.

There were alliances to build, invites to send out, and extensive streams of complicated rules holding the tower together.

Phoenix was still out there somewhere, either stuck in the tunnels or more likely on his way to one of the other towers. If he took his undead plan, which she still didn't even really understand, to the other towers and they supported him, it would bring about the unthinkable.

The whole situation clouded in her mind like an oncoming storm, but even that couldn't dim her smile.

If I can survive Storm Talie, I can probably survive the rest.

ACKNOWLEDGEMENTS

A huge thank you to every reader who has walked with me through Faerie and is still coming back for another visit! To those who've shared on social media, done ARC reads or just given me compliments about the book to keep me going, thank you!

To my family and also my writing family as always, your support means everything to me – Aerin Apeltun, Katina Wright, Estelle Tudor, Maria Oliver, Anna Britton, Sally Doherty, Marisa Noelle, Emma Finlayson-Palmer, writing Twitter, the amazing ARC readers (who have caught so many printing blips it's not even funny…), the wider writing community and everyone who joins #ukteenchat, WriteMentor, SCBWI, and especially libraries and schools who've taken a chance on the previous books, shops that are still stocking them and giving this indie author a chance to reach more readers *deep breath* and most importantly to the readers who will find these books in the future:

THANK YOU!

ABOUT THE AUTHOR

While always convinced that there has to be something out there beyond the everyday, Emma focuses on weaving magic realms with words (the real world can wait a while). The idea of other worlds fascinates her and she's determined to find her own entrance to an alternate realm one day.

Raised in London, she now lives on the UK south coast with her husband and a very lazy black Labrador who occasionally condescends to take her out for a walk.

Aside from creative writing studies, an addiction to cake and spending far too much time procrastinating on social media, Emma is still waiting for the arrival of her unicorn. Or a tank, she's not fussy.

For the latest news and updates, check the website or come say hi on social media:

www.emmaebradley.com
@EmmaEBradley

www.ingramcontent.com/pod-product-compliance
Lightning Source LLC
Chambersburg PA
CBHW050545190726
48283CB00007B/2011